"What makes you think you can help my son?"

The contempt in Lincoln Korda's voice was unmistakable. "Surely you can't blame me for doubting your potential?"

Sara's pride argued that this man didn't deserve an answer. But no matter how objectionable Lincoln might be, his son Jeff still needed her help. She couldn't abandon him without even trying.

"Probably I am naive," she answered. "But haven't all the more sophisticated means at your disposal failed?"

"Jeff won't let you help him." His face showed the strain he was feeling. "He won't let anyone help him. No one can get through to him."

"Is that why he took an overdose?" Sara inquired pointedly, then flinched at his look of fury.

"We'll talk again, Miss Fielding," he declared as he stood up. "In the morning. And you'll need all your strength then, believe me!"

D1357971

Dear Reader,

This month we celebrate the publication of our 1000th Harlequin Presents. It is a special occasion for us, and one we would like to share with you.

Since its inception with three of our bestselling authors in May, 1973, Harlequin Presents has grown to become the most popular romance series in the world, featuring more than sixty internationally acclaimed authors. All of the authors appearing this month are well-known and loved. Some have been with us right from the start; others are newer, but each, in the tradition of Harlequin Presents, delivers the passionate exciting love stories our readers have come to expect.

We are proud of the trust you have placed in us over the years. It's part of the Harlequin dedication to supplying, contemporary fiction, rich in romance, exotic settings and happy endings.

We know you'll enjoy all of the selections in this very special month, and in the months to come.

Your friends at Harlequin

ANNE MATHER

night heat

Harlequin Books

TORONTO • NEW YORK • LONDON
AMSTERDAM • PARIS • SYDNEY • HAMBURG
STOCKHOLM • ATHENS • TOKYO • MILAN

Harlequin Presents first edition August 1987
ISBN 0-373-11003-0

Original hardcover edition published in 1987
by Mills & Boon Limited

CHAPTER ONE

SARA hadn't felt much like going to the party. In fact, after what had happened that afternoon, it was probably the last place she would have chosen to go. But Vicki had been determined that she should, when she had hinted as much to her, and perhaps it was sensible, as Vicki said, not to stay at home and mope.

All the same, it wasn't going to be easy to put on a cheerful face, when what she really felt like doing was crying her eyes out. It was so unfair, she thought, for the umpteenth time since Doctor Walters had given her the news. All those years of work for nothing. A slip on the stairs, and her whole life was ruined. Or the most important part of it, she amended, not being given to lying, even to herself.

It didn't help to know that it could have been worse, that she could have been left with a permanent limp, or, heaven forbid! callipers on her leg. And it was little consolation at this time that she had a job which was not dependent on her being able to effect an *arabesque* or perform a *pirouette*. But all her life she had wanted to dance, ever since she was able to walk, and to know now that her dancing days were over was a bitter pill to swallow.

Her earliest memories were of tottering round on wobbly legs, to the delight and admiration of her parents. She had loved to perform for friends and relations alike, and when other children had been playing with dolls or acting out their fantasies, she had been content to practise at the barre.

But now the dream she had had, that one day she might become more than just a member of a chorus line, was over. The ankle she had thought only strained had, in fact, been broken, and in spite of a belated plaster cast and

5

weeks of therapy, she was never going to regain the strength that had been there.

Of course, if she was brutally honest with herself, she would accept that the chances of her ever becoming really famous had been slim. It was true that when she was ten years old, she had been the star pupil at her ballet class. But her parents' deaths in a multi-car pile-up, and a subsequent move to live with her aunt and uncle in Warwickshire, had done much to retard the modest success she had had. Her aunt, who was her father's older sister, did not regard becoming a dancer as either a suitable or a sensible career, and not until Sara was eighteen and old enough to make her own decisions was she able to devote all her time to her art.

Much against her aunt's and uncle's wishes, she had used the small legacy her parents had left her to move to London and enrol at a dance academy. But after two years of attending auditions and tramping from agency to agency in the hope that someone might be willing to give her a chance to prove herself, she had had to admit defeat. A temporary office job had provided funds to take a course in shorthand and typing, and in spite of her misgivings, she discovered an unexpected aptitude for secretarial work. Her speeds at both shorthand and typing assured her of regular employment, and the comforting rise in salary enabled her to move from the tiny bed-sitter, which had been all she could afford. She had answered an advertisment asking for someone to share the rent of a two-bedroomed flat, and that was how she met Vicki Hammond.

It was later that Vicki had explained she had chosen Sara because she was a Libran. 'Librans are compatible with Geminis,' she said, revealing her reasons for asking Sara's date of birth, and whatever the truth of it, they had become good friends.

Vicki was a photographic model, though she was quick to point out that she did not take all her clothes off. 'Mostly layouts for catalogues, that sort of thing,' she explained, when Sara asked what she did. 'I get an occasional trip to Europe, and once we went to Florida, which was exciting. But mostly we work in a studio in Shepherd's Bush. It's not very glamorous, but the money's good.'

She had tried to get Sara interested in modelling. 'With those eyes and that hair, you'd be a natural!' she exclaimed, viewing Sara's slender figure with some envy. 'And you're tall, too, and that's always an advantage. I'm sure if I spoke to Tony, he'd be willing to give you a try.'

But Sara had refused, flattered, but not attracted by the world of fashion. She had still not given up hope of becoming a professional dancer, and she had exercised continually, keeping her limbs loose and supple.

Curiously enough, when her break did come, it was quite by accident. It had happened at a party she had attended with Vicki—much like tonight's, she reflected ruefully. A young man had invited her to dance, and discovering her ability to follow his every move, he had put on a display for the other guests. The music was all guitars and drums, a primitive rhythm that demanded a primitive response. And Sara, who had always considered herself a classical dancer, found her vocation in the disco beat.

It turned out that the young man was himself a dancer, one of a group famous for their television appearances. To Sara's delight and amazement, he told her that their choreographer was always on the lookout for new young talent, and in spite of her initial scepticism, an audition had been arranged.

That had been exactly ten days before Sara slipped on the stairs in the apartment building and hurt her ankle. It had been bruised and stiff, it was true, but she had never dreamt it might be anything more serious than a sprain. It had been such a little slip, but, a week later, the pain had driven her to seek medical treatment. That was when the tiny splintered bone had been discovered, not too serious in itself, but compounded by the fact that she had used the foot without support.

Of course, the television audition had had to be cancelled, and as if that wasn't enough, six weeks later she had been told that the bone was not mending correctly. Further treatment had been arranged, more weeks of rest and frustration, before the cast had finally been removed and therapy could begin.

And now, today, when she had been sure her ankle was almost cured, when she had convinced herself it would soon be as strong as it had ever been, Doctor Walters had broken the news that she should never dance again—not professionally, anyway. 'The ankle simply wouldn't stand it,' he told her regretfully. 'Haven't you found already that even standing for long periods makes it ache?'

Of course Sara had, but she had believed that sooner or later the strength would return. To learn that that was not going to happen had been a bitter blow, and she had left the hospital in a daze. She remembered dragging herself to Regent's Park, and sitting in the gardens there for over an hour, trying to come to terms with what this would mean. The future she had planned for herself was never going to materialise. All her hopes and dreams were shattered. She was condemned to working in an office for the rest of her life. Anything less sedentary was not recommended.

As usual, Vicki had been philosophical. 'It's not the end of the world,' she had said, when she had come in from an assignment to find her friend slumped on the sofa. 'It could be worse. You could have been scarred for life. As it is, you'll simply go on as before. There's more to living than working, you know.'

'I know.'

Sara had tried to equal the other girl's stoicism. So far as Vicki was concerned, working was merely a means to earn money, and her affairs with the opposite sex were legion. Sara, on the other hand, had never had a steady boyfriend, and her experience of men was therefore limited. Besides, she had always been too single-minded in her ambitions to regard men as anything more than a passing diversion. She had never been in love, and if she had ever thought of getting married, it had been at some far distant time, when she was too old to continue her career.

'Well, at least you're not out of work,' Vicki had commented, referring to the part-time secretarial post Sara had been obliged to take, while waiting for the results of the therapy. The long weeks of wearing a cast had curtailed her mobility, and she had had to leave the permanent job she had had as personal assistant to a solicitor in Gray's Inn. But her finances were not so healthy that she could afford not to work at all, and her present place of employment was only a few yards from the apartment.

Her response to Vicki's attempts at encouragement had not been enthusiastic, and that was when the party had been mentioned. It was being held to celebrate the twenty-first birthday of one of Vicki's fellow models, and was exactly what she needed to take her mind off her problems—or so Vicki said.

'Come,' she said wheedlingly. 'You'll have fun! You can't stay here on your own—not tonight!'

Even so, Sara was still undecided as she followed her friend into the apartment where the party was being held. The tears she had shed before Vicki got back had left her with a dull headache, and although she had taken some aspirin before leaving home, she could still feel it.

The noise in the apartment was terrific, and the room was full of people talking and laughing and having fun. Judging by the amount of empty glasses strewn around, alcohol was flowing freely, and as if to emphasise this assumption, a glass was thrust into her hand as she came through the door.

An hour later, Sara was wishing she had stuck to her original intention of having an early night. The noise had not abated, indeed it had been supplemented by music from a sophisticated hi-fi system, and in the lulls between the records, someone could be heard strumming an electric guitar. Two glasses of fairly cheap champagne had not assisted her headache, and although food of a kind was on offer, it mainly consisted of nuts and crackers and tiny stuffed olives.

At least no one would notice her white face here, she reflected. White faces were quite fashionable among this crowd, and compared to some of the outrageous costumes she had seen, they were reasonably conservative. Her own beige silk flying suit looked almost unbearably plain, she felt, and with the lustre of her hair confined in a single braid, she was unlikely to attract anyone's attention.

She was wondering if she could make good her escape without Vicki's noticing when one of the men she had not discouraged with a freezing glance came to sit beside her. She had noticed him watching her earlier with a faintly speculative stare, and now he came to sit on the arm of her chair, apparently immune to her cool indifference.

'You're Sara, aren't you?' he remarked, and she glanced round instinctively, expecting to see Vicki close at hand. But her friend was not in sight, and she turned back to the casual stranger with faint resignation.

'She told you, I suppose,' she declared, noticing he was older than most of the other guests. His light brown hair, which she suspected owed its curl to a bottle rather than to nature, showed evidence of tinting at the roots, and his dissipated face spoke of years of experience.

'No, I guessed,' he said now, offering to refill her glass from the bottle he was carrying, but she covered the rim with her palm. 'Vicki described you to me, and she's generally accurate. You are beautiful, and you have a certain—touch-me-not air, which isn't very common in this company.'

Sara sighed. 'You're very kind,' she said cynically, wishing he would just go away. She was not in the mood for compliments, no matter how well meant, and his presence was preventing her from making an anonymous exit.

'I'm not kind at all. I'm honest,' he retorted, running his hand over the knee of his pants before offering it to her. 'Tony Korda,' he added, when she reluctantly responded. 'Your friend Vicki works for me.'

'The photographer!' Sara was scarcely flattering in her description of him, and he winced. 'I'm sorry,' she murmured, with a rueful smile. 'But you do take marvellous photographs!'

'Thank you.' He inclined his head. 'I'm glad you think so.' He paused. 'I'd like to photograph you some time.'

'Oh, no!' She held up a regretful hand. 'I appreciate the compliment, but I'm not interested in modelling. Besides——' She broke off at that point, silencing the involuntary desire to confess her impediment. The disability she had suffered would not interest him, and so long as she was seated, he could not observe the way she still favoured her right foot.

'Besides?' he prompted, but she shook her head, and as if sensing her anguish, he said gently: 'Vicki told me about the accident. If you don't want to talk about it, I'll quite understand. But I wondered if you'd made any plans—you know: what you're going to do now that that particular avenue is barred to you.'

Sara drew in her breath. 'You don't pull your punches, do you, Mr Korda?'

'Tony. And no; not if I don't consider it necessary.'

'And you don't?'

He shook his head. 'There are other things in life besides dancing.'

Her lips twisted. 'You have been talking to Vicki,' she conceded ironically.

Tony Korda shrugged. 'As I said a few moments ago, Sara, you're a beautiful girl. Perhaps you weren't meant to waste your life in hot theatres and even hotter studios.'

'That's your assessment of it, is it?' Sara was trying very hard to be as detached as he was, but his ruthless candour was tearing her to pieces.

'I think you're allowing emotion to colour your judgement, yes,' he said frankly. 'So—you had an audition coming up. So what? You could have fluffed it!'

Sara bent her head, angry with herself for allowing him to upset her. 'Do you mind going away?' she exclaimed huskily, groping for a tissue from her bag. 'I'm sure you think you know what you're doing, but I can do without your amateur psychology.'

'I'm no amateur psychologist,' he asserted flatly. 'I'm just trying to make you see that——'

'——there are more things in life than dancing. I know. You already said that.'

'That wasn't what I was going to say, actually,' he retorted, without heat. 'I was going to tell you that sitting here feeling sorry for yourself is a form of self-indulgence. There are people much worse off than you are, believe me!'

Sara felt the warm, revealing colour fill her cheeks. 'I'm sure there are . . .'

'And I don't just mean the millions who die every year from disease and malnutrition,' he continued, his tone hardening. 'You hurt your ankle, and it's going to limit your career. But how would you have felt if you'd been completely immobilised?'

She held up her head, forcing herself to listen to him. 'You said that with some feeling,' she ventured at last. 'Is there a reason?'

Tony Korda studied the amber liquid in his glass. 'Yes,' he admitted eventually. 'Yes, there is a reason. My nephew had a car accident six months ago. He was only eighteen at the time. Now he's paralysed from the waist down. It looks like he'll be stuck in a wheelchair for the rest of his life.'

Sara caught her breath. 'I'm sorry . . .'

'Yes. So's Jeff.' Tony sounded bitter. 'Unfortunately, being sorry doesn't help at all.'

She flushed. 'I didn't mean——'

'I know, I know.' Tony was instantly contrite. 'I'm sorry, too. I didn't mean to sound as if I was blaming you. I was only trying to show you how futile a situation like that can seem to a boy of Jeff's age.'

Sara nodded. 'I'm sure it must.'

Tony sighed, his face taking on a brooding expression as he refilled his glass. There was silence for a pause, and then, as if compelled to go on, he added: 'It doesn't help that Link and Michelle—that is, my brother and his wife—seem to ignore his existence.' He grimaced. 'I guess your parents want you to go back home, eh? Didn't Vicki say you came from up north somewhere?'

'I lived in Warwickshire for a number of years,' admitted Sara, after a moment. 'But my parents are dead. They died in a car crash when I was eight.'

'Aw, hell!' Tony swallowed the contents of his glass at a gulp. 'Trust me to put my foot in it yet again! You're going to have to forgive me. I guess I've had more of this stuff than I can handle.

'It's all right.' And Sara meant it. Curiously enough, Tony had achieved his objective. Right now, she was more intrigued with his story than with her own. She wanted to ask him to go on, to explain what he had meant about his brother and sister-in-law ignoring their son's existence, but of course she couldn't. Nevertheless, his words had stirred a sympathetic chord inside her, and she felt for the youth whose future had been laid waste.

'I didn't mean to depress you, you know,' Tony muttered now, filling his glass again. 'God, I'm such a clumsy bastard!'

'You haven't depressed me,' Sara assured him swiftly. 'As a matter of fact . . .' She hesitated before continuing, but then silencing her conscience, she added, 'I'm interested.'

'In Jeff?' He blinked.

'Well, in the reasons why you think his parents don't care about him.'

'Oh,' he shrugged, 'I don't say they don't care about him. I guess they do. They must, mustn't they? But Michelle has her—commitments, and Link—well, I guess he's too busy making money to care that his son's bleeding to death!'

'Bleeding to death?' Sara exclaimed, appalled.

'Emotionally, I mean,' Tony explained himself. 'The kid's neglected! Left alone in that big house, week after week, with only the paid help for company—I'm surprised he doesn't go round the bend!'

She moistened her lips. 'Your brother lives out of London, then.'

'Out of London?' Tony blinked. 'Hell, yes. He lives in New York.'

'I see.'

'I doubt you do.' He took another mouthful from his glass. 'My brother married an American, Sara. He's lived in the States for almost twenty years. Jeff was born there.'

Sara frowned. 'But your nephew lives in England, now——'

'No! Jeff lives in Florida,' amended Tony impatiently. 'My brother owns a property there. A place called Orchid Key, about twenty-five miles north of Miami.'

'Oh . . .'

Sara was beginning to understand, but before she could say anything more, Vicki's faintly-intoxicated tones broke into their conversation. 'You two seem to be hitting it off,' she declared, leaning over the back of Sara's chair and regarding the pair of them with evident satisfaction. 'I thought you would. When are you going to come and work with us, Sara? Don't tell me Tony hasn't asked you, because I won't believe it.'

Sara sighed, turning to survey her friend with some regret. Vicki's intervention had terminated Tony's narration, and she guessed from the way he greeted the other girl that he was not averse to the interruption. He was probably already regretting the fact that he had confided personal details to someone he barely knew, and she suspected that without his liberal intake of alcohol, he would never have spoken so frankly. As if to confirm that fact, Tony excused himself a few moments later, and Sara was left with the unpleasant feeling that she was to blame.

Even so, she could not resist the temptation later that night to quiz Vicki about her boss's nephew. Having persuaded the other girl that she was tired, Sara offered to make a cup of hot chocolate when they got back to the flat, carrying it into Vicki's room as she was creaming off her make-up.

'Did—er—did you know Tony Korda's nephew had been injured in a car accident?' she asked casually, perching on the end of Vicki's bed, her cup cradled in her hands. 'He was talking about it tonight.'

'Was he?' Vicki had sobered considerably since encountering the cool October air, and her brows arched inquisitively at Sara's well-schooled expression. 'Yes, I knew.'

Sara's lids fell defensively. 'You didn't mention it.'

'No.'

'Why not?'

Vicki hesitated. 'I thought it might upset you. Your parents, and so on.'

'Oh, I see.' Sara's head lifted. 'That was sweet of you, but honestly, it is more than ten years since the accident. And I'm not a child any more.'

'No.' Vicki grimaced. 'Oh, well . . .' She picked up another pad of cotton wool. 'So what was Tony saying? Did he tell you the boy is only a teenager?'

'Mmm,' Sara nodded. 'It's a tragedy, isn't it?'

'It's very sad,' conceded Vicki slowly. 'But I can think of worse fates.'

'Vicki!'

'Well! I should live in such idyllic surroundings, waited on hand and foot!'

Sara gasped. 'You don't mean that!'

'I do.' Vicki reached for her cup of hot chocolate. 'I've been there. I know.' She paused. 'Do you remember me telling you, we once did a shoot in Florida? That was where we did it. Lincoln Korda's place: Orchid Key!'

Sara's eyes widened. 'Go on.'

'Go on—what?'

'Tell me about it—Orchid Key, I mean. Is it very exotic?'

'Very.' Vicki's tone was dry. 'It's an island, actually, just off the coast. You could swim there from the mainland, if they'd let you. But of course they don't. It's virtually a fortress. Guards—*armed* guards—everywhere. I guess Lincoln Korda owns a lot of expensive stuff.'

Sara couldn't resist. 'Did you meet him?'

'Who? Lincoln Korda? No chance. He seldom uses the place. According to Tony, he's a workaholic.'

'Yes.' Sara was thoughtful. 'He told me his brother lives in New York. But what about Mrs Korda? Doesn't she prefer Florida?'

'Maybe. As long as Lincoln Korda's not there, of course. They're separated, you know. Have been for years.' Vicki finished her chocolate and got up from the dressing table stool. 'You know,' she said, viewing Sara's concerned face with wry sympathy, 'people like that shouldn't have children. They can't afford them—emotionally speaking.'

Three weeks later, Sara had practically forgotten all about Jeff Korda, when she unexpectedly got a telephone call from his uncle.

'Sara!' Tony Korda sounded distraught. 'Thank God I've managed to get hold of you. Where've you been all day? I've been ringing since one o'clock!'

Sara blinked, glancing at the plain gold watch on her wrist. It was barely six. 'I do have a job, Mr Korda,' she reminded him drily. And then as she remembered her friend was away, in Scotland, her stomach contracted. 'It's not Vic——'

'This has nothing to do with Vicki,' he forestalled her swiftly. 'Look, could you meet me? In—say—half an hour?'

'Half an hour?' Sara was taken aback. 'Mr Korda, I don't think——'

'This isn't an assignation,' he declared flatly. 'I just want to talk to you, that's all.' And when she demurred: 'It's about Jeff. My nephew, remember?'

Half an hour later, entering the pub in Charing Cross which Tony had suggested, Sara wondered why the mention of the boy's name should have provoked such an immediate response. And the right response, too, judging by Tony Korda's reaction. He had known she would respond to an appeal of that kind. But was Jeff Korda the real reason why he wanted to see her?

She had not bothered to stop and change, but her black and white tweed suit, with its calf-length skirt and thigh-length jacket, was not out of place in the smoky atmosphere of the White Lion. Worn with a high-necked blouse and a man's narrow tie, it successfully disguised her unusual beauty, the tight coil of hair at her nape merely adding to her severe image.

Tony Korda was standing at the bar, but when he saw her, he picked up the two drinks he had ordered and urged her into the quieter surroundings of the lounge. 'I'm afraid it's only lager,' he remarked, setting the two glasses down on a low table, and squatting on the stool opposite. 'But I didn't know what to order, and at least it's long and cold.'

'Lager's fine,' said Sara, who secretly hated the stuff. And then: 'So—why have you brought me here? What's wrong? You said it was something to do with your nephew.'

'It is.' Tony hunched his shoulders, looking even more world-weary than he had at the party. Casting a glance over his shoulder to make sure they were not being overheard, he went on: 'Jeff took an overdose yesterday evening. They rushed him into the hospital in Miami, but for a while there it was touch and go.'

Sara was horrified. 'How terrible!' She shook her head. 'Is he going to be all right?'

'So they say. He's still in the hospital, of course—something to do with testing the toxicity of his blood. But he'll be home in a day or so. I'm flying out there tomorrow to see how he is for myself.'

Sara nodded. 'It must have been a terrible shock!'

'It was. When Link rang to tell me, I could have wrung his bloody neck!'

She hesitated, not quite knowing what was required of her. Then, awkwardly, she put out her hand and squeezed his arm. 'Thanks for feeling you could tell me,' she murmured. 'I appreciate your confidence.'

'My confidence?' Tony's expression was suddenly even grimmer. 'Is that why you think I rang? Just to share this confidence with you?'

She moved a little nervously on her seat. 'Didn't you?'

'No!' He leant across the table towards her. 'Sara, I rang because I thought you might be willing to help. You seemed—sympathetic when I spoke to you at Chris's party. Or was that an act?'

'No!' She was indignant. 'I just don't see——'

'I want you to consider a proposition I have to put to you,' said Tony swiftly, and the sudden input from a juke-box in the bar made what he was saying almost inaudible. 'I've spoken to Link, as I've said, and he's agreeable. How does the idea of spending the winter months in Florida appeal to you?'

'In Florida?' Sara was sure she had heard him wrong, but Tony was nodding.

'As a companion—a friend, if you like—for Jeff. You'd get a salary, of course. A more than generous one, I can guarantee that. And all expenses paid, naturally——'

'Wait a minute!' She held up a dazed hand. 'Why would you think I can help your nephew? Surely a psychiatrist——'

'He's had psychiatrists,' Tony interrupted her harshly. 'And psychologists, and psycho-therapists, and goodness knows what else! That's not what he needs.' He paused, before continuing urgently: 'Sara, what Jeff is missing is someone *young*, someone of his own generation, someone who understands what he's going through. Someone like you.'

Sara gulped. 'You can't compare my injury——'

'I know that. But you're the closest Jeff's going to come to facing the truth about himself, to dealing with it.'

'But I know nothing about nursing!'

'I've told you—Jeff has had all the nurses and doctors he can cope with.'

She was finding it difficult to believe what she was hearing. 'But, Tony,' she said, trying to speak reasonably, 'I have a job——'

'What job? Secretary to some small-time businessman, with offices in Kilburn High Street? It's hardly high-priority!'

She stared at him. 'How do you know where I work?'

'How do you think? I asked Vicki.'

Sara struggled with a feeling of indignation. 'She had no right to tell you.'

'Why not? She didn't know why I was asking.'

'You've spoken to her today?'

'Yes,' Tony grunted. 'Don't worry, I didn't tell her why I wanted to know. I just slipped it into the conversation.'

She shook her head. 'Well, you must know I'm going to refuse.'

'Why?'

'Why?' She made a helpless gesture. 'Well—because it's

crazy! Asking me to go out to Florida to meet someone I don't even know! Someone who might take a dislike to me at first sight.'

'He won't.'

'How do you know that?'

Tony sighed. 'Haven't you looked at yourself lately, Sara?'

She was running short of excuses, and she wondered rather impatiently why she felt she needed one. It was a ludicrous idea, asking her to go to Florida, to try and reason with some boy who, despite his injuries, was probably far more capable of handling his own life than she was. But she hadn't tried to kill herself, a small voice reminded her insistently. She wasn't alone in some palatial Southern mansion which, no matter how luxurious, apparently bore all the hallmarks of a prison.

'But what about your brother?' she persisted, fighting the insidious demands of compassion. 'And your sister-in-law? Don't they have any ideas of their own?'

Tony was silent for so long that Sara began to wonder whether the noisy juke-box had drowned out her words. But, eventually, he spoke again. 'Michelle's no good around sick people,' he admitted at last. 'It's not her fault, she's always been that way. And Link just doesn't have the time.'

'For his own son?'

'For anyone,' said Tony obliquely. 'Well? What do you say? Is typing someone's letters really more important than saving someone's life?'

CHAPTER TWO

Put like that, there had really been no answer to it, reflected Sara some ten days later, feeling the rush of adrenalin as the big jet made its approach to Miami International Airport. Melodramatic, maybe; unfair, perhaps; but Sara had acknowledged that she really could not refuse.

Oh, it was easy enough to argue that Tony had had no right to ask her, that he had put her in an impossible position by insisting that she was the only one who could help. And in all honesty, she should have refused because of the responsibility he was putting on her. But from the beginning she had been interested in the boy's case, and shouldn't she really blame herself for being tempted by the challenge?

Besides, once she accepted the inevitability of her decision, she had been unable to deny a sense of anticipation at the prospect of leaving England in November for the tropical warmth of this most southerly state. Even Vicki's somewhat uncharacteristic lack of enthusiasm had been unable to douse her excitement, and only now, as she approached her destination, did more practical considerations gain the upper hand.

What did she know about psychological problems, after all? It was all very well for Tony to assure her that Jeff was looking forward to her arrival, but what faith could she put in that when in the next breath he had told her the boy was morose and well-nigh unapproachable! He had said that both his brother and his estranged wife were enthusiastic about her arrival, but he had also said that she shouldn't take any notice if tempers sometimes got frayed. Emotions could apparently run high in the Korda household, and on those occasions she should make herself scarce.

It was all a little daunting to someone who had never even left England before, let alone to cross the vastness of the

Atlantic, and only the knowledge of the return ticket in her handbag gave her the confidence to leave the plane.

If only Tony had been able to accompany her, she thought. If only he had been around to introduce her to his relatives, or at least ease her entry into the household. But Tony had only been able to spend a couple of days in America. He was a busy man, and he had had to get back to England to fulfil his obligations; or so he said.

'My guess is he's as eager to pass the buck as his brother!' Vicki had commented acidly. 'Making time with a teenage schizophrenic can't be fun for anyone. I think you're crazy for letting him put you on the spot!'

Sara had argued that Jeff was not a schizophrenic, that there was no question of a split personality, but what did she really know? What kind of person—what kind of *teenager*—swallowed an overdose of some highly dangerous substance, that only the prompt action of the hospital medics had prevented from proving lethal? His situation seemed harrowing, it was true, but it was not desperate. There were obviously thousands—millions—of people worse off than he was. But as he had probably heard that particular argument many times before, it was going to require much ingenuity on her part to make it sound convincing.

Sara was not immediately aware of the humidity when she left the plane. The airport buildings were all air-conditioned, and only the scent of overheated humanity gave her an inkling of what she might have to face outside. The airport was crowded, too. A sea of dark, Hispanic faces, with only a smattering of Caucasian among them. Two flights—one from Puerto Rico, and the other from Colombia—had landed ahead of the British Airways jet, and in the confusion, Sara despaired of ever finding whoever had come to meet her.

Amazingly enough, she eventually found herself in the baggage collection area, and rescuing her suitcase and the rather scruffy carpet bag that contained her personal belongings from the carousel, she made her way to the exit. If no one had come to meet her, she was contemplating taking the next flight back to England, and she half hoped the worst would happen. Just for a moment, the unfamiliarity of her surroundings caused a wave of homesickness to sweep over her, and she would have given anything to be back in London, fog and all.

The man in the chauffeur's uniform, carrying the card that read 'Sara Fielding', almost passed her by. She didn't know what she was looking for exactly, but it was not a cardboard notice displaying her name.

'I—er—I'm Sara Fielding,' she admitted reluctantly, stopping in front of him. 'Do you—I mean—have you any means of identification?'

The tall black man thrust his hand inside his jacket, and briefly Sara was reminded of all those television series, where such an action heralded the producing of a gun. But all the chauffeur produced was a driver's licence, showing his photograph and giving his name as Henry Isaiah Wesley, and a letter introducing the man from someone who signed himself Grant Masters.

'If you'll follow me,' the chauffeur suggested, after Sara's faint smile had assured him that his credentials had been accepted, and taking her suitcase and carpet bag from her, he set off across the concourse.

The car—a huge black limousine, with smoked glass windows—was waiting, double-banked, in a no-waiting area. But apparently its size, or perhaps its owner, warranted some respect, for the police patrolman who directed them out into the stream of traffic paid no heed to any offence which might have been committed. And to Sara, bemused by the switch from air-conditioned terminal to equally air-conditioned limousine, with a blast of hot humidity in between, it was all part and parcel of the chaotic confusion of her arrival.

Nevertheless, she couldn't help but relax in the cushioned comfort of the car. With her feet resting on a carpet, with a pile as thick as any she had ever seen, and her limbs responding to the yielding softness of fine leather, she was hardly aware of what was going on outside the windows; and not until they turned into the multi-laned elegance of a highway, lined with stately palms and bordering the ocean, did she give her surroundings her attention.

Although the flight had taken the better part of ten hours, the change in time zones meant that it was still only late afternoon in Miami. And with the sun casting long shadows across the avenue, and the blue-green waters of what she later learned was Biscayne Bay—and not the Atlantic, as she had innocently imagined—shimmering invitingly between the masts of yachts and other sailing craft, she felt a rekindling of the excitement she had felt when the Embassy official in London had stamped her visa.

It was an effort, but summoning her courage, she leant across the seemingly vast expanse of space that separated the rear of the car from the driver's seat. 'It's very hot, isn't it?' she ventured, in what she hoped was an encouraging tone. 'It was raining back in London.'

'I'll turn up the conditioner,' responded the chauffeur at once, and immediately, the pleasant waft of cool air emanating from the grilles beside her became a chilling draught. Within seconds, the car was reduced to a temperature bordering on freezing, and Sara sighed unhappily, before attempting to explain that that was not what she had meant.

'I was talking about the temperature here—in Florida,' she mumbled, after the air-conditioning had been restored to its usual level, but receiving no reply, she concluded that the chauffeur did not consider it part of his duties to make polite conversation with a paid companion.

Finding the monotonous row of high-rise hotels and office buildings on her left of little interest, Sara concentrated her attention on the recreation areas beside the beach. Acres of grassy parks and walkways, some less attractive than others, she had to admit, were nevertheless more interesting than the commercial aspects of the city, particularly as from time to time she glimpsed causeways heading out to places called Treasure Island or Indian Creek or Bal Harbor.

North of Miami, they left the impressive interstate highway for the less hectic route along the coast. Sara had read somewhere that this area was called the Gold Coast, and she could understand why. An almost unending vista of sandy beaches contoured the road, and their progress was observed by graceful seabirds, sweeping down to the breakers that lapped the shore.

Beyond the busier centres of Fort Lauderdale and Boca Raton, with their golf courses and high-rise condominiums, they entered the quiet streets of Cyprus Beach. Hiding behind high clipped hedges, a handful of luxury dwellings made Sara aware of the exclusivity of this resort, and long before they

reached the harbour, with its neatly-staked pier and expensive
shops, she guessed they were nearing their destination. If the
chauffeur had been more approachable, she could have shared
a little of her sudden apprehension with him. But after her
abortive attempt to be friendly, they had spent the whole
journey in silence, and she was hardly surprised when he
made no attempt to reassure her now.

The long, luxurious limousine was drawn to a halt as close
to the pier as possible. Once again, their arrival was marked
by an armed policeman, leaning against the bonnet of his
squad car. But, once again, he made no move to stop them
parking in what would appear to be a no-parking area, and
when Wesley opened the car door for Sara to alight, she
scrambled out with alacrity.

Her appearance did generate a mild response from the
policeman. He was probably unused to seeing rather travel-
worn young women emerging from the Korda family limousine,
Sara reflected wryly, brushing down the creases in her wine-
coloured corded pants suit. If she had only thought about it in
the car, she could have re-touched her make-up and re-coiled
her hair before meeting her employer—if that was the correct
way to regard the young man who was to be in her charge.
As it was, she was obliged to hope that the strands of hair
escaping from her chignon would not look too untidy, and
that her nose was not as shiny as she imagined it to be.

Wesley slammed the car door, but didn't lock it. Why
bother, reflected Sara wryly, with a policemen to stand guard
over it? But then she saw the boat that was apparently to
transport her and her belongings to Orchid Key, and the
luxury of the car distinctly faded by comparison.

The yacht moored at the pier was the kind of vessel Sara
had hitherto only seen in advertisements. The *Ariadne*, as she
was called, was at least fifty feet in length, with cabins fore
and aft, and the sun reflecting from its gleaming hull
accentuated its look of controlled power. A ribbed gangway
gave access to its polished deck, and as Wesley indicated that
Sara should precede him aboard, another man came forward
to greet her. This man was less formally dressed, in white
pants and a short-sleeved white shirt, his blond good looks in
no way diminished by the deepness of his tan.

'Miss Fielding,' he said, his smile warm and friendly. 'Or

can I call you Sara? I'm Grant Masters, Mr Korda's personal assistant.'

'How do you do?' murmured Sara, relieved, responding to his smile. 'You're the person who wrote the letter that—that the chauffeur——'

'Wesley, yes.' Masters' gaze moved past her to the black man who was presently depositing her luggage on the deck. 'That's okay,' he dismissed him. 'I'll take care of Miss Fielding from here on in.' And then, returning his attention to Sara, 'Come into the saloon. I'm sure you wouldn't say no to something long and cool and thirst-quenching.'

'Oh, no.' In all honesty, Sara was beginning to feel the heat, and wishing she had thought to bring another set of clothes to change into on the plane. The corded suit was decidedly too heavy for this climate, and with a murmured word of thanks after the departing chauffeur's back, she followed her host into the forward cabin.

Above her—or was it below her, she couldn't be exactly sure—engines fired to life, and glancing round, she saw another man casting off the lines that had moored the *Ariadne* to the pier. But her own attention was immediately absorbed by the luxurious appointments of the cabin, and as Masters poured drinks at a refrigerated bar, Sara shed her jacket and looked about her.

The cabin was panelled in oak, with a curved elevation forward, and smoked glass all round. There were long cushioned banquettes, and onyx lamps with pleated shades, and the soft carpet underfoot gave the feeling of walking on velvet. As in the car, the air supply was controlled, and the presence of both a television and a hi-fi system assured her that the yacht had its own generator too.

'There you are. I think you'll like it,' Masters was saying now, and turning somewhat bemusedly, Sara took the tall tumbler from his hand.

'Er—what is it?' she asked, looking down into a glass frothing with a creamy fluid, and frosted with sugar.

'It's just fruit juice with a little coconut milk added,' Masters declared smoothly, and as the movement of the craft caused her to take an involuntary step, he gestured to the banquette behind her. 'Won't you sit down? The trip only takes a few minutes, but I think you'd feel safer.'

Sara subsided on to the cushions gratefully. It was all a little too much to take in and, sipping her drink, she wondered if anyone ever got used to such luxury.

'Did you have a good flight?'

Masters was speaking again, and she turned to him almost guiltily. 'Very good, thank you,' she answered, wiping a film of foam from her lip. 'Um—this is lovely.'

Masters himself was not drinking, she noticed. He had draped his elegant frame on the banquette opposite, and was evidently enjoying the novelty of watching her. From time to time, he cast a thoughtful glance in the direction in which they were heading, but mostly he studied her, which was a little disconcerting.

'Have you ever been to Florida before, Sara?' he asked, his confident use of her name seeming to indicate that in his employer's absence, he had the authority. It made her wonder if perhaps he was the person with whom she would be dealing. After all, if Tony Korda's brother spent most of his time in New York, it was possible that he employed someone like Grant Masters to act as his deputy.

'This is my first trip to the United States,' she answered honestly, and as if anticipating her reply, he inclined his blond head.

'You worked as a secretary in London, didn't you?' he probed, after a moment. 'But that wasn't what you really wanted to do.'

'No.' Almost unconsciously, Sara moved to tuck her right foot behind her left, and although he said nothing, she sensed Masters had noticed.

'What do you know about Jeff?' he asked now, and she was glad of the glass in her hands, which acted as a convincing diversion.

'Not a lot,' she admitted, lifting her shoulders. 'I—I was told he had had a car accident. And—and that there's some paralysis.'

'There's total paralysis from the waist down,' Masters told her, with some emphasis. 'Jeff is wholly incapacitated. He can neither walk, nor dress himself; he has negative control over his bodily functions, and because he refuses to co-operate, he has to be washed and groomed and fed, just like a baby!'

Sara stared at him aghast. Tony had told her none of this.

From the little he had said, she had assumed the boy was depressed and unhappy, suicidal even, but not outwardly aggressive. After all, taking an overdose was not such an exceptional thing these days. Lots of people took drugs, some of them using attempted suicide as a cry for help, without any real intention of taking their own life. Not that she'd actually believed that Jeff Korda's overdose had been a cry for help—heavens, with his background, he could want for nothing—but she had thought it might have been a spur-of-the-moment decision, a desperate fit of depression culminating in a desperate act.

But now, listening to Grant Masters enumerating the boy's disabilities, she was horrified by her own inadequacy. In heaven's name, why had Tony sent her here? What did she know of a mentality that defied all normal precepts? How could she expect to reason with someone who had already spurned all attempts to rehabilitate him? How could she help the boy when he evidently had no desire to be helped?

'You look a little pale, Sara,' Masters remarked now, and for a moment she wondered if he had deliberately tried to disconcert her. He might be exaggerating, she told herself without conviction, and in any case it was too late to turn back.

'I expect I'm tired,' she responded, refusing to let him think he had upset her. 'After all, although it's only early evening here, my body tells me it's almost bedtime.'

A trace of faint admiration crossed Masters' face. 'Of course,' he said, taking his cue from her. 'It's after eleven in England. It's just as well we're almost there. I expect you'll be glad of a rest before dinner.'

Won't I just? thought Sara fervently, swallowing the rest of her drink, and when Masters suggested they go out on deck so that she could see the island, she was eager to accept his invitation.

Her first view of Orchid Key was disappointing. After the car and the yacht, she had expected something more inspiring than the rocky shoreline that confronted them, and the line of barbed wire fencing running right around the headland seemed to confirm Vicki's assertion that the island was inaccessible without an invitation. There was a guard, too, waiting for them on the stony jetty, with a snub-nosed automatic pistol tucked into his belt.

The yacht was berthed and the gangway slung across, and instructing one of the crew to bring her luggage, Masters strode off the boat with Sara close behind him. Shades of Alcatraz, she thought gloomily, thinking she understood why Lincoln Korda spent all his time in New York.

A shallow flight of stairs, dug out of the cliff, lay ahead of them, and Sara followed her guide up the steps. They emerged on to a grassy plateau, with an all-round view of the island, and her impression of a barren outcrop swiftly changed. Ahead of them now at this, the narrowest, end of the island, were acres of sand-dunes, sloping away to a shell-strewn beach. An uneven line of palms framed the blue-green waters of the Atlantic, and not even the thought that some security guard was probably patrolling the shoreline could rob the scene of its natural beauty.

Closer at hand, a single-storied building with several jeeps parked outside served as a kind of guard station. Although the island was not big—no more than two or three square miles, Sara estimated—the jeeps would prove invaluable in an emergency. But as well as the utility vehicles, there was also a sleek silver convertible, and it was to this that Masters led her after acknowledging her approving gaze.

With her bags securely stowed in the back of the convertible, Sara joined Masters in the front. No chauffeurs here, she thought, not without some relief. She wasn't used to the presence of so many helping hands, no matter how deferential they might be. She breathed a sigh of relief as they drove off along a gravel track, and Masters gave her a thoughtful look as he swung the wheel through his hands.

The island was roughly triangular in shape, with access by boat only available at the narrowest point. 'We're situated above a sandbar,' Masters explained. 'The ocean to the east of the island is too shallow to allow a craft of any size to approach that way, although windsurfers have been known to come ashore in rough weather.'

Sara lifted a nervous shoulder. 'Are they allowed to?'

'We're not running a top secret establishment here, Sara,' he responded drily. 'Visitors have been known to arrive and depart without any hassle. We don't encourage intruders, it's true, but Mr Korda has to protect his property.'

Sara made no comment. It was not up to her to question her employer's security arrangements. If they made her feel a little like a prison visitor, that was her hang-up. She was not here to make her opinions felt—not about security anyway.

The centre of the island, which was flat, apparently served as a landing pad. Across a stretch of rough turf, she could see two hangars, one of which had its doors open to reveal the tail of a helicopter. Of course, she thought cynically. There would have to be a helicopter. It was all part and parcel with what she had seen so far.

The Korda house was situated above a stretch of golden sand. Three stories high, it rose majestically from a pillared terrace, its white-painted grandeur far more redolent of the 1920s than more than half a century later. Surrounding the house were gardens that reminded Sara of the gardens of an Italian villa she had once read about. There was a profusion of waterfalls and statuary, and a stone-flagged fountain splashing sibilantly in the foreground. She guessed a small army of gardeners would be required to keep the place in order, and her nerves prickled anxiously at this further evidence of her employer's wealth.

Grant Masters brought the car to a halt and thrusting open his door, got out. At the same time, a woman of perhaps forty emerged on to the terrace, and Sara's escort went to speak to her. Left briefly to herself, Sara too vacated the vehicle, leaning into the back to rescue her bags, just as Masters turned back and saw her.

'Leave them,' he called, and although the words were spoken carelessly enough, it was an order. 'Come and meet Mr Korda's housekeeper. She'll show you to your rooms and explain about dinner and where we eat.'

Sara was tempted to bring her carpet bag anyway, just to show she preferred to be independent, but the older woman was watching their exchange, and she decided not to argue. Instead, she looped the jacket of her suit over one shoulder and, making a determined effort not to drag her right foot, she climbed the steps to the terrace.

'This is Sara Fielding, Cora,' said Masters, performing the

introduction. 'Cora will take care of you, Sara,' he added. 'Anything you need, just ask her.'

'Thank you.'

Cora was polite, but Sara was aware that the housekeeper was regarding her rather guardedly. She probably thinks I'm as incapable of helping Jeff as Grant Masters evidently does, Sara reflected unhappily. And why not? If the best brains in medicine couldn't help him, how could she?

At Cora's summons, a young black boy appeared, and after directing him to fetch Miss Fielding's luggage, she invited Sara to follow her. 'Go ahead,' said Grant Masters, pushing his hands into his trouser pockets and giving her a vaguely sympathetic grin. 'I'll see you later.'

They entered the house through double doors that stood wide, but which had fine-meshed screen doors in their place. 'The insects are attracted by the light,' said Cora, who spoke with a decidedly Southern accent and seldom actually finished off her words. 'The house is air-conditioned, but Mr Link, he likes for the breeze to blow right through on days like this. He says it's more healthy, and what Mr Link says goes.'

She smiled as she made this statement, proving she had a sense of humour, and Sara felt a little more reassured. If the housekeeper could joke about her employer, the atmosphere at Orchid Key couldn't be all bad. Nevertheless, it did prompt her to wonder exactly what Tony Korda's brother was like. Up until then, she had been more concerned in anticipating his son's reaction to *her*, but now she found herself speculating what manner of man cared more about his business than his family. Physically, she assumed, he would resemble his brother. Tony Korda was not a handsome man, but she supposed he might be attractive to some women, who didn't mind his affectations. Still, without the curl in his rather mousy hair, and the stylish clothes he seemed to favour, he would have been rather nondescript, and that was how she had pictured Lincoln Korda. A man of medium height and medium build, possibly running to fat, with that certain look of avidity that went with material success.

The entrance hall was marble-tiled and impressive, with an enormous chandelier suspended above their heads. There was a semi-circular table, flanked by two crystal blue armchairs, set against the far wall, and two alabaster plinths, on which

were set two enormous bowls of flowers, in the foreground.
The hall was filled with the fragrance of the flowers and,
admiring their waxed petals, Sara was compelled to ask if
they were orchids.

'Miss Michelle's father used to cultivate them in the
glasshouse out back,' said Cora, after acknowledging that they
were. 'It was Mr de Vere who built this house and named the
island Orchid Key.' She shrugged. 'I guess he spent too much
time cultivating his orchids. Things went bad, and after Mr
Link married Miss Michelle, he bought it from her father.
But Mr Link doesn't have time to grow orchids. These days,
the gardeners do that.'

'I see.'

Sara felt a pang of pity for the man who had evidently
spent so much time and effort in making this such a beautiful
home. Was that why Michelle and Lincoln Korda had split
up? Because they wanted different things from life?

She was being fanciful, and pushing her unwarranted
thoughts aside, she hurried up the stairs after the housekeeper.
But, in spite of her haste, she found her progress hindered by
her need to take in her surroundings, to absorb them, to tell
herself somewhat incredulously that for the next few weeks—
possibly *months*—this was to be her home.

The hand-wrought iron balustrade curved above arched
recesses giving access to the ground floor apartments of the
house. A corridor disappeared to the right, with windows
overlooking the gardens at the front, and beneath the stairs
another passageway led towards the back. A gallery of pastel-
tinted watercolours mounted the silk-covered wall beside her,
and she didn't need to examine their legendary signatures to
see for herself that they were originals. She doubted there
was anything in the house that wasn't totally authentic, except
perhaps its occupants, she reflected somewhat cynically.

The rooms which had been allotted to her overlooked the
beach. A large sitting room, with its own dining area, was
adjoined by an equally large bedroom, the colonial-style
fourposter set on a shallow dais, allowing its occupant to view
the ocean without even sitting up. Sara was still absorbing the
view from the balcony outside when Cora left her, announcing
that she would send up a tray of tea.

'You might like to have dinner in your room this evening,'

she added, and Sara wondered if the suggestion was as innocent as it seemed. But it probably would be wiser to have this time to take her bearings, she conceded shrewdly. Not to rush into anything until she knew exactly what was expected of her.

Her suitcase and carpet bag were delivered as she was rinsing her face in the bathroom. She had spent some time admiring the circular bath, with its jacuzzi attachment, and delighting in the gold-plated luxury of the taps, but the sound of the outer door closing was a sobering signal. Casting a regretful glance at tinted mirrors and intriguing crystal flagons, set on a fluted crystal shelf, Sara went to unpack her belongings, promising herself a more thorough exploration when she had the time.

As well as her luggage, a tray of tea and some tiny shortbread biscuits resided on the table beside the bed. Evidently, whoever had brought the tea had assumed she could drink it while she unpacked her cases, and Sara blessed their thoughtfulness as she poured herself a cup.

Fifteen minutes later, with the more crushable items of her wardrobe hung in the capacious walk-in closet, Sara decided the rest could wait. Stepping out of her trousers, she tossed them on to the pale green velvet chaise-longue that was set between the long windows, and doffing her shirt, stretched on the bed in only her bra and bikini briefs. She felt so weary, suddenly, and the fading light was very restful. If she could just close her eyes for a few minutes, she thought, and knew no more . . .

She awakened, chilled, to the dazed lack of awareness strange surroundings invariably invoked. She lay for several minutes in the darkness, struggling with a sense of panic, and then relaxed again at the soothing, sucking sound of the ocean, just beyond the bedroom windows. Of course! She was in Florida. At Lincoln Korda's house on Orchid Key, to be precise. But what time was it? And how long had she slept? She had taken off her watch to have her wash, and she evidently hadn't replaced it.

Shivering, she groped for the lamp beside the bed, which she was sure she had noticed earlier. Its light was attractively muted by a Thai silk shade, a shade she noticed—quite inconsequently at this moment—which matched the coverlet on her bed and the long drapes at the windows.

There was a clock beside the bed, too, and blinking, Sara discovered it was almost twelve o'clock. *Midnight!* she breathed, inaudibly. She had slept for almost six hours! What must the rest of the household be thinking of her? Not least, Jeff himself!

She was hungry, too, ravenously so, the kind of hunger that comes from not having eaten a proper meal for more than twelve hours. It had been approximately two p.m. London time when lunch had been served on the plane and, apart from the fact that she had been too excited to do justice to what was offered, that was almost fifteen hours ago now. Oh, there had been a few sandwiches offered as afternoon tea before they landed at Miami, but nothing to satisfy an appetite sharpened by anxiety. Even the tray of tea, which she had enjoyed earlier, had been taken away as she slept, preventing her from salving the ache inside her with the few shortbreads that were left.

The arrival of a rather large moth curtailed her remorseful musings. Realising that the door to the balcony was still open and that the light was attracting unwelcome visitors, she scrambled off the bed to go and close it. But before she did so, she stepped out on to the balcony, delighting in the unaccustomed warmth of the night air. Cooler than in the day, obviously, but far more appealing, the sky overhead absolutely bedizened with stars. She couldn't see the ocean, but she could hear it more clearly here, the shushing sound she had identified earlier accompanied by the deeper vibration of the waves. What a heavenly place, she thought romantically. How could anyone choose to live in New York when this place was waiting?

Resting her hands on the iron railing, she looked down, and as she did so, she saw the sudden flaring of a cigarette in the darkness. She was momentarily shocked, was instinctively drawing back, when her common sense told her that whoever it was could not see her. She didn't have the glow of a cigarette end to give her away, and sheltered by the balcony, the illumination from her room was visible only to the insects. The man—*woman?*—whoever it was, was seated directly below her, and forcing her eyes to adjust themselves to the gloom, she was astounded to make out the unmistakable lines of a wheelchair. *A wheelchair!*

Her heart flipped over. Was it Jeff down there? Did he find it difficult to sleep, and use this time to exercise the abilities he spurned during daylight hours? It was a tantalising thought. And it could be true. Was it possible his refusal to accept rehabilitation was only an act? Had she inadvertently stumbled on his secret?

She stepped back from the rail, breathing unevenly. She had to find out. There was no way she could mention her suspicions to Grant Masters without at least trying to prove that she was right. Pulling the balcony doors closed behind her, she drew the curtains and then put on the corded pants she had shed earlier. A pink sweat shirt was easier than the shirt she had worn to travel in, and fretting at the time she was wasting, she spent more precious minutes brushing the now mussed length of her hair. Deciding she couldn't afford to wait while she plaited her hair, she tied it back with a silk scarf and after slipping her feet into low-heeled sandals, she opened her door.

She had no definite idea about how to reach the back terrace, but trusting her instincts, she made her way to the galleried landing. Low lights illuminated the hall below, and trying to control her breathing, Sara sped silently down the stairs.

Rejecting the corridor at the front of the house, she headed for the archway beneath the curve of the stairs, feeling a thrill of excitement at the unmistakable draught of air that greeted her. She was on the right track, she was sure of it, and as if to confirm her belief, she turned a corner and saw the darkness of the terrace only a few yards ahead of her.

Immediately, her feet slowed, and in spite of the silence all around her, she felt unbelievably exposed. She glanced back over her shoulder, half expecting someone must be following her, but she was alone in the lamplight shadows. All the same, there was something uncomfortably alien about what she was doing, and a sudden twinge in her foot reminded her she was unused to abusing her ankle in this way. Running down the stairs, she had given little thought to its weakness, but now she leaned against the wall, wishing she had not been so precipitate.

Still, she was here now, and unless she wanted Jeff to come upon her as he returned to his room, she had to make an effort. Having come so far, it would be foolish to return to her room without at least trying to see him, and moving slowly, she edged towards the terrace.

A mesh door, similar to the ones that protected the front of the house, stood ajar, and guessing the progress of the wheelchair made opening doors difficult, she was encouraged. Besides, the open door enabled her to emerge unnoticed, though her heart was beating so loudly, she was sure it must be audible.

Ahead of her, something glinted in the darkness, and she realised it was a swimming pool. It was just as well she hadn't tumbled into that, she thought wryly. What a way to announce her presence! She could just imagine Grant Masters' anger if she crowned her arrival by destroying Jeff's efforts to cure himself

Inching forward, she found herself on a flagged patio, which was doubtless a suntrap in daylight. The ribbed outlines of low chairs around the pool seemed to point to this conclusion, though the obvious absence of any cushions gave them a skeletal appearance. But where was the wheelchair? she wondered uneasily. Surely, after all her efforts, Jeff had not abandoned his vigil.

And then she saw it. Set some yards along the terrace, the chair still rested below the level of the balcony, and even as she gazed towards it, she saw the revealing circle of fire as his cigarette was drawn to his mouth.

If only she could see more clearly, she thought frustratedly, cursing the moonless night. She wondered what he would do if she spoke to him. Would he be shocked, or angry, or both? Dared she intrude on his isolation? Or might she, as she had thought earlier, destroy any desire to recover his strength by exposing the frailty of his efforts?

'Why don't you come and join me?' he asked suddenly, evidently aware of her quivering observation, and Sara gulped. His voice, coming to her in the darkness, was low and harsh and attractive, and undeniably mature for a boy of his age. 'What were you hoping to see, I wonder?' he added, turning his head towards her. 'Will you be making a habit of sneaking about the place, when you're supposed to be in bed? If so, I'll have to watch I don't do anything to shock you!'

'I wasn't sneaking . . .' Sara took an unsteady breath, and then continued: 'How—how did you know I was here? How did you know it was *me*?'

'Call it—intuition.' He shifted slightly towards her, and moving closer, she saw the long, useless legs stretched in front of him. 'Miss—Fielding, isn't it? Tony's final solution! Forgive me if I beg to doubt his confidence. He always was hopelessly romantic!'

The harsh disturbing voice scraped on Sara's senses, but in spite of the cynicism of his words, she knew a kindling surge of encouragement. Surely if Jeff could speak to her like this, he was not the grim, despairing youth she had been led to expect. If, by exposing his nightly ritual, she had pierced the surface shell he evidently presented to the other members of the household, surely she must stand some chance of reasoning with him.

Her excitement was blunted somewhat, however, by the sudden reminder of why she was here. If Jeff was making such obvious progress, why had he attempted to take his own life less than two weeks ago? Why, if he could speak so philosophically about his uncle, had Tony told her no psychiatrist could reach him?

She was still pondering this enigma, when the wheelchair squeaked and its occupant rose easily to his feet. 'Forgive me.' The tall, lean man who had vacated the seat sent the remains of what he had been smoking shooting away in an arc across the terrace. And as Sara backed away in sudden panic, he came towards her holding out his hand. 'I should have introduced myself,' he finished easily. 'I'm Lincoln Korda. And you, I believe, are a friend of my brother.'

CHAPTER THREE

SARA lay awake for the rest of the night. She told herself it was because she had slept for six hours already and she wasn't tired any longer, but in all honesty, it was neither of those things. Meeting Lincoln Korda had been such a shock, and try as she might, she could not dispel the trembling in her knees which had gripped her when he rose up out of the wheelchair. Dear God! he had scared her half to death in that moment, and then he had completed the process by inviting her into his study and offering her a drink.

She had accepted a brandy in the hope that it might restore her shattered defences, but of course it hadn't. It would take more than an albeit generous measure of cognac to help her regain her confidence, and in spite of Lincoln Korda's solicitude, she had wished quite desperately that she had never left her room.

Apart from the obvious strain that his careless deception had caused, she had had to cope with an entirely different reaction. Lincoln Korda bore no physical resemblance to his brother whatsoever, and although Sara knew he was three years the elder—and therefore forty, or thereabouts— he had the litheness and physique of a man ten years younger. He was tall, as she had noted when he was sitting in the wheelchair, and much darker-skinned than his brother. His hair was dark, too, and only lightly touched with grey, longer than she would have expected, and lying thick and smooth against his head. His eyes were grey and deep-set, probably the only characteristic about him that she had anticipated, in that they were cool and remote. Otherwise, his features were lean and intelligent, with narrow cheekbones and a thin-lipped mouth, and a nose which she suspected had been broken, and which gave his attractive face more character. Unlike Tony's, his stomach did not strain at the waistband of his pants, and in black jeans and a black cotton tee-shirt, she could have been forgiven for mistaking him for one of his employees. But not his son, she added silently, acknowledging her anger with both of them for creating such an embarrassing situation.

'I know—you thought I was Jeff. I'm sorry,' he had said, after they had entered the book-lined elegance of his study. 'Sit down. You look as if you've had a shock.'

She had. But although she felt like telling him what she thought of his methods of introducing himself, she did not need the ruby-set signet ring on his little finger, or this luxuriously-appointed apartment, to remind her that from everything she had heard, Lincoln Korda was not a man to tangle with. It was her own fault. She had thought she was being clever, when she wasn't. And now she had to deal with the unwelcome realisation that she had made a complete fool of herself.

He poured her a brandy from a crystal decanter set on a silver tray. The tray itself was residing on a cherrywood cabinet, whose definitive design was echoed in the scrolls of the leather-topped desk, and repeated in the armrests of the comfortable sofa. The carpet was of Persian design, the desk flanked by two leather recliners, and a pair of club chairs were grouped about a chess table, set with elaborate chess pieces. The room was generous in proportion, but the clever combination of furniture enabled its owner to create whatever kind of atmosphere he chose. Right now, Sara was uncomfortably aware that she felt distinctly overpowered by her employer's nearness, and she was irritatingly conscious of him in a way that was neither cool nor logical.

He allowed her to swallow the better part of her drink before speaking again, but when he did she was compelled to answer. 'You had no dinner, I understand,' he remarked, hooking his thigh over a corner of the desk. 'Cora tells me you didn't eat in your apartments, and as you didn't join the rest of us . . .'

Sara's tongue rescued a pearl of brandy from the corner of her lip, and then she said: 'I didn't realise you were

here, Mr Korda. I—was given to understand you were in
New York.'

'Who told you that?'

His eyes were intent, and meeting their cool deliberation,
Sara wished she still had the darkness of the patio to hide
her blushes. She was acutely conscious of her bare face and
carelessly-tied hair, and the corded pants had not benefited
from their discarded sojourn on the chaise-longue. If she
had anticipated meeting Tony's brother—and it had not
seemed an imminent possibility, from what he had said—
she had assumed she would be prepared for the event.
Encountering him now, and finding him so different from
what she had expected, had unnerved her, and she thought
he might have allowed for that—and the lateness of the
hour—instead of regarding her with such disparagement.

'No one actually told me,' she admitted now, replying to
his question. 'But your brother——'

'Yes? What did Antony tell you?'

Antony! Sara blinked. It sounded strange, hearing Tony
Korda referred to as *Antony*. Gathering herself, she
murmured quickly: 'He implied you spent most of your
time in New York.'

'Did he?' Lincoln Korda inclined his head. 'Did he also
believe I would allow some—girl-friend of his into the
house, without first meeting her myself? Particularly when
that girl is supposed to work some magic with my son?'

Sara held up her head. 'I am not one of your brother's
girl-friends,' she declared stiffly. 'If he told you I was, then
you've been misinformed.

'What are you, then? A failed model?' The contempt in
his voice was unmistakable. 'I suppose being lame would
limit one's capabilities. Still, I'd have thought with your
looks they'd have found something for you to do.'

Sara's lips compressed. 'You don't pull your punches, do
you, Mr Korda? Is this a crash course in how to be
successful in business? First disable your opponent, then
move in for the kill! Only in my case, the disablement was
there to begin with. Are you going to fire me now, or wait
until tomorrow; just to give it some credence?'

He had the grace to colour slightly at her words, and the
spasmodic palpitation of her heart steadied a little. *The*

bastard! she was thinking, wondering how she could ever have allowed Tony to talk her into this. After all, she had been against it from the beginning. She might not agree with Lincoln Korda's methods, but she certainly agreed with his scepticism.

She was preparing to walk out of the room when his harsh voice stayed her. 'All right,' he said, and she realised it was the closest she would get to an apology for his sarcasm, 'maybe I was a little rough on you, but you have to admit, it's a rough situation. Hell, what makes you think you can help my son? If your behaviour outside was anything to go by, surely you can't blame me for doubting your potential. God, you thought I was Jeff! Wasn't that hopelessly naïve?'

Sara was tempted to refuse the overture. Her pride argued that this man didn't deserve an answer, and it would have given her the utmost pleasure to tell him to stuff his opinion; but something wouldn't let her. No matter how objectionable Lincoln Korda might be, she had not come here to make friends with the family. Jeff still needed help—possibly her help—and could she really abandon Tony's faith in her without even meeting the boy?

Putting down her empty glass, she linked her hands together. 'Probably it was,' she answered, meeting his assessing gaze with enforced composure. 'But I thought you expected that. Isn't it true that all the sophisticated means at your disposal have failed?'

Lincoln Korda's mouth twisted. 'Antony told you that too, I suppose.'

'He told me a little, yes.' A lot more than she wanted to remember, she thought uneasily. Tony had said that the boy's parents didn't care about him. But Lincoln Korda was here because she was. So what did that mean? Did he care more for his son than the boy's mother did?

He shook his head now, and she came to attention. 'Do you have any real idea of what you're taking on?' His face showed the strain he was feeling. 'Jeff won't let you help him. He won't let anyone help him. No one can get through to him.'

'Is that why he took an overdose?' enquired Sara

pointedly, then flinched at the look of fury he cast in her
direction.

Sliding off the desk, he straightened, his superior height
an added disadvantage. 'We'll talk again, Miss Fielding,' he
declared, terminating the interview. 'I hope you sleep well.
You'll need your strength in the morning, believe me.'

Now, slipping from beneath the crisp cotton sheet which
was all that covered her, Sara trod across the shaggy pile of
the carpet to the windows. It was early, but as she'd been
awake for most of the night, it didn't seem so. Nevertheless,
it was reassuring to see the sun fingering its way between
her curtains, and somehow nothing seemed as desperate
then as in those early pre-dawn hours.

Just looking out on a view, which might have been taken
from a travel brochure, simply wasn't enough, and discarding
the disturbing remembrance of what she had last observed
from her balcony, she stepped outside.

It was deliciously cool, the air not yet overlaid with the
sticky heat of the day. The sun's rays still lacked the
strength to burn her shoulders, and its golden benediction
spread fingers over the ocean. Closer at hand, a handful of
seagulls pecked among the flotsam thrown up on the shore
by the tide. Sara could see seaweed strewn along the
narrow bar of sand, and dwarf palms edging the beach
where a low stone wall marked the garden's boundary.

Almost beneath her windows, but a few yards to her left,
the sickle-shaped pool was another unwelcome reminder of
the night before. Perhaps it would have been better if she
had stumbled into the pool, she reflected cynically. Lincoln
Korda might have had some sympathy for her then.

She didn't want to think about Lincoln Korda, not when
she had so many other, more important, things to think
about, but she couldn't help it. She disliked him; she
considered he was rude and autocratic, but she couldn't
forget him. He was the most infuriating man she had ever
met, and she pitied Jeff Korda for being his son. All the
same, he was a disturbingly attractive man, and she
wondered again why he and his wife had parted. Perhaps
his attraction for the opposite sex was part of the reason.
No doubt with his money and his connections, he could

have any woman he wanted. Except me, thought Sara drily, ignoring the obvious fact that he wouldn't want her.

Discovering it was barely seven o'clock, she had a refreshing shower in the fluted-gold luxury of the cubicle beside the jacuzzi, and she finished with an all-over pummelling that acted much the same as a massage. She emerged from the shower feeling infinitely sharper, and physically prepared at least to face the other pressures of the day.

After drying her hair with the hand-drier, also provided, she brushed it out and regarded its tawny length with some misgivings. Perhaps, now that any hope of her becoming a dancer had been squashed, she should have it cut, she mused doubtfully. After all, the present fashion was for short, spiky hairstyles, or smooth Twenties-style bobs. Long hair might be attractive, but it also took a lot of looking after, and what was the point? Who cared—except herself? All the same, as she plaited it into the single braid which she thought might be most suitable for the job that was facing her, she had come to no definite conclusion, and for the present it would have to stay as it was.

She dressed in cream cotton pants and a lime green vest, putting on a pair of comfortable trainers instead of the sandals she had worn the night before. She found trousers most easily disguised the lameness Lincoln Korda had so ruthlessly exposed, and besides, she was here to do a job of work, not to laze about in the sunshine.

Her rooms were off a wide corridor which led from the galleried landing, and although it had not been dark when she arrived the previous afternoon, she had been too overwhelmed to really absorb the beauty of her surroundings. She had an entirely different perspective, too, from the way she had felt the night before, and in broad daylight, she was half inclined to believe she had exaggerated the night's events.

A maid was using a buffing machine on the hall tiles, but she switched it off at Sara's approach had wished her good morning. 'You want something to eat, Miss Fielding?' she enquired, in the same Southern drawl that Cora used. 'There's a table set out by the pool, if you'd like to help youself.'

'So early?' Sara was surprised.

'Mr Lincoln left for New York about a quarter of seven,' replied the maid smoothly. 'I'll bring you some fresh coffee. You go take it easy.'

'Thank you.'

Sara managed to be polite, even though her thoughts were racing. So Lincoln Korda had left as unexpectedly as he had come. She was not going to have to face his remorseless appraisal as she took her first steps towards getting to know his son. Whatever his misgivings, he was prepared to give her a chance. So why did she feel so depressed all at once, as if all the excitement had gone out of the day?

Outside, under a striped umbrella, a round, glass-topped table was laid for breakfast. Fresh orange juice, with ice still floating in the jug, croissants keeping warm over a small flame, butter, preserves, and a jug of thick cream. Hearing her tummy rumble in anticipation, Sara poured herself a tall glass of juice, and after savouring its texture, she buttered a crisp golden roll.

It was a heavenly spot, she thought, looking about her. The flagged patio was set with tubs of geraniums, fuchsias, and lilies, smilax spilling its trailing fronds over tub and paving alike. A scarlet hibiscus rioted over a trellis separating the patio from the lawned area beyond, and beside the pool, wooden *cabanas* were disguised beneath a patchwork of bougainvillaea. The bare bones of the pool furniture she had a glimpsed the night before were now comfortably covered with cushions, which matched the awning over her head. There were chairs and loungers, and even a swinging sun-bed, its pillowed couch swaying in the breeze.

The light from the pool was dazzling, and she didn't realise the maid had returned until the jug of coffee she had brought was set down on the table 'Now then,' she said, 'how would you like scrambled eggs, or French toast, or waffles? Or maybe you'd prefer some pancakes, with a nice jug of maple syrup——'

'Oh, no!' Sara shook her head. 'No, thank you. This is fine, honestly.' She indicated the croissant she was eating. 'These are delicious!'

'Made this morning,' agreed the maid, with a grin. 'You sure now? It's no trouble.'

'I'm sure,' said Sara, with an answering smile, and the woman shrugged expressively before sauntering away.

Sara poured herself some coffee, added cream, and then resting her elbows on the tabletop sipped the aromatic beverage slowly. The food she had consumed, the warmth of the day, the unspoiled beauty of her surroundings, soothed her, and she thought how delightful it would be to just soak up the sun. Even Jeff could do that, she reflected thoughtfully, feeling an unwelcome sense of apprehension at the daunting task ahead of her.

'Good morning!'

Once again she had not heard anyone's approach, and she looked up to find Grant Masters striding across the patio towards her. In an open-necked shirt and Bermuda shorts, he looked more like a tourist than she did, and she wondered if Lincoln Korda had spoken to him before his dawn departure.

'Good morning,' she answered, putting down her coffee cup as he pulled out the chair beside her and lounged into it. 'It's a beautiful morning, isn't it?'

'That's why people like Florida,' he agreed, helping himself to some juice. 'Did you sleep well? You must have been exhausted.'

Sara didn't know how to answer him. 'I—er—I woke up around midnight,' she offered, giving him the opportunity to tell her he knew that, but he didn't. 'I'm sorry if I caused a problem. I—er—I didn't realise Mr Korda was here.'

'Link?' Masters gave her a swift look. 'How do you know Link was here? You didn't meet him—did you?'

Oh, lord! Now what? Sara moistened her lips. 'The—er—the maid said something about—about him leaving early this morning,' she mumbled, feeling the colour mount in her cheeks. For heaven's sake, why hadn't she just told him outright that she had mistaken Lincoln Korda for his son in the wheelchair? The wheelchair which, she saw with a hasty turn of her head, had disappeared this morning. 'Um—was I supposed to meet him?'

Grant Masters frowned. 'I wouldn't have thought so, but he did arrive here last night with that intention.'

'Last night?' Sara couldn't hide her astonishment, and Masters shrugged.

'A trip down here is no big deal to a man like Mr Korda,' he remarked, reaching for the coffee pot. 'I guess you're not used to someone flying over a thousand miles to see his son, and flying back the next morning, huh?'

'Not very,' admitted Sara wryly. Then, remembering the conversation she had had with him, she commented: 'He mustn't need a lot of sleep.'

'I guess he sleeps on the plane. It does have a bed.' And at her astounded expression: 'The plane belongs to Mr Korda, Sara. He doesn't have the time to use the scheduled service.'

'Oh! Oh, I see.' But it was a bit too much for her to take in. Private planes; private yachts; private *islands*: it made her wonder how she had had the nerve to stand up to him.

'So . . .' Masters buttered a croissant. 'Have you settled in? Are your rooms comfortable?'

'Very,' Sara assured him, glad to get on to firmer ground. 'I've never slept in a bed on a pedestal before!'

'And it's quite some view, isn't it?' Masters agreed. 'If I owned this place, I don't think I'd ever want to leave.'

'No.' Sara silently endorsed his words, content for the moment just to gaze at the ocean.

'Of course, it depends who you share it with,' Masters commented after a moment. Wiping his hands on a napkin, he gestured towards the house. 'I guess this place doesn't have too many happy associations for Link.'

Sara turned to look at him. 'No?' she ventured enquiringly, and consoled her conscience with the thought that the more she knew of the boy's background, the easier it would be to understand his personality.

'Mmm.' Masters seemed to be thinking. 'You see, the house and the island used to belong to Mrs Korda's parents.'

'I know.' And in explanation: 'Cora told me.'

'Ah.' He grimaced. 'Well, that's true. Link stepped in when Michelle's father got into financial difficulties. If he hadn't, the old man could have ended up in jail. He was an attorney. He used to handle wills, probate, that kind of thing. But he'd been defrauding his clients for years, setting up trusts in his own name, and using clients' funds to finance his fancy life style. He was facing an indictment for grand larceny when Link bailed him out. Don't ask me how he did it, because I don't know. Maybe he bought up the jury, or the judge—or both.' He grunted. 'All I know is, old man de Vere was allowed to live out his days here, on Orchid Key.'

Sara moistened her lips. 'He's dead now?'

'The old man? Yes. I guess he should never have married Michelle's mother. She's years younger than he was, and my guess is it was Mrs de Vere who spent all the money.'

She hesitated. 'Does she still live here?'

'Hell, no!' Masters snorted. 'Mrs de Vere's like her daughter. Orchid Key's too quiet for her.' He paused. 'She never comes here now.'

'Now even to see her grandson?' Sara frowned.

'Not even for that,' replied Master wryly. 'She married again some years ago, and I somehow think a nineteen-year-old grandson would cramp her style.'

Sara was amazed, but she kept her own counsel. She still had questions, of course, dozens of them, not least how Jeff came to have his accident, where he was living at the time, and if it was his choice to live at Orchid Key, or his father's. But they could wait. Right now, it was time to make the acquaintance of her charge.

Taking a deep breath, she said: 'Tell me about Jeff: where are his rooms? On the ground floor, I suppose, if he's confined to bed.'

'Jeff?' Grant Masters grimaced. 'No, Jeff's rooms aren't on the first floor—they're upstairs. There's a lift at the other end of the hall. I'll get Cora to show you around later, so you can find your way about without it being a problem.'

'Thank you.' But Sara had less interest in the house than its occupant. 'When can I see Jeff?'

Masters finished his coffee before replying. But then, putting aside his napkin, he made a careless gesture. 'Whenever you want, I guess. But there's no hurry.' His eyes moved speculatively over her shining hair and slim

figure. 'What say I show you over the island this morning?
We could swim and get some sun. You do swim, don't
you?'

'Oh, yes, I can swim,' Sara agreed diffidently. 'But I
think I ought to meet Jeff first, don't you? I mean, he is
the reason I'm here.'

He sighed, his expression hardening. 'If you like,' he
essayed, abruptly getting up from the table. 'Okay, let's go.
Right about now, Keating should be getting him his
breakfast. It's probably a good idea for you to meet him
while he's still comatose.'

Sara blinked. 'Comatose?'

'He needs barbiturates to sleep. How do you think he
got the pills to take an overdose?'

'Oh.' She felt hopelessly ignorant. Lincoln Korda was
right, she was naïve; and stupid.

Accompanying Grant Masters across the splendid hall
and along the carpeted corridor she had observed the
previous day, she tried again. 'Who is Keating?' she asked,
grasping at the name.

'Keating looks after the patient,' replied Masters rather
scathingly, and Sara couldn't decide whether his contempt
was for Keating or the boy. 'He's English, as a matter of
fact. He came over with Link in the sixties. He used to
work in the Manhattan apartment, but when Jeff was
injured, he took over here.'

'So he's a sort of valet?'

'Valet, nurse, cook, you name it, he can do it. Looking
after Jeff suits him just fine. Link never relied on him like
Jeff does.'

Sara looked at him cautiously. 'You don't like him.'

'It's that obvious, huh?'

'But why?'

'Keating's an old woman! He treats Jeff like he was
made of glass. You may find your job doubly difficult with
Keating looking over your shoulder. He won't welcome
someone who's going to try and take his patient away from
him.'

Sara swallowed a little convulsively as she stepped into
the wide lift—surely designed with an invalid's needs in
mind. At every turn she seemed to encounter some new

complication. Tony would have a lot to answer for when she finally got back to London.

The lift transported them up one floor—to the *second* floor, as Grant Masters described it. 'Wouldn't it be simpler if Jeff's apartments were on the ground floor?' she asked, as they rode up, and her companion bestowed her with a mocking smile.

'Much,' he agreed flatly. 'And if it were left to me, that's where they'd be.'

'Then why——?'

'Jeff doesn't want to be near the ocean. He doesn't want to hear the ocean, and he certainly doesn't want to see it. It reminds him that he's paralysed, that he'll never swim again. That's why he's shut away up here. That's why he nurses his neuroses in a darkened room.'

The lift doors slid back to reveal a similar corridor to the one Sara's rooms opened from. But this was the main corridor which led from the landing, and Grant Masters explained as they went that Jeff's rooms were at the far end.

'As far from his father as possible,' he intimated carelessly. 'You might as well hear it from me: Jeff and his father don't exactly hit it off.'

'Why not?' Sara couldn't prevent the question, and Grant Masters shrugged.

'You'll find out,' he responded annoyingly, halting before a pair of double doors. 'Well, here we are. Are you sure you're ready for this?'

CHAPTER FOUR

A WEEK later, Sara shifted her position on the sun-bed beside the pool, rolling on to her stomach and lifting her hair so that the single braid curled about her neck and shoulder, leaving her back exposed. She had already acquired a slight tan. Although her skin was fair, if she took care it didn't burn, and this past week she had had plenty of time to take all the care she needed.

Pressing her cheek against the fluffy texture of the towel she had spread over the cushions after her swim, Sara tried not to think about all the time she had wasted. It was eight days since Grant Masters had collected her from the pier at Cyprus Beach and brought her to the island; eight days, during which time she had swum and sunbathed, and allowed Grant—he had told her to call him that—to drive her all over Orchid Key.

But at no time during those eight days had she laid eyes on Jeff Korda. Every morning she had presented herself to his servant, Keating, and every morning he had told her that Mr Korda was not well, that he was sleeping, that he didn't want to see her. There was no way she could get past the officious little man, and although she would have liked to have disagreed with Grant, she had had to concede that Keating was impossible.

Of course, it was conceivable that Jeff had refused to see her. From what she had heard about him—and since she had spent so much time in Grant's company, it was quite considerable—he had been, and probably still was in Grant's opinion, a spoiled brat. He had apparently spent most of his time charging about the country in his high-speed sports car, and Grant said everyone had known it was only a matter of time before he smashed it—and himself—to pieces. He was a high-school drop-out, a typical under-achiever, with an intelligence quotient far higher than his grades would suggest. 'At least, that's what they say,' Grant had added bitingly. 'I'm more inclined to believe the kid's a psycho. I guess I don't have a lot of time for the poor-little-rich-kid syndrome!'

For her part, Sara was inclined to reserve judgement. It wasn't that she didn't *like* Grant exactly, but she was wary of him. He talked a lot, and she sometimes wondered if Lincoln Korda had left him here deliberately to keep an eye on her. He had confided that like Keating, he used to work in New York before Jeff's accident, but he wasn't grumbling about this extended vacation. All the same, she occasionally wished he wasn't *always* around to share her leisure. Sometimes she liked to be alone, as she was now, and she welcomed the fact that this morning he had gone over to the mainland, to mail some papers to his employer.

'Would you like a drink, Miss Fielding?'

The maid's familiar voice brought Sara up on her elbows, and then, grimacing, she dropped down again to fasten the bra top of her bikini. 'Oh—thanks, Vinnie,' she murmured, pushing her sunglasses up into her hair, and reaching for the frosted glass of iced tea from the maid's tray. 'Mmm, this is just what I needed! You must be a mind-reader.'

'It's a hot one, all right,' agreed Vinnie, gesturing at the day. 'It would be, just when we got extra work and all. Mr Keating, he must be real glad he chose today to go into Miami.'

Sara stiffened. 'Mr—Keating's away today?'

'Like I said, he's gone into Miami with Mr Masters.'

Sara shook her head, her mind racing. 'I didn't know.'

'No—well, how could you?' Vinnie shrugged her ample shoulders. 'Mr Keating doesn't take that many days off. I guess, left to himself, he wouldn't take any time off at all, and that would suit us just fine. But Mr Link, he insists that Mr Keating takes at least one day off every week—and this is it.'

Sara licked her lips. 'So—who is looking after Jeff?' she asked, affecting a casual tone.

'Well, Rosa's going to give him his lunch, I guess, and with a bit of luck, he'll sleep most of the afternoon. Mr

Keating'll be back around five. Whatever else, *he* insists on
settling the boy down for the night.'

Sara came up on her knees and pushed herself to her
feet. 'Er—perhaps I could help,' she ventured, trying not to
sound too eager. She knew the number of servants Lincoln
Korda kept in the house, and no way could any of them be
regarded as overworked. But it could work to her advantage
to let them think she thought they were. What a marvellous
opportunity! she thought, hardly daring to believe her luck.
Keating and Grant Masters both away! It was too good to
miss.

'Well . . .' Vinnie sounded uncertain now, 'perhaps you
ought to speak to Cora.'

'Yes, perhaps I ought,' murmured Sara softly. 'Okay.
Thanks, Vinnie. For—er—for the iced tea, I mean.'

The maid sauntered away and Sara snatched up her
cotton wrapper and slipped it over her shoulders. It matched
the all-over pattern of pink, lilac and white of her bikini,
and was an attractive foil for the honey-gold texture of her
skin. She was barefoot, and in spite of her weakness, she
strode swiftly into the house, her long legs moving lithely
as she made her way upstairs.

She had intended to go to her own rooms, and bathe and
dress before visiting Jeff's apartments. But at the head of
the stairs, where the corridors parted, her pace slowed. It
would be just her luck if Grant came back unexpectedly
early, maybe even bringing Keating with him. She doubted
Lincoln Korda could protest if Keating chose to spend his
leisure time on Orchid Key, and as it was so hot, it was a
definite possibility. Which left her in a quandary. What
should she do? Vinnie's suggestion that she should ask
Cora, she had silently vetoed. Cora would not want to take
responsibility for any change in Jeff's routine, and she
might get the older woman into trouble if she involved her
at all. Her best chance—her *only* chance—was to take the
initiative herself. And the sooner the better, before she
chickened out.

Jeff's rooms were not difficult to find. After passing the
lift she and Grant had used the previous week, she had all
the confirmation she needed, and swallowing her doubts,
she halted at his door. She knew that beyond these doors

was a comfortable sitting room—she had glimpsed it over Keating's shoulder on the numerous occasions she had attempted to reach Jeff—and beyond that was Jeff's bedroom, which she had never seen.

She knocked first. Her sense of bravado would not allow her to burst into his suite unannounced, but, as she had hoped, there was no response from within. Evidently it was too early yet for Rosa to bring him his lunch, and in Keating's absence, there was no one to guard the inner sanctum.

As she had expected, the sitting room was empty. Not even a magazine littered the cream satin cushions of the window seat, or disturbed the polished surface of the table, where Keating presumably took his meals. Silk-hung walls, a soft cashmere carpet underfoot, a high-backed sofa, with a striped Regency pattern: the room looked nothing like the kind of living quarters she would have expected a boy of nineteen to have. It was elegant, but impersonal; luxurious, but lacking in any character; that was what was wrong, there was no imprint of its occupant on this room. It was like a suite in a hotel, cooled by air-conditioning, all the windows tightly closed behind half-drawn Roman blinds.

As she picked her way across the silky carpet, Sara's toes curled appreciatively. But her nerves were taut and anxious, and when she reached the door which must lead into Jeff's room, her courage almost deserted her. What if she upset him by coming here? What if her intervention caused some irreparable damage? What did she know of the mental state of failed suicides? What if her bungling efforts precipitated a crisis?

Pushing thoughts like these to the back of her mind, she reached for the handle. What was the point of coming here, if she was going to think so negatively? She had to believe that she might have something new to offer. Hadn't Tony Korda told her that the doctors had tried every way to reach him? If she gave up now, what alternative did they have?

The bedroom was shadowy, the blinds here drawn almost totally, bathing the room in a milky light. The low buzz of the cooling system successfully drowned out any external sounds, and Sara felt astonished that anyone could live like this.

The bed was angled away from the door, and she was able to let herself into the room without its occupant being able to see her. But she had hardly taken a step before a harsh voice halted her, its resemblance to another voice she had heard only tempered by its lack of maturity.

'Who's there?' he demanded, and she heard him swear as he attempted to turn and see. 'If it's you, Rosa, you can get lost. I don't want anything to eat. I'm not hungry.'

'It's not Rosa,' said Sara abruptly, taking her courage in both hands, and moving swiftly around the bed so that he could see her. 'It's Sara. Sara Fielding.'

For what seemed a long moment—but which was probably only a few seconds—he gazed at her with a mixture of indignation and fury. For a heart-stopping space of time, his eyes—brilliant blue eyes, she noticed inconsequently—surveyed her with a crippling look of injustice, before dark, stubby lashes dropped to block their expression. 'You can get out, too,' he stated then, without emphasis, and rolling on to his side, he turned his head away from her.

Sara felt an overwhelming surge of compassion. She wasn't absolutely sure what she had expected, but after Grant Masters' description of his employer's son, she had been prepared to dislike Jeff Korda on sight. But somehow, the image of the spoiled selfish rich kid Grant had described was difficult to hold on to when she was faced with the reality of Jeff's condition. It was such a waste, she thought, her heart aching at the sight of the thin wrists poking from the sleeves of his silk pyjamas; such a tragedy that someone with undeniably attractive features and sun-bleached blond hair should have such lines ingrained in his face and such bitterness twisting his mouth.

'Jeff . . .'

She said his name almost involuntarily, and his eyes snapped open to gaze at her with dislike. 'I said get out!' he repeated harshly. 'If you don't understand polite English, I can use a coarser expression.'

Sara swallowed, but she stood her ground. 'I bet you can,' she remarked steadily. 'I know a few of those words myself. And I've used them on occasion—particularly when I don't get my own way.'

The epithet he used to describe his reaction to this amateur attempt to reason with him was both coarse and crude, and Sara knew a quite uncharacteristic desire to respond in kind. But it was a fleeting impulse, just as swiftly squashed, and she blamed herself for her ignorance in imagining that approach had not already been tried.

'Did—er—did Mr Keating tell you I was here?' she began again, hoping for more success this time. 'Your uncle—your uncle Tony, I mean, asked me to come. I live in London, you see, and just recently I had an accident too.'

It sounded patronising and it was, and inwardly Sara groaned. But it wasn't easy talking to someone who wouldn't even look at you, and when he resumed his position with his head turned away from her, she felt like giving up. Still, he hadn't ordered her to leave again, and taking courage from that small advantage, she moved a little further round the bed. Now, if he opened his eyes, he would be forced to look at her, and choosing her words carefully, she made another attempt.

'I was beginning to think you didn't really exist,' she ventured lightly. 'I've been here for over a week and I've tried to visit you every day, but Mr Keating always had an excuse why I couldn't. Either you were ill, or you were sleeping, or you—wouldn't see me——'

'Look, butt out, will you?' Jeff was abrupt and the term he used to endorse his words made Sara wince. 'Did nobody bother to tell you? I don't *have* visitors! I don't like them, and I don't need them. And if this is some idea my father's dreamed up to stimulate my interest, then tell him he's wasting his time. God, if he's had to stoop to buying up cheap talent to try and arouse my libido, he must be desperate!'

'That's not why I'm here!' Sara was horrified.

'No?'

'No.' She felt her spine stiffening in anger, and she had to force herself to remember who he was and why he was saying these things. Taking a deep breath, she said: 'My being here has nothing to do with your father. At least, only indirectly. I've told you, it was your uncle who asked me to come. He thought we might have something in common.'

'Really?' Jeff said contemptuously. 'Is that why you came here half naked? Is that why you're wearing nothing under that robe?'

'You——' Sara caught back the epithet that sprang to her lips. 'You're—mistaken.' Pulling the cord of her wrapper free, she allowed the two sides to part, revealing the bathing suit beneath. 'I was by the pool when Vinnie told me you were on your own, and I came straight up. I was afraid Mr Keating might arrive back from Miami at any moment, ready to re-establish his role as your watchdog!'

Jeff's mouth twisted. 'Well, you've seen me now, so you can go back to your sunbathing. And thanks for the offer, but no, thanks!'

Sara's fists clenched, but she was unable to prevent the automatic retaliation. 'You flatter yourself!' she declared, striding towards the door. 'I may be lame, but I'm not desperate. And I'd have to be to throw myself at a nasty-minded little prig like you!'

'You can't talk to me like that!' he exclaimed furiously.

'Can't I?' Sara halted in the doorway. 'I just have.' Ignoring the hollow feeling in her stomach, she lifted a careless shoulder. 'Sorry if I've scraped a nerve, but you shouldn't think you've cornered the market on self-pity!'

She heard his angry use of her name as she stalked across the sitting room, and again as she let herself out of the suite; but she didn't go back. Her indignation carried her all the way to her bedroom, and by then it was much too late to have second thoughts.

Sara went down for dinner that evening with some reluctance. She invariably shared the meal with Grant Masters, in the small primrose yellow dining room that overlooked the ocean at the back of the house, and she was not looking forward to having to tell him of her abortive exchange with Jeff.

She had thought about what she should do during the long afternoon hours, when it had been too hot to go outside and she had been compelled to remain in her room.

In the normal way, she didn't mind her own company. But not today. Today, she had the memory of that awful scene on her conscience, and no matter how she tried, she couldn't justify her behaviour. It was all very well telling herself that everything Grant had said about him was true, that he was morose and mean-spirited, and his attitude did not encourage sympathy. But nothing could excuse her own appalling lack of self-control, or defend the urge to use his weakness against him.

However, Grant was not waiting for her this evening as she had expected. The table was laid for two, as it usually was, but he had not yet put in an appearance, and Sara felt an unwelcome twinge of apprehension, which she swiftly put away.

Crossing her arms across her body, she cupped her elbows in her hands and walked to the long windows. The palest of yellow curtains framed a view of the terrace, with a low stone wall edging a sloping garden bright with trailing rock plants. It was getting dark, and the ocean looked grey instead of blue—a reflection of her mood, she thought disconsolately, wondering if Lincoln Korda would come to dismiss her or if he would leave that to his assistant.

The sound of brisk footsteps in the hall brought her about face, but whoever it was did not approach the dining room. Instead, she heard low voices, a muffled conversation, and then their passage on the stairs as whoever had arrived made their way upward.

Frowning slightly, Sara started towards the door, only to halt uncertainly as Vinnie appeared in the entrance. The woman was carrying a tray, which she set down efficiently on a marble-topped side table, then gestured Sara to her seat, placing a juicy slice of fresh fruit in front of her.

'There you are,' she said, straightening, and moved to take another dish from the tray. 'Melon, baked snapper, and I've got a mess of home-made ice-cream cooling in the freezer. You want me to pour the wine?'

'No, I can manage, thank you.' Sara didn't immediately sit down, but regarded Vinnie withh some misgivings. 'I—er—isn't Mr Masters back from Miami?'

'Heck, yes.' Vinnie picked up the tray. 'He was back

about five o'clock.' She walked towards the door. 'You got everything you want now?'

Sara put out her hand to stop her. 'Isn't—isn't Mr Masters joining me?'

'Not right now, Miss Fielding.' Vinnie looked as if she would have preferred not to be asked. 'Enjoy your meal. I'll be back later with——'

'Why isn't he joining me?' asked Sara urgently, suddenly convinced there had to be a reason. 'Is something wrong?'

'You don't know?' Vinnie sounded sceptical, and Sara stared at her.

'No. How could I?'

'I thought you might,' Vinnie shrugged. 'It's Jeff—he's got a fever.'

'A fever!' Sara's mouth felt dry. 'Is it serious?'

'It could be.' Vinnie was regarding her with wary eyes, and Sara wondered what she was thinking. Did the woman know she had gone to Jeff's apartments that morning? Or did she only suspect?

Swallowing, Sara endeavoured to speak casually. 'Is Mr Masters with him?'

'Mr Masters and the doctor both,' agreed Vinnie tautly. 'Fevers can be dangerous for a boy in Jeff's condition. Maybe they'll take him into the hospital. Maybe they won't.'

Sara nodded. 'I'm sorry.'

'Yes, so'm I,' returned Vinnie obliquely, and walked away before Sara could ask her what she meant.

Needless to say, Sara did not enjoy her meal. She tasted the melon, but the fish—a speciality of the area—returned to the kitchen untouched. She was too tense to eat, too anxious to think about anything but the boy upstairs possibly fighting for his life. She did drink some wine, two glasses of the chilled white Chablis that was no doubt delectable, but which she scarcely tasted, except as a texture on her tongue. For the first time in her life, she felt completely helpless, and more than a little apprehensive of Lincoln Korda's reaction when he discovered she was to blame for the deterioration in his son's condition.

Not that he could blame her any more than she blamed herself, she thought unhappily. Dear God, why had she taken the liberty of interfering in matters of which she was so ignorant? Why hadn't she simply continued to enjoy her unaccustomed freedom, as anyone else would have done when provided with such idyllic surroundings?

Refusing the ice cream Vinnie produced for a dessert, Sara made another attempt to find out what was going on. 'Has—er—has this happened before?' she asked the servant. 'I mean, have you heard what's going on? Are they moving the patient to hospital?

'I guess Mr Masters will tell you, when he comes down,' replied Vinnie non-committally. 'You want your coffee here or on the terrace? Or I can bring it to your room, if you'd rather.'

Sara sighed. 'Forget the coffee,' she said wearily, getting to her feet. 'I'll be outside, if Mr Masters wants to see me. Will you tell him that?'

She was sitting on the sun-bed, rocking it gently to and fro, when she heard a car departing. The doctor, she assumed, her nerves tightening, and as if to confirm her suspicions, a few moments later Grant came strolling across the terrace towards her. After dark, the area around the pool was lit by Japanese lanterns and Grant, in dark trousers and an open-necked shirt, was clearly visible as he made his way towards her. He seemed strained, she thought, his usual complacency replaced by a look of gravity, and her heart sank even lower at the prospect of what he had to tell her.

But he didn't initially tell her anything. Instead, he cast an admiring gaze over the simple elegance of the white silk shirt and matching pants she was wearing, and touched her cheek with a careless hand.

'You're getting quite a tan,' he remarked, subsiding on to the couch beside her. 'I envied you today. The air in Miami was like a blast from a furnace!'

Sara allowed her breath to escape in a rush. 'How is he?' she asked, not prepared to play a waiting game. 'Vinnie said Jeff has a fever. Is it true? Is he going to be all right?'

Grant hooked his elbows over the back of the couch and regarded her tolerantly. 'Look,' he said, 'I've just spent two hours with Doc Haswell and Alan Keating debating that very issue. Do you think you could give me a break?'

Sara swallowed. 'Surely you can tell me if he's going to survive?'

'*Survive!*' Grant uttered a disbelieving snort. 'What are you talking about? There's never been a question of him not surviving! It's only a raise in temperature; not a life-or-death crisis!'

Sara felt weak. 'But Vinnie said——'

'Yes? What did Vinnie say? Did she tell you Jeff was in a critical condition?'

'No. No, not exactly . . .' Sara felt foolish, and Grant pulled a wry face.

'I guess you overreacted, eh?' he remarked, allowing the arm closest to her to descend along the seat at her back. 'He'll be okay. I just wish I knew what precipitated the attack in the first place.'

Her tongue circled her upper lip. 'You don't know?'

'No.' Grant shook his head, and she had the feeling he was more interested in the wisps of hair escaping from her braid than in his charge's health. 'So tell me: what have you been doing all day?'

Sara baulked. 'This and that.' Then, unable to leave the subject, she added: 'What did Doctor Haswell say? Is Jeff conscious?'

'Aw, come on . . .' groaned Grant, his breath whistling warm against the curve of her neck. 'Can we leave that subject alone?' And then, at the determination in her face, he conceded: 'The doctor says it's probably a chill, brought on by the cooling system they have up there. And what do you mean—is Jeff conscious? Why wouldn't he be?'

She took a deep breath. 'Well, didn't he say anything?'

He grimaced. 'I've told you, Jeff doesn't communicate. At least, not often. And certainly not in any way that could be construed as helpful. Now, can we leave it?'

Sara's shoulders sagged. Jeff hadn't reported her visit to his room! The mental torment she had been putting herself through had all been for nothing. For reasons best known to himself, Jeff had apparently said nothing about their conversation, and if that was the reason for his sudden relapse, they were the only ones who knew it.

'Hey . . .' Grant tugged gently at her braid, and she turned dazed eyes in his direction. 'Did you miss me at dinner? Vinnie said you didn't eat much. You're not sickening for something, are you?'

'Oh—no.' She dislodged his hand from her hair and stood up. The last thing she needed was that kind of complication. 'I—was worried.'

'About the kid?' Grant's lips thinned. 'You know something? You're getting to be like the rest of the folks around here. You think the world revolves around Jeff Korda. Well, it doesn't. Believe me, it doesn't. God, you don't even know him!'

Sara took a breath. Now was her opportunity. Now was her chance to confess that she did know him, or at least that she had met him. But she didn't. Something, some cowardly impulse, she suspected, kept her silent, and Grant scuffed his foot against the flags and set the couch swinging.

'Anyway,' he cast her a belittling glance, 'have you decided what you're going to tell Link when he arrives? I mean, he might think you're not making much of an effort to fulfil your purpose in coming here. Oh, I mean, *we* all sympathise with your predicament. Link might not.'

His tone was mocking, but Sara was more concerned with what he was saying. 'Mr Korda—is coming here? When?'

'When he can find the time,' Grant shrugged indifferently. 'The weekend, maybe. Haswell insisted on phoning him. My guess is he'll be here Friday night. You haven't met him yet, have you? I bet you wish it could have been under happier circumstances.'

Friday! Two days yet! Sara breathed more easily. Surely Jeff would have recovered by Friday.

Now she smoothed her damp palms down her thighs and lifted her shoulders. 'Well,' she said, endeavouring to sound casual, 'I'm tired. Would you mind if I went to bed? Thank you for telling me about Jeff. I'm really glad to hear it's nothing serious.'

Grant frowned. 'Yes, you are, aren't you?' he remarked, suddenly thoughtful, and she felt her colour rising.

'Goodnight,' she said, not responding to the latent query in his voice, and hoped like mad that her hasty exit would not arouse any more suspicions.

CHAPTER FIVE

The following morning Grant appeared to have forgotten his irritation of the night before. 'Why don't we go sailing?' he suggested, joining Sara as she was eating her breakfast on the terrace. 'There's nothing spoiling here. Cora can handle any calls, and Jeff is hardly likely to send for you today, is he?'

'Oh, but——' Sara wetted her lips, 'I think I should stay around—just in case.'

'In case of what?' Grant said dismissively. 'Keating's not going to let you near the kid today. He's fussing like a mother hen!'

'You've seen him? Jeff, I mean?'

Grant's expression cooled. 'And if I have?'

'Well, how is he?'

He moved his shoulders in a careless gesture. 'How is he ever?' And then, with resignation: 'His temperature's down. Almost normal, in fact. Whatever it was, he's gotten over it.'

'Thank goodness!' Sara was fervent, and he looked at her curiously.

'For someone who's never even met the kid, you seem pretty concerned,' he observed drily. 'Anyone would think you were to blame for what happened.'

Sara looked down into her cup. 'Perhaps I am,' she ventured, the urge to confess overcoming discretion, but Grant did not allow her to finish.

'Look,' he said, 'no one expects miracles, least of all me. What you need—what we both need—is to get away from this place for a couple of hours. We could ask Cora to make us a picnic lunch and have it on the boat. Sun, sea, and—isolation.'

It was doubtful whether Sara would have agreed. The

sun and the sea were attractive enough, as was the yacht,
but the isolation was something else. It wasn't that she
didn't trust Grant exactly, but she did have the feeling that
he thought, because of her background, that she was more
experienced than she was. And fending off his advances
was not going to make her job any easier. If indeed she
had a job after Friday.

But to her relief, she did not have to make the choice.
While she was struggling to answer him, he was called to
the phone, and when he came back his expression said it
all.

'I guess we'll have to take a rain check on that trip,' he
remarked gloomily. 'That was a call from Link's bankers in
Miami. There's some complication with the figures I gave
them yesterday. I've got to go see them this morning, so
we'll have to go sailing some other time.'

'Oh.' Sara tried to hide her relief. 'Well, never mind. I
have a letter I should write anyway.'

Grant frowned. 'To your family?'

'I don't have any family,' she admitted ruefully. 'Except
for an uncle in Leamington.' And at his blank expression,
she elaborated: 'That's in Warwickshire, about a hundred
miles north-west of London.'

'I see.' Grant's brows arched. 'You've got a boy-friend,
then.'

Sara was tempted to say yes, and thus alleviate the
problem she suspected she might have with Grant, but she
didn't. Lying did not come naturally to her, and besides,
she felt he would make a better friend than an enemy.

'I have—male friends, yes,' she conceded. 'But not a
boy-friend, as such. In any case, I was going to write to
Vicki. She's the girl I share a flat with.'

Grant seemed satisfied with her answer, and after he had
gone Sara took up her usual position by the pool. After
smoothing a protective cream over the exposed places of
her bikini-clad body, she determinedly turned her attention
to the writing pad and ballpoint pen in her hands, but it
was surprisingly difficult to think of how to begin. Bearing
in mind that whatever she wrote to Vicki would doubtless
find its way to Tony Korda eventually, she could hardly
confide her anxieties to her friend, and without that freedom

she was in a cleft stick. Should she lie and say that she
hadn't as yet communicated with the patient and risk
Tony's frustration? Or should she simply avoid all mention
of the reason why she was here? Both alternatives seemed
equally unsatisfactory, and she half-wished she hadn't felt
the need to identify her correspondent to Grant.

The sun was hot, and after an abortive half hour, she
laid the pad aside and gave herself up to supine lassitude.
The letter to Vicki would have to wait until she had some
positive news to tell her. Right now, she had to decide
what her next move was going to be.

The morning slipped away. Sara grew too hot lying on
her back and rolled on to her stomach, loosening the bra of
her swimsuit so that the straps did not mark her tan. She
was sweating freely, her whole body bathed in heat, her
brain numbed and listless. It was too hot to think; it was
almost too hot to breathe; the only sounds the distant ones
of ocean, birds, and aircraft, making for the international
airport at Miami . . .

She suspected she must have fallen asleep for a few
moments. After the upheaval of Jeff's sudden relapse—and
her part in it—she had slept badly the night before, and it
was hardly surprising that she should have lost consciousness
for a short time. It was not something she had done before,
always conscious of the dangers of over-exposure to the hot
Florida sun, but when she opened her eyes and found
herself in the shade of a huge beach umbrella, she could
think of no other explanation. She struggled up, clutching
the shreds of her bra to her chest, only to find the terrace
was deserted. Whoever had shifted the umbrella had gone,
and she blinked somewhat resentfully at the thought of
someone watching her as she slept. It must have been
Grant, she decided tautly, fastening the straps of her bikini.
Thank goodness she hadn't written anything incriminating
in her letter. Her 'Dear Vicki' was all that marred the
naked page.

It was the unexpected splash of water that alerted her to
someone's occupancy of the pool behind her. Of course,
she thought, impatiently, turning her head to see a dark
shadow gliding beneath the surface of the water, Grant
wouldn't have been able to resist a cooling dip after his trip

to Miami. It must be later than she thought. For heaven's sake, why hadn't Vinnie awakened her?

The emergence of a dark head sent all her preconceptions spinning. *Jeff!* she thought incredulously. Jeff had actually left his bed to swim in the pool! How fantastic! Scrambling to her feet, she hurried to the poolside, blinking back the sunspots that dazzled her eyes. Was this her doing? she wondered excitedly. Had their argument forced the breakthrough his doctors had been striving for? She couldn't wait to ask him. She couldn't wait to find out.

Squatting on her haunches, she opened her mouth to voice her enthusiasm—and then closed it again. Feeling somewhat foolish, and not for the first time, she rose uncertainly to her feet again, suddenly—and embarrassingly—conscious of her near-nudity. For it was not Jeff Korda who was reaching up to pull himself out of the pool; not a boy, who pressed his hands down on the tiled surround and levered his long lean body out of the water. It was Jeff's father, Lincoln Korda, who rose like an avenging god beside her, his dark muscled body barely clothed in a pair of wet-clinging shorts.

'You don't learn, do you, Miss Fielding?' he greeted her without warmth, reaching for the towel she now saw he had left on the arm of a cushioned lounger. 'Don't tell me—you thought I was my son again. Now why would you make that mistake? Is Jeff in the habit of coming down here to swim?'

Sara drew a steadying breath. 'You know he's not.'

'Do I?' Lincoln Korda raised one eyebrow. 'But I understood you were here to effect a sea-change. Isn't that what you told me the last time we spoke together?'

She took a deep breath. 'Are you saying you're not satisfied with—with my being here?'

There was silence for what seemed an inordinate length of time, and then Lincoln Korda dropped the towel he had been using on to the tiles at his feet and regarded her critically. 'I'm glad you didn't say—with developments,' he remarked sardonically. 'I'm told you haven't spoken to my son since you took up residence, and while I can appreciate your reluctance to abandon your present surroundings, this is not a charitable institution, Miss Fielding.'

Sara's face burned. 'I never thought it was.'

'No?' His eyes dropped insolently over her scantily-clad figure. 'So why do you spend your days improving your tan instead of attempting to justify your position?'

Sara had never felt so humiliated. It might have been less painful if she had been fully clothed; as it was, she could hardly deny his accusation when the truth of it was there for him to see.

'I've tried,' she said at last, endeavouring to ignore the ignominy of her appearance. 'But Mr Keating always has an excuse why your son should not be disturbed. Ask him. He can hardly deny it.'

'You're putting the blame on Keating, then.'

'Not exactly.' She pursed her lips. 'But if I can't get to see Jeff, how am I supposed to help him?'

'A good question.' Lincoln Korda's lips twisted grudgingly. 'Keating is an old woman, and I imagine he does guard his position jealously. But surely someone with as much ingenuity as you led me to believe you had could have found a way to circumvent his authority—if you'd tried.'

Sara held up her head. 'Is this your way of telling me I'm fired?'

'Have I said so?'

She held on to her crumbling dignity with an effort. 'You didn't need to.'

'Why?' He shrugged. 'Because I stated the obvious?' Giving her a sidelong look, he lowered his weight on to one of the cushioned lounges and stretched his length upon it. 'You can hardly deny it, you don't look as if you're earning your keep, do you?'

'Perhaps not.' She quivered. 'So—do you want me to leave?'

'How you do persist in that! Do you want to leave?'

'I didn't say that.'

'So . . .' He gave her a wry glance. 'Suppose you tell me why you think my son suddenly developed this fever.'

Sara moistened her lips. 'How would I know?'

'That's not an answer.' He ran an exploring hand across his midriff. 'Surely you must have a theory, at least.'

Her knees felt decidedly unsteady now, and reaching for her cotton wrapper, she took some time over putting it on.

But her mind was racing. She didn't like this turn in the conversation, and while logic told her that if Jeff hadn't confided in either Grant or Mr Keating, or the doctor, he was unlikely to have confided in his father, she still felt uncertain. Grant had said that Jeff and this man didn't get on, yet Lincoln Korda had again flown over a thousand miles just to assure himself of his son's welfare. That was not the action of an indifferent father.

Choosing her words with care, she said: 'Doctor Haswell said it might have been caused by the air-conditioning.'

'Did he?' Lincoln Korda shifted a little impatiently, she felt.

'And—and Grant agreed with him.'

'How convenient!'

Sara sighed. 'Mr Korda, what do you want from me? I'm not a doctor; I'm not even a nurse! What earthly use is my opinion to you?'

There was silence for a few pregnant moments, and then Lincoln Korda looked up at her, his eyes glacial. 'Perhaps I'm waiting for the truth, *Miss* Fielding,' he told her harshly. 'Perhaps I'm waiting for you to admit that you may have been responsible for Jeff's rise in temperature. You did go to see him, didn't you? Yesterday some time.'

Sara thought of denying it. Unless Jeff had told his father, he could have no proof. But the relief was so great, she barely hesitated before asking quietly: 'How did you find out?'

Lincoln Korda swung his legs off the chair and got to his feet again before saying roughly: 'It wasn't difficult. Only the kind of upheaval caused by a deviation in his routine would have affected his condition, and as soon as I learned Keating had been away for the day, I guessed what must have happened.'

She gazed at him, a feeling of outrage stirring at the calculating way he had allowed her to incriminate herself. But it wasn't easy fuelling her abused senses in the present situation. His proximity disturbed her, the whole aggressive length of him, taut with anger and contempt, evoked completely different feelings inside her. She couldn't remember any man ever having such a devastating effect on her before, and although she knew it was crazy, she was becoming emotionally aroused. It was resentment, she told herself fiercely, fighting her awareness of his maleness with something akin to desperation. Lincoln Korda was old enough to be her father, for heaven's sake, and he was making no secret of the fact that he despised her. His expression said it all, and just because the circumstances of this exchange were unusual, it was no less unpleasant because of it.

'I'm sorry,' she said at last, avoiding his gaze, hoping he would accept her apology—however grudgingly given—and that would be the end of it. But of course, it wasn't.

'What happened?' he demanded. 'What did you say to him? None of your homespun philosophy, I trust. He's not a fool, and he's had enough psycho-analysing to last him a lifetime!'

Sara took a breath. 'Why should I tell you what happened?' she returned, stung by his attitude. 'Can't you guess? You seem to have anticipated everything else!'

Lincoln Korda's mouth compressed. 'You want me to fire you, is that it?' he enquired scathingly. 'Of course; that way you can go home to brother Antony and tell him *I* threw *you* out!'

'No——' Sara spoke involuntarily, then bit her lip when she realised the impulse had cost her a possible means of escape.

'No?' Dark brows descended over eyes that mirrored a scornful incredulity. 'You mean you want to go on? Why? Did I miss something?'

'No.' Sara shook her head, but now her eyes were caught and held by the interrogative depths of his. 'Oh, you might as well hear it. He—I—we—we quarrelled. Jeff was rude, and I lost my temper. Now are you satisfied? Your misgivings have all been justified.'

Lincoln Korda frowned. 'You—lost your temper?' he echoed, and then the glimmer of something which might have been humour, but which Sara was sure could not be, briefly softened his gaze.

'Yes, I lost my temper,' she confirmed tensely, wrapping her arms about herself, as if to ward off the effects of his disturbing appraisal. 'I know it was wrong. I know I behaved badly. But so did he. He was—he was insulting——'

'My God!' To her astonishment, Lincoln Korda sounded almost relieved. Releasing her from his belittling inspection, he turned away to gaze somewhat ruefully across the rippling expanse of the pool, only swinging back to face her when she had had the time to recover her equilibrium. 'I knew it,' he said, running an impatient hand along the back of his neck and allowing it to rest there. His action caused the slipping waistband of his damp shorts to expose the arrowing of dark hair on his flat stomach, but he seemed unaware of it. 'My instincts were right. I admit, I wasn't enthusiastic about your coming here, but losing your temper, treating him like a normal human being, may be exactly the kind of treatment Jeff needs. You shook him out of his apathy. You proved it can be done. That hasn't happened before.'

She frowned. 'But his fever . . .'

'Probably psychosomatic. He was upset; frustrated, if you like, over something you said—or did. In his condition, any kind of stress, mental or physical, is enough to send his temperature soaring. When Grant rang and told me what had happened, I wondered if you could be involved. But when I asked you and you denied it, I guess I lost *my* cool. What can I say? I'm sorry.'

Sara moistened her lips. 'It doesn't matter.'

'It does.' He moved to close the gap between them, his expression softening. 'Look, maybe I have been a little hard on you. I've hurt your feelings, right? Hell, when you know me better you'll learn that if I'm wrong, I'm the first to admit it.'

If she had not been so aware of him and his nearness, she might have taken his apology at face value, and thus avoided any further exchange between them. But her expression revealed her uncertainty, and as if to reinforce his argument, Lincoln Korda put a reassuring hand on her shoulder. At his touch, she panicked, jerking back from him with more urgency than good sense, forcing herself to come down heavily on her injured right foot. The pain that shot through her ankle caused her to lose her balance, and she was teetering near the edge of the pool when he saved her. Using both hands this time, he hauled her back from the brink, and in the clumsy struggle that followed, Sara felt the muscled hardness of his body braced against her.

'Are you crazy?' he grated, as she pushed against him, and as he released her abruptly, his hands fell loosely to his sides.

Sara, endeavouring to accomplish the twin tasks of tightening the belt of her wrapper and calming her scattered senses, did not answer him, and balling his fists, he added harshly: 'Just what was that all about?'

She forced herself to look past him. 'I—I have a weak ankle, as you know,' she replied hastily, realising he had been unaware of her reactions. 'I—er—I slipped. You startled me.'

Lincoln's mouth compressed. 'And this all came about because I laid a hand on you.'

'You startled me,' she insisted feebly. 'I told you——'

'I know what you've just said,' he conceded bleakly. 'But you didn't slip. At least, not until I touched you. For pity's sake, you didn't think I was making a pass, did you?'

'No——' Sara was dismayed at his ability to interpret situations. 'Why would I?'

'Why indeed?' he agreed, watching the colour deepen in her cheeks. 'But you did think that, didn't you? You actually believed I might find you irresistibly attractive.'

'No,' she said again, convinced now she had undone all the good she had done herself by admitting her involvement with Jeff, and as if to confirm that fact, Lincoln swore.

'For God's sake,' he demanded. 'What do you take me for?'

Sara shook her head. How could she tell him how it really was? How could she admit that far from wanting to reject his overture, she had been afraid of showing how she really felt? It was her own unwilling attraction to him which had precipitated that involuntary withdrawal, and she was still trying to come to terms with a situation she had never expected.

'I'm sorry,' she said now, struggling to retrieve her nerve. 'Whether—whether you believe it or not, it wasn't how you think.' That, at least, was true.

Lincoln's nostrils flared. 'Really?' Clearly he didn't believe her. 'I suppose, then, there's no need for me to point out to you that I'm a married man.'

Sara held up her head. 'None at all.'

'Good.'

With a gesture of impatience, he snatched up his towel and

strode away towards the house. He was angry, and she knew it, and she could only hope that by behaving so foolishly she had not jeopardised her position. So much for capitalising on his approval, she reflected bitterly. Instead of using his approval of her encounter with his son to her advantage, she had probably alienated any confidence he might have had in her. And made a fool of herself into the bargain.

Closing her eyes for a moment, she allowed the whole scene to replay, in all its embarrassing detail, behind her lids. He *had* only been trying to save her from falling into the pool, and it wasn't his fault that the involuntary contact with his lean body had had such a sensual effect on her. She didn't know what was the matter with her. It wasn't as if she was completely ignorant of the opposite sex. She had had some experience; but she had probably convinced him she was one of those awful females who saw promiscuity in every innocent gesture.

While she was showering and changing for lunch, she was plagued with the suspicion that she had probably made her position here untenable. What man in his right mind would want some raging feminist associating with his son, and if he ever suspected her real feelings, any success she might have had with Jeff would count for little. His announcement that he was a married man was no more reassuring. Unless Vicki had made a mistake, and he and his wife were still living together, it was just another way of proving he wasn't interested.

Choosing what to wear posed something of a problem. She usually wore tee-shirts and shorts, when she wasn't wearing her swimsuit, and she had lost much of her self-consciousness over her lameness. But today she felt obliged to dress a little more formally, and eventually she put on a pair of loose cotton pants and a man's navy silk shirt. She turned the cuffs back to the elbows and filled the open collar with a chunky gold necklace. Then, with thick gold rings swinging from her ears, she felt more ready to face whatever decision Lincoln Korda might have come to, and for once she hoped Grant would be there to ease the situation.

In fact, it was Grant, and only Grant, who awaited her in the primrose dining room. The long windows were open to the terrace outside, and he turned from his surveillance of the

sun-drenched patio when he heard her nervous footsteps.
Immediately, his expression changed to take in her efforts at
sophistication, and his lips twisted in wry approval.

'Very nice,' he applauded, leaving the window to come and
meet her. 'But not for my benefit, unless I'm very much
mistaken.'

Sara controlled her colour with an effort. 'Well,' she
defended herself swiftly, 'Mr Korda is my employer. Um—
where is he? Isn't he joining us?'

'No,' Grant said bluntly. 'As a matter of fact, Link's taking
lunch with Jeff. Or at least, in his apartments. You can never
anticipate Jeff's mood.'

'I see.' Sara didn't know if she was disappointed or relieved.

'I guess you're pretty peeved, eh?' commented Grant,
pulling out her chair and assisting her into it. 'You've not met
the great man yet, have you? Who told you he'd arrived?'

'As a matter of fact, I did meet him earlier,' she admitted,
realising it would be foolish to prevaricate. 'I—er—I was
sunbathing by the pool when he—joined me. It was quite a
shock. I never imagined he'd appear so—unexpectedly.'

'Nor did I,' averred Grant shortly, taking the chair at right
angles to hers. 'It's not like Link to neglect his empire in
favour of his family. So—what did you think of him?'

She looked down at the colourful slices of melon, pineapple
and grapefruit on her plate, choosing her words with care.
'He—he seems very nice,' she murmured, picking up her
fork. 'Hmm, this fruit is chilled. How delicious!'

'But what did he say to you?' exclaimed Grant, not
prepared to be sidetracked. 'Didn't he ask about Jeff? Did
you tell him you hadn't seen him yet?'

'We discussed Jeff, of course.' Sara had no wish to get into
an argument over her conversation with Lincoln Korda. 'I—
er—perhaps that's why he's having lunch with his son. Maybe
he's trying to persuade Mr Keating to be a little more—co-
operative.'

'Link doesn't persuade; he *tells*,' averred Grant drily.
'Besides, he and Keating have a special kind of relationship.
They've known each other a lot of years. In any case, Jeff's
unlikely to go along with any *suggestion* his father might
make.'

Sara put down her fork. 'So why doesn't Mrs Korda take a

hand? I've been here almost two weeks, and she hasn't even telephoned to ask how Jeff is, has she?'

He shrugged. 'Michelle's no good with sick people. Besides, I doubt if Link knows where she is. She took off for Tahiti about ten weeks ago, and nobody's heard from her since. Nobody here, that is.'

Sara stared at him. 'You mean—she didn't even tell her husband where she was going?'

'Link?' Grant gave her an old-fashioned look. 'Didn't his brother tell you? Link and Michelle don't live together. They've been separated for—oh, I don't know exactly—ten, maybe twelve, years.'

'They have?' Her stomach contracted. So Lincoln had been lying after all. 'I wasn't sure.'

'Oh, yes.' Grant was expansive. 'That's why Jeff's such an objectionable little bastard! Michelle brought him up. He lived with her until he had the crash. Then, of course, she couldn't wait to be rid of him. Michelle doesn't like responsibilities of that kind. Who knows?' He grimaced. 'Maybe I'd be pretty messed up if I'd had Jeff's kind of upbringing.'

Sara hesitated. 'But didn't Mr Korda—I mean, well, surely he must have seen his son during that time; spent some time with him? Even if the boy was living with his mother, that's no reason why his father——'

He shrugged. 'Don't ask me. All I know is, Link kept out of the way while Jeff was growing up. I guess that's why Jeff hates him.'

'Jeff hates his father?' She was appalled.

'Yeah. Cosy little household, isn't it?' remarked Grant sardonically, and Sara was glad of Rosa's intervention with their next course to give herself time to absorb this latest development.

'Hmm, pita salad—my favourite!' added Grant, exchanging his usual banter with the dark-skinned serving girl as she produced two bowls, lined with shells of pita bread and filled with shredded lettuce and cheese. He broke off a square of the crisp shell and munched enthusiastically. 'You must have read my mind.'

'It's just as well I can't,' retorted Rosa, setting dishes of various sauces on the table. 'Now, if there's anything else you want, you're gonna have to call.'

He grinned. 'What would we do without you?' he teased, loosening the tie of her apron, and Rosa tossed her head as she sauntered out of the room.

The salad nestling in its edible casing looked very appetising, but Sara's thoughts were not occupied with food. She was still thinking about Lincoln Korda, and his wife, and wondering why a man who was concerned enough about his son to abandon his business affairs and fly down here to see him just because his temperature had taken a rise should have neglected the boy for the better part of his life.

'Aren't you hungry?' Grant asked now, realising she was just staring at the food. 'Don't worry, Link will work it out. He knows what Jeff's like. He doesn't expect miracles.'

'Doesn't he?' Sara turned her attention to the salad with some determination. It was no wonder Tony's story had been so vague. No matter what he had said, nothing could have prepared her for this strange household, or the disturbing personality of her employer.

CHAPTER SIX

SOMETIMES, in the early evening, Sara took a dip in the ocean. The water was warmer at that time of day than at any other, and it was extremely pleasant to feel the faintly abrasive movement of salt water against her limbs. In addition to which, after a day of applying screening creams to her skin, it provided an excellent way of removing oil from her body, and a shower afterwards left her feeling distinctly cleaner and fresher.

So far as she knew, no one was aware of her nightly exertions. It was at this time that Grant usually telephoned his employer in New York, and Keating and the other members of the staff were employed about their own duties. In consequence, it was a period Sara guarded gratefully, a brief spell in the day when she could be completely herself.

This particular day was no exception. Indeed, after an afternoon spent waiting for Lincoln Korda's summons—which incidentally never came—she was all the more eager to shed her problems and immerse her overheated flesh in the cool water. She had kept out of the sun all day since his arrival, but the pants and shirt she had been wearing had become unbearably hot. She was glad to leave them, with her towel, on the beach.

The pull of the tide was strong this evening, the undertow almost sweeping her off her feet as she waded into the water. She could imagine how rough it must be out in mid-Atlantic, and she marvelled at the comparatively gentle swell that surged about her thighs.

She dipped down once to wet her shoulders, and then dived fearlessly into the waves. The sudden chill almost took her breath away, but it was marvellously invigorating,

and as the tension eased from her body she realised that
since Lincoln Korda's arrival, she hadn't been able to relax.

She was a strong swimmer, due in no small part to her
professional training. She had always had slim, yet strong,
legs, and in the water the weakness in her ankle didn't
matter. Glad to expunge the frustration that had been with
her all afternoon, she swam purposefully out from the
shore, turning on to her back to rest only when she was
satisfied she was unlikely to be observed.

What a day it had been! she reflected broodingly,
wondering what was going to happen now. Grant had little
confidence in her, Jeff didn't like her, and Lincoln Korda
didn't trust her—so what point was there in staying? And
why, when since she came here she had felt such a fraud,
did the prospect of returning to England no longer have
such appeal?

She sighed, refusing to associate her sudden restlessness
with Lincoln Korda's appearance. He was a disruptive
influence, it was true, but she must not allow him to upset
her. She had already made a fool of herself at least twice in
his presence, and if she truly wanted to help Jeff, she had
to forget all about his father.

Nevertheless, she couldn't help thinking about what
Grant had said about Michelle Korda. What kind of woman
was she, to abandon her son just when he needed her
most? No wonder Jeff was so bitter, if he had been left
with his father, just because there was no one else willing
to care for him.

Noticing that the sea around her was getting choppy, she
abandoned her cogitations, and started back for the shore.
She could drown out here without anyone being the wiser,
she mused a little self-pityingly, ignoring the fact that she
had only herself to blame if she did get into difficulties.
But, if the worst happened and she had to be rescued, how
much smaller could she be made to feel?

Predictably, she thought, she reached the shallows again
without mishap. Wading up on to the sand, she squeezed
out the sodden rope of her hair, which had wound itself
about her neck, then picked up her towel to rub briskly at
her chilled flesh. The bra and pants she was wearing were
not strictly a bikini; in fact, they were simply two items of

underwear. But, as they were cream, and made of cotton, she had adopted them as such when her other bikini was still wet. Now, however, they clung rather uncomfortably to her cold skin, and realising she could wear the pants and shirt without anything underneath just to go up to her room, she swiftly took them off.

It wasn't until she was actually fastening the belt of her pants that she became aware that someone was watching her. In her haste to shed one type of clothing for another, she hadn't given a thought to the fact that the person that Grant invariably phoned was actually here, on the premises. And there he was, standing silently by the low wall that separated the gardens from the beach, one foot raised to rest upon the roughly-built stones.

Sara was glad it was dark enough to hide her embarrassment. Had he seen her? She rather thought he had. For heaven's sake, did he think she made a habit of stripping off on the beach? He certainly made a habit of coming upon her when she least expected it. Or wanted it, she acknowledged tensely, wondering what had been going through his mind as he watched her little tableau.

Picking up her towel and the two offending scraps of cotton, she realised she had no choice but to find out. He was making no attempt to leave and spare her blushes, and pressing her lips together, she crossed the sand and climbed the two shallow steps to where he was waiting. If he didn't mention it, nor would she, she decided as she reached the lamplit terrace, her features schooled to politeness as she wished him a good evening.

'Wait,' he said, as she would have passed him, swinging his raised foot to the ground and turning to face her. 'I want to talk to you, and now would seem to be as good a time as any.'

Sara halted with evident reluctance, conscious of her wet hair and bare feet, and the nervous erection of her breasts against the damp texture of her shirt. If she had known she was going to have to face an interview with Lincoln Korda, she would have kept her bra on, she thought childishly. As it was, she felt hot and exposed.

He was formally dressed this evening, the expensive elegance of his pale grey suit in sharp contrast to her own dishevelment. They should have had this conversation at lunchtime, she thought rebelliously. She had been ready for him then; she was not ready for him now.

'You do realise how dangerous it is to swim without warning anyone of your intentions, don't you?' he remarked, as she shifted uneasily a few feet away from him. 'Particularly at dusk, when shadows can be deceptive.'

Sara made no comment, other than to lift her slim shoulders in assent, and as if made impatient by her attitude, he added sharply: 'You should always tell someone where you're going. Apart from the current, which can be turbulent, you could get cramp. Even the strongest swimmers have drowned because of cramp!'

Sara took a breath. 'I'll be careful,' she responded stiffly. 'Is that all?'

'No, that's not all.' There was a distinct edge to Lincoln's tone now. 'Why don't you sit down? I might get to the point that much sooner if I wasn't anticipating your disappearance at any moment.'

'I can't sit down. I'm wet,' she said coolly, daring him to argue with her, and he moved his shoulders almost wearily.

'No, you're not,' he said, making no attempt to avoid the fact. 'I saw you dry yourself just a few minutes ago. Now, will you sit down?'

Sara swallowed. 'You watched me!' she exclaimed, making a bid for indignation, and his lean mouth turned down.

'Yes, I watched you,' he conceded. 'You saw me doing so. I admire your persistence, but I must repeat—you're wasting your time!'

Her lips parted. 'You think I undressed deliberately to shock you!' She didn't need to pretend indignation now.

'That isn't the word I would have used, but something like it,' he agreed drily. Then, observing the nervous rise and fall of her breasts, he added quietly: 'Look, we're getting away from what's important here. I don't give a damn about your motives——'

'My motives?' Sara was astounded.

'All I care about is that we should understand one another,' he continued, as if she hadn't spoken. 'I guess it can be a bit frustrating for a girl like you, living down here, miles from anywhere, with no shops, no entertainment——'

'Why don't you say—*and no men*?' she interrupted him hotly. 'That's what you're implying, isn't it? You think I'm attracted to you, don't you? You think that's why I took my clothes off just now; to show you what you're missing!'

Lincoln pushed one brown hand into the pocket of his trousers, sweeping back the dark weight of his hair with the other. His expression mirrored his impatience with the scene that was taking place, and she wondered why he didn't simply tell her she was unsuitable and be done with it.

There was silence for a few pregnant moments, and then he spoke again. 'If I tell you I don't care why you took your clothes off, will you believe me?' he enquired flatly, his grey eyes impassive. 'This may sound arrogant, and I'm sorry, but believe me, the sight of another naked female form is no novelty.'

She flinched. 'Thank you.'

'Oh, God!' The sudden imprecation was unexpected, but she knew better than to be moved by it. This must be very inconvenient for him, she thought bitterly. Not only a failure, but an hysterical one as well.

'You don't understand,' he continued, just as she was on the point of making some excuse and escaping. 'I don't want to hurt you. I just don't see how I can avoid it. Not if you persist in pretending you don't know what I'm talking about. I live in New York, remember? Crass though it sounds, sex is pretty cheap in that city. Even for a married man. Besides—well, money is a powerful aphrodisiac.'

Sara's lips twisted. 'You think I'm attracted to your money?'

'I think you've thought about it. And, on reflection, I'd guess Grant hasn't exactly been discreet about my relationship with Michelle.'

She gasped. 'You flatter yourself, Mr Korda!'

'I dare say. It's not true, then?'

'What's not true?' She was deliberately obtuse.

'That you don't find all this . . .' he indicated the terrace and the lamplit colour tones of the house itself '. . . appealing.'

She faltered. 'Anyone would find this place appealing,' she protested. 'That's not to say——'

'I disagree,' Lincoln interrupted her. 'I know a lot of people who don't care for Orchid Key at all. Michelle's one of them.'

Sara sighed. 'Well, I'm sorry——'

'Why are you sorry?' Lincoln's thick lashes narrowed the probing gleam of his eyes. Then, scornfully: 'Oh, yes, of course, I almost forgot. You're going to offer me sympathy now. That is the next ploy, isn't it? The offer of a consoling shoulder to cry on? You see, Miss Fielding, I know all the moves. Unfortunately for you, I've been this way before.'

'You—you swine!' Sara was stunned at the strength of her own revulsion. 'I don't know what kind of women you usually associate with, Mr Korda, but rest assured, they're only what you deserve!'

His lips twitched. 'You still insist that—that that striptease was innocent?'

'Yes.'

'Okay.' His jaw hardened. 'Let's find out, shall we?'

Without giving her time to apprehend his intentions, he reached for her, dragging her close against him, and capturing her throat in a choking grasp. As she fought to free herself from that suffocating hold, his mouth sought the parted convulsion of hers, and she realised that that had been his intention. Gasping for breath, she was in no state to prevent the intimate invasion of his tongue, and she sagged against him as its hot wetness blocked what little air she had left.

As if he realised she was nearly unconscious, the pressure on her throat eased, and the hand that had previously bruised the tender skin below her jawline moved sensuously down the opened neckline of her shirt. Only then was she able to clench her teeth on his tongue, and he swore volubly as it was withdrawn.

Fortunately for him, she thought frustratedly, she was still too weak to do much damage, and although he did not kiss her again, he did not release her either. Instead, he studied her flushed face while allowing his thumb to rub intimately over the hardened crest of her nipple, palpable beneath the thin silk of her shirt. There was mockery in his gaze, and insolence too, and Sara had never hated anyone as she hated him at that moment.

'Well,' he said provokingly, 'don't you have anything to say? Or are you biting your tongue, too?'

She seethed, but she refused to answer him. He should not gain any more amusement from her, she thought, and as if he sensed her withdrawal, his hand stilled.

'You may be mollified to hear that you hurt me just now,' he remarked, but if it was an attempt at mitigation, it failed. 'So,' he murmured, as a drop of water fell from her hair on to his hand, 'You're giving up the fight. Shame on you! I was just beginning to enjoy it.'

Sara's jaw clenched, and she contemplated what he would do if she resorted to more physical methods. She might conceivably succeed in hurting him with her knee, but what might he do in retaliation? Vicki had always said you should never push a man too far, not unless you were prepared to take the consequences, and the situation was quite volatile enough without inflaming it further.

'Will you let go of me?' she ventured at last, and Lincoln's lips parted.

'Of course,' he conceded, inclining his head, but when she attempted to move out of his arms, he prevented her. 'In a moment,' he appended, bending his head towards her, and her startled protest was lost beneath the searching pressure of his mouth.

It was not like the other time he had kissed her. Even though she fought him just as vehemently, his lips moved insistently on hers, and in spite of herself, she was disarmed. He didn't force her, although his hand wound into the soaking tangle of her hair bound them together. Nevertheless, it was the potent caress of his mouth on hers that stifled her resistance, and giving herself up to the wild sweet fire, she linked her arms around his neck.

His arms slid around her, moulding the narrowing curve of her waist, before his hands cupped the firm swell of her buttocks. She was brought intimately against him, so intimately she could feel the sudden stirring of his body, and when she pressed herself even closer, his tongue once again sought possession.

It was arguable what might have happened had Grant's

voice not rung out at that moment. He was talking to Cora, and the sound carried easily on the still night air. 'Where?' he was saying. 'Oh—outside. Okay, Cora, thanks. I'll find him.'

Lincoln set Sara free only seconds before Grant walked out on to the terrace. She just had time to gather her wits before the younger man came to join them, but obviously he was not surprised to see her, and she realised he would have no suspicion of what had happened. Why would he? she asked herself unsteadily. She wouldn't have believed it herself less than an hour ago. She hardly believed it now, and she had been a participant.

'Hey, Sara,' said Grant, after greeting his employer, and Sara had to steel herself to meet his casual gaze. 'What's going on? Isn't it time you changed for dinner?'

'It's my fault,' said Lincoln coolly, and looking at his lean, impassive face, Sara wondered if she had imagined what had happened after all. Certainly there was no evidence of passion in his expression now, and his tone when he addressed Grant was lightly apologetic. 'I'm afraid I kept Miss Fielding talking,' he added, as if daring her to contradict him, and she knew a blinding anger at his smug self-congratulation.

'Yes,' she said now, and she knew she had startled him by the sudden gleam that entered his eyes. 'Mr—er—Mr Korda was just telling me that it will probably be better for all concerned if I leave right away. I'm sure you'll agree with him, Grant. Jeff and I are getting nowhere.'

Before Grant could speak, however, Lincoln intervened. 'Did I say that?' he countered, the grey eyes warning now. 'Oh dear, Miss Fielding, you do seem to have misunderstood me! I can't deny the idea of sending you back to England hasn't crossed my mind.' He allowed that little barb to find its mark before continuing: 'But my son's unpredictability is nothing if not predictable. When I happened to mention, in his hearing, that I thought you were wasting your time here, he actually got quite animated. It seems he wants you to stay. He wants to see you. Tomorrow.'

Sara blinked, her throat closing on her protest. 'You're not serious!'

'Oh, but I am.' Lincoln's features hollowed, and she wondered for a moment what he was really thinking. 'I've given Keating orders that you're to have a free hand where

Jeff is concerned. I think I can promise you, you'll receive no further obstruction from that quarter.'

Sara shook her head. She didn't know what to say. After what had happened, he must know it was the last thing she had expected. Was that what he had come to tell her? Had she really jumped to the wrong conclusion?

'Well—um—thank you,' she mumbled now, and Grant came to lay a familiar arm across her shoulder.

'Hey, you did good!' he exclaimed, embarrassing her still further by planting a kiss at the corner of her mouth. 'You can relax now. You're staying on.'

Sara didn't know whether that was a reason for relaxation or not. She rather thought not. And for all his words of endorsement, there was no trace of compassion in the enigmatic gaze Lincoln was bestowing on her.

'Say, Cora tells me you're dining out this evening, Link,' Grant said now, withdrawing his arm, much to Sara's relief. 'You're not flying back to the city tonight, are you?'

She tensed, waiting with some apprehension for Lincoln's answer, but when it came, she didn't know whether to be glad or sorry. 'No,' he said, parting his jacket to push his hands into the pockets of his trousers. 'I'm dining with the Steinbecks, that's all. And,' he glanced pointedly at the slim gold watch circling his narrow wrist, 'I should be leaving right now.'

Sara heard the car come back around two a.m. She hadn't been to sleep. She had been lying listening to the ocean, and anticipating her meeting with Jeff the next day—and trying not to think about where Lincoln was and who he was with.

It was Grant's fault that she had found sleep so elusive, she told herself. Until tonight, she had known nothing of Lincoln Korda's private affairs, except the fact that he was separated from his wife. And she hadn't wanted to know, she thought tensely. After what had happened this evening, the less she knew about Lincoln Korda, the better. If it hadn't been for the fact that Jeff himself had asked to see her, she would have handed in her resignation there and then, but her sympathy for his son far outweighed any personal grievance she might have towards Lincoln Korda. A man who had neglected his own flesh and blood for so long could have no real affection for the boy, and she had no intention of collaborating in yet another betrayal of his responsibilities. She would stay, at least until she had convinced herself that there was nothing more she could do. And if that meant confronting Lincoln Korda's ego, then so be it.

But her brave defiance took a definite battering when Grant chose to tell her where his employer had gone. 'Old man Steinbeck owned the investment bank on Wall Street where Link got his first break. That's how he made his money, you know. He started out as a tax consultant, but he soon graduated to investments. I've heard him described as a financial genius, but Link insists it was all luck!' He grimaced. 'Anyway, these days he has his own trust company, and a seat on the board of several other corporations, including Steinbecks. Which is very convenient considering the old man is hankering for Link to become a fully-fledged member of the family.'

Sara had known it was nothing to do with her, but Grant's revelations had been couched in such a way that she couldn't resist the automatic: 'What do you mean?'

'Rebecca Steinbeck,' Grant had responded gratuitously. 'The old man's granddaughter. He had no daughters, you see, only one son, and he died in a yachting accident when Rebecca was three. Unfortunately, Link was married himself by that time, but the old man's kept a close eye on the relationship, if you know what I mean.'

Sara knew what he meant, and in spite of her reluctance, she had to ask: 'Does Rebecca live with her grandfather, then?'

'No,' Grant shrugged. 'She has a place of her own in New York. But she spends a lot of time down here, with her grandfather. He's virtually retired now, of course, and it's common knowledge that Link's expected to get the presidency next year.'

'I see.'

Sara had absorbed this information without comment, and to her relief, Grant had found another topic for discussion. But she had wondered why he had chosen now to reveal so much about their employer, and she wondered if it was his way of warning her off. Of course, he knew nothing of what had passed between her and Lincoln Korda that evening, but perhaps he had seen something in her nervous expression to alert his suspicions. After all, he knew, as well as anyone, that his employer was an attractive man. And he might be trying to get his own back at her for the way she had persistently held him at bay.

Whatever the reason, he had turned to her prospective meeting with Jeff as an alternative, and she had been shocked by the derision he had shown. 'You don't honestly believe he means to co-operate with you, do you?' he had scoffed. 'Just you wait until Link goes away, then you'll see what happens. So long as Link's here, so long as Jeff believes his father thinks you're wasting your time, he'll make a fuss. But once Link's safely back in New York, you may find you're not so popular.'

'You're very pessimistic,' she had exclaimed, wishing he had not voiced his opinion at all. But although she changed the subject, she could not forget what he had said, and like their conversation about Lincoln Korda, it remained a bone of contention between them.

And that was why she was still lying awake when her employer returned home. She hadn't wanted to think about Lincoln's dinner engagement, or about who had invited him, but at that time of night, her resistance was at its lowest. She couldn't help recalling how easily he had overcome her oposition to his lovemaking, or remember her submission without a feeling of revulsion. He had treated her abominably. He had tormented and provoked her into a gesture of defiance, and then used his not inconsiderable skills to pervert her plea for dignity. He had *used* her—but as what? A rehearsal for his encounter with Rebecca Steinbeck, perhaps? Or an endorsement of his belief that he was irresistible to women?

Sara eventually fell asleep about three o'clock. She had some inkling of what time it was, because at a quarter to three, she fetched herself a glass of water from the bathroom. She had wished it was brandy. She could have done with something to numb the feeling that nothing would ever be the same again.

CHAPTER SEVEN

SARA was still on tenterhooks when Keating let her into Jeff Korda's suite after breakfast the next morning. She had rung down and asked Cora if she could have coffee and rolls in her room at eight o'clock, to avoid any possible encounter with the boy's father, but when Rosa delivered her tray, she also delivered the information that Mr Link had already left for New York.

'He's flying up with the Steinbecks,' she continued, conversationally. 'You know—them people he dined with yesterday evening? Seems like he offered the use of his plane to Miss Becca, and her granddaddy decided to go along for the ride.'

Sara managed a smile in return, but her happy expression only lasted until Rosa had gone out of the door. Apart from the unpleasant realisation that she was upset about Lincoln leaving, she had the additional anxiety of wondering if Grant was going to be proved right sooner than he had anticipated.

'You will remember Mr Korda is easily disturbed, Miss Fielding,' Keating greeted her, and for a moment she wondered who he was talking about.

'Oh, you mean Jeff!' she exclaimed, refusing to call the boy *Mr* Korda to anyone. 'Yes, I know that,' she added, smoothing her palms down the seams of her cut-off white jeans. 'Don't worry. We have met and—I think we understand one another.'

That was a massive piece of optimism, but she refused to let Keating see she was nervous. She would get nowhere with Jeff if Keating baulked her at every turn, and while she might be apprehensive, what had she to lose?

'Very well, Miss Fielding.' He backed off. 'I presume you do know where to find him.'

'In his bedroom?' Sara lifted one shoulder in a gesture of

84

assent. 'Oh, well, wish me luck. I'm sure you hope this works as much as the rest of us.'

His smile was decidedly frosty, but like the good servant he was, he didn't contradict her. Instead, he disappeared into what she assumed to be his apartments, which adjoined the suite on the other side, and Sara was left to take the initiative herself.

It was like a repeat of that other time she came here, only this time she had his consent, she reassured herself. All the same, she did wonder if Jeff had been told his father had already departed. And if so, would his attitude change as Grant had predicted?

He was lying in exactly the same position as before, the sheet folded neatly across his chest, his arms stretched over it and resting by his sides. It was as if he was completely paralysed, thought Sara, somewhat daunted. She had hoped he might have made an effort and greeted her from his wheelchair.

'Hi,' she said uncertainly, coming round the bed, and he looked up at her unsmilingly.

'Hi.'

She was encouraged. 'You were expecting me, then?'

'I sent for you,' responded Jeff challengingly. 'I knew you'd come if my father asked you.'

A little of Sara's nervousness evaporated. 'You didn't have to get your father to ask me,' she retorted smoothly. 'I'd have come just the same if you'd invited me. That's what I'm here for.'

Jeff's thin face was sulky. 'That's not true!'

'What's not true? Why else do you think I'm——'

'It's not true that you'd have come if I'd asked you to. You ignored me. I called your name and you ignored it.

She blinked. 'You mean a couple of days ago?'

'When else?'

She shook her head. 'As I recall it, you told me to get out. And in no uncertain terms.'

Jeff's jaw clenched. 'You startled me. I thought you were Rosa.'

'But you soon found out I wasn't,' Sara reminded him drily. 'Anyway, I'm here now, so perhaps we should start again.'

'Start what?' he asked sardonically.

'Start being friends, of course.'

'Friends!' His lips twisted. 'I don't have friends.'

'Like you don't have visitors, hmm?' suggested Sara tensely. 'Look, Jeff, don't you think this is getting a bit ridiculous? I'm here. We're talking. Can't we at least try and find a bit of common ground, before you lapse back into that well of self-pity that's drowning you?'

His eyes glittered suddenly. 'What are you?' he snapped. 'What particular branch of medicine did you qualify in? No, let me guess—psychology or psychiatry, am I right? They're certainly turning out better-looking doctors, I'll give them that.'

'I'm not a doctor,' exclaimed Sara at once. 'Honestly, I'm not. I wouldn't know how to psychoanalyse anyone. As a matter of fact, I—I *was* a dancer. Or at least, I hoped to be.'

'A dancer?' Jeff stared at her. 'What kind of a dancer?'

'Well, I trained as a classical dancer first, but then I found modern dancing was more my scene.' She hesitated. 'It was a terrible blow when I had to give it up.'

He frowned. 'Why did you?'

'Because I broke my ankle.'

'Oh yeah,' he grunted, 'I remember. You said that you were lame.' He levered himself up on his elbows and looked down at her feet. 'You don't look lame to me.'

'That's because I try not to be,' replied Sara carefully. 'There's a weakness there, but I don't give in to it.'

He uttered a short laugh and flopped back on to his pillows again. 'Oh, God!' he muttered. 'How noble of you!' His voice was raw with sarcasm. 'You break your ankle and it mends again, and you're here to tell me the story of your sacrifice! What does it really mean to you? Instead of spending your life trying to make it big in some small time theatre company you've got to find yourself a sedentary occupation. Big deal!'

'It wasn't like that!' Sara was indignant. 'I had an offer to work on TV!' It was an exaggeration, but what the hell!

'Puppets work on TV,' replied Jeff disparagingly. 'It's not a life-and-death situation. You do have a life left to lead.'

'So do you!'

'Oh, grow up, will you? I don't need platitudes, from you or anyone else.'

'What you need is reality!' retorted Sara, without hesitation. 'This isn't reality, this——' she gestured about her, '—this padded cell you've ensconced yourself in! You don't even know what day it is up here. You don't know if it's wet or dry; you don't even know when the sun's shining!'

'That's the way I like it.'

'Why?' She had started, so she argued that she might as well finish. If she was fired now, at least she could console herself with the knowledge that she had said what she wanted to say. 'You don't really like living up here, remote from what's going on around you, but the truth is, you're scared to do anything else.'

'Scared?' Jeff started up on his elbows. 'I'm not scared!'

'Aren't you? Aren't you really afraid to face things as they really are?' Sara shook her head. 'Oh, I know you're going to tell me that if you're not scared of death, you can't be scared of life, but it's not true! It takes a hell of a lot more courage to face living than it does dying!'

He was angry now. 'What would you know about it?' he sneered. 'Have you ever taken an overdose?'

'No.' Sara was honest. 'But that's not to say I haven't thought about it. Everybody does, at some time or another. But we don't all look for the easy way out.'

'Easy?' Jeff flopped back again. 'You sure as hell don't avoid the jugular, do you?'

She took a breath. 'All right, maybe I don't. Maybe I'm wrong, and you're right. But I'll tell you this, there isn't a great deal of difference between the way you're living and—and dying. This room is like a mortuary!'

He groaned. 'Did no one ever tell you, you don't speak that way to a sick person?'

She knew a moment's contrition. And then she said quietly: 'Are you?'

'Am I what?' Jeff gave her a lacklustre gaze, and she realised his momentary surge of anger had exhausted him. It made her wonder if she was not simply hurting him in an effort to justify her own existence, but it was too late now to call back her words.

'Are you a sick person?' she replied softly.

He shook his head. 'Are you crazy?'

'No, I mean it.' She moved nearer to the bed and looked

down at him. 'What's really wrong with you now? Apart from the paralysis, I mean.'

'Apart from the paralysis?' Jeff's lips curled. 'Oh, well, if we dismiss the paralysis, let's see: I guess I'm pretty fit, wouldn't you say?'

'Don't be sarcastic!'

'Well, don't you be so bloody stupid!' he retorted. 'I'm paralysed, for God's sake! That's it! Period!'

Sara sighed. 'And you're prepared to lie here until you either grow old or succeed in what you didn't succeed in a few weeks ago.'

'Until I succeed in killing myself. Why don't you say it right out? You've said everything else.'

She hunched her shoulders, pushing her hands into the waistline pockets of her jeans. 'You feel pretty sorry for yourself, don't you?'

He gasped. 'Don't you ever give up?'

'I'm only telling you the truth. That's what you wanted, isn't it?'

He bit his lip. 'I think you'd better get lost now. I'm tired.'

'Okay,' Sara shrugged resignedly. She had known it was an outside chance at best. She backed away from the bed. 'Goodbye, then. I hope you achieve what you're aiming for.'

'What do you mean?' Jeff dragged himself over to stare after her. 'That sounded final.'

'It was.' She halted with her hand on the door. 'I've tried everything I can think of, but you don't want to know. The sooner I use my return ticket for London and stop wasting your father's money——'

'He can afford it.' Jeff plucked impatiently at the sheet. 'Look, I don't want you to leave. Not yet, at least. Come back tomorrow. We can talk some more then.'

'I don't think——'

'Dammit, I don't care what you think!' he snapped, and there were beads of perspiration standing on his forehead now. 'My father's paying your wages, for God's sake! I didn't ask you to come here, but you came. At least have the decency to stay as long as you're needed!'

Although Grant was obviously curious about her conversation with Jeff, Sara managed to evade his most pointed questions.

She was loath to discuss what had happened with anyone, and although she supposed she had scored a minor success by getting Jeff to ask her to come back, it didn't much feel like it. As usual, as soon as she had had time to think about what she had said, she was plagued with misgivings, and she waited apprehensively for the repeat of what had happened before. But the rest of the day passed without incident, and she actually ate her dinner that evening with something akin to enthusiasm.

However, when Keating let her into the suite the next morning, he was evidently less than pleased to see her. 'Oh, it's you, Miss Fielding,' he greeted her offhandedly. 'Does Mr Korda expect you?'

'I think so.' Sara quelled the urge to be impatient with the man. 'Shall I go straight in?'

'No. That is—Mr Korda's not ready for you,' declared Keating hastily. 'He—he—he's still having breakfast. Could you come back later?'

'How much later?' she asked suspiciously.

'Oh—an hour?'

'An hour!' Sara stood her ground. 'Surely it doesn't take him an hour to eat his breakfast?'

"Keating!"

Jeff's peremptory summons broke into their conversation, and looking anxiously over his shoulder, the little man clucked his tongue. 'Look, I've got to go,' he said, turning back to Sara, but she was not so easily diverted.

'I'll wait,' she said, sliding past him and seating herself on the upright chair by the door. She dredged up an appealing smile. 'You can tell him I'm here, if you like.'

Keating was evidently torn between the desire to get rid of her and the equally strong need to attend to his patient's wishes. 'Oh, very well,' he muttered ungraciously, as Jeff called again, and slamming the door, he hurried into Jeff's bedroom.

He was out again with a tray some ten minutes later. 'You can go in now,' he said grudgingly. 'But don't stay too long. He tires easily.'

'Thank you.'

Sara waited until he had disappeared into the adjoining

apartment, and then sauntered as casually as she could into the other room.

During the minutes she had been kept waiting, she had wondered if Jeff's lateness could have anything to do with what they had been talking about the previous day. She had allowed herself to dream of how she would feel if she walked into Jeff's room and found him sitting in his wheelchair, maybe even dressed, although that was carrying things a little too far. However, it had been just a dream, she acknowledged, and she tried not to look too disappointed when she found he was still as immobile as ever.

'Hello,' she greeted him cheerfully, approaching the bed. 'How are you?'

Jeff's nostrils flared. 'How do I look?'

She shrugged. 'Pale.'

'Gee, thanks.' His response was ironic, but not unfriendly. He nodded towards a chair set against the wall. 'You'd better sit down.'

'Thank you.' Sara pulled the chair towards the bed and subsided on to it. 'Did Keating tell you I've been waiting?'

'He grumbled that you were here,' agreed Jeff, with a trace of humour. 'Keating doesn't like his schedules to be disrupted.'

She grimaced. 'Did I disrupt his schedules?'

'Your coming here disrupts his schedules,' said Jeff drily. 'I'm the only one allowed to do that.'

She bent her head. 'Well, he'll just have to put up with it.'

'That's what I said,' he remarked carelessly. 'So, forget about Keating. Let's talk about you.'

'We talked about me yesterday,' murmured Sara. 'Why don't we talk about you?'

Jeff scowled. 'As you said yesterday, I'm a drag!'

'I didn't say that.' She stared at him.

'As good as.' His hunched thin shoulders beneath the cream silk pyjamas. 'Anyway, it's true. I'm boring. You're not.'

She sighed. 'I've told you about me.'

'Only that you trained to be a dancer. What do you do now? Apart from counselling failed suicides?'

So Sara told him about her life; about Vicki, and the flat, and the job she had given up to come out here. She even mentioned his uncle, although she noticed Jeff shied away from any discussions of his family.

Even so, the morning passed quite quickly, and when Keating appeared with Jeff's lunch on a tray, she was astonished to realise it was almost twelve.

'You can come back this afternoon, if you like,' Jeff invited casually, but now Keating intervened.

'Don't you think Miss Fielding should be allowed a little time to herself, Jeff?' he asked, swinging out the legs of the tray and setting it across the boy's knees. 'Besides, you know you have to rest after lunch. I think tomorrow morning would be quite time enough.'

'I could come back this evening,' suggested Sara, prepared to endorse Keating's assertion that Jeff should rest for a while during the heat of the day, but the manservant shook his head.

'Mr Korda retires early, Miss Fielding,' he declared firmly, and Sara, meeting Jeff's strangely defensive gaze, did not argue.

'Okay, tomorrow then,' she said, giving the boy a reassuring smile, but he hunched his shoulders and looked away, as she walked out of the room.

By the end of the week following, Sara felt as if she was beginning to make some headway. The progress they had made was slow, but positive, and although there were times when she despaired of ever persuading him he had something to live for, these times were less frequent, and usually in the wee small hours. Much like the times she thought about his father, she admitted reluctantly. Despite her efforts with Jeff, and Lincoln's absence, she still thought about him far too often, and perhaps that was why she put such energy into her work.

Of course, Jeff still resisted any attempt to get him to use his wheelchair. So far as she knew, Keating still attended him, like the baby Grant had described. But she had discovered he now fed himself on occasions, instead of forcing someone else to do it if they didn't want him to starve.

Still, the black moods he suffered were decidedly fewer, and he was not so negative in his outlook. She realised he had begun to look forward to the time they spent together,

and because of having an interest in something, he was
definitely getting stronger. Talking didn't tire him, as it had
done in the beginning, and even the occasional argument had
no adverse effect on his temperature.

There were limits to what they talked about, of course. Jeff
didn't like any personal questions about himself or his family,
and if he sometimes revealed more than he had intended, he
quickly changed the subject. Nevertheless, Sara did learn
more about his childhood, and a picture slowly emerged of a
lonely little boy, brought up by servants, and ignored by his
father. How could Lincoln do that? she asked herself time
and time again. It was obvious that the boy's mother had had
little time for her son, by Jeff's inadvertent remarks concerning
holidays and the like. He had evidently attended a private
residential school, and his free time had been spent with a
series of minders. He had attended ball games with people
called Buzz or Mac, and only rarely did Michelle figure in his
reminiscences. Lincoln must have known this. He must have
realised what kind of existence he was condemning his son to.
Yet he had done nothing to change the situation, and not
until Jeff was lying paralysed in a hospital bed had he
belatedly remembered his responsibilities.

Because of the taboos concerning these relationships, the
conversations Sara had with Jeff usually turned more to
outside interests. They talked about music and art and
entertainment, and they had some lively discussions concerning
the relative merits of rock versus heavy metal. The kind of
music Jeff said he preferred made Sara pull a face, but they
did agree on some things and agreed to disagree on others.

Then, one morning, about ten days after Sara had begun
her regular visits to his suite, she discovered Jeff actually
listening to a tape, played on the hi-fi which had hitherto
stood idle in a corner. After that, they played music a lot.
Jeff had an enviable library of tapes, and when Sara suggested
they ought to watch television sometimes too, it received
consideration.

A couple of days later, a television was installed, and with
it a stereo video recorder. 'It's mostly repeats of game shows
in the mornings,' Jeff explained, somewhat sheepishly,
revealing how he had spent at least some of his time before

the crash. 'I thought we might get some pre-recorded tapes. Sort of have our own movie premiere!'

Sara didn't object. Anything that encouraged Jeff to take an interest in what was happening in the outside world was to be applauded, and she was warmed by the thought that she had instigated it.

At least, she was, until the night the whole household was awakened by a series of screams and agonised yells coming from Jeff's rooms. It was after midnight, and Sara had been reading a book she had borrowed from the library downstairs. It was a dated thriller; not the sort of thing she would have normally chosen to read, but her mind hadn't really been on it anyway. She had chosen the book at random, just something to put her to sleep, she had thought, and she had been feeling pleasantly sleepy when the unearthly rumpus began at the other side of the house.

There was something eerie about shrieks and cries at that hour of the night, and when Sara dived out of bed, dragging on her cotton wrapper, she had half believed that burglars had invaded the premises. It wasn't until she emerged into the corridor and located the direction the screams were coming from that she realised it was Jeff who was making them.

Shocked into action, she stumbled in the direction of the noise, only to discover that half the household was there before her. Rosa and Vinnie, their ample forms wrapped in striped bathrobes, Cora, similarly attired, trying to hold a garbled conversation with Grant, and Keating, barring the way to the suite, and endeavouring to reassure everyone that he could manage.

The screams had ceased now. An uneasy silence had fallen in the apartment, and Sara gazed anxiously at the manservant, willing him to tell them what had happened.

'Crazy kid!' muttered Grant, as he noticed her arrival. 'For God's sake, I thought there must be a fire, at least!'

'What happened?' exclaimed Sara, her eyes wide and troubled. 'Does anyone know? What's going on?'

'Oh, Keating said something about Jeff falling out of bed,' replied Grant irritably. 'He was probably getting out to change the tapes in that bloody recorder you've had installed in his room.'

But she wasn't listening to him. 'Falling out of bed?' she echoed faintly, her eyes turning back to Keating, but he was already closing the door and she dared not intrude right now.

'It's all over,' declared Cora, ushering the two maids back along the corridor. 'There's nothing more to be done. Let's all get back to bed, huh?'

'But what happened?' Sara persisted. 'Do you know, Cora? Those screams—they were—they were——'

'—too loud! Selfish little bastard!' grunted Grant Masters peevishly. 'Waking up the house like that. Just because he doesn't have to get off his butt from morn till night, it doesn't mean the rest of us——'

'Don't say that!' Sara was disgusted by his attitude. 'For heaven's sake, do you think Jeff wants to—to stay on his butt, as you put it? It's not his fault he can't get up.'

'Just tell me who was at the wheel of the car, then, if it wasn't him?' Grant retorted angrily. 'God, is that what you have to do around here to get some attention? Get yourself half killed?'

She refused to answer him. She knew he was getting at her for spending so much time with Jeff. Apart from a couple of hours in the afternoon, which she generally spent soaking up the sun, and the short period between dinner and bed, he saw little of her; and she couldn't deny she often used Jeff as an excuse to avoid any prolonged period with him. It wasn't that she disliked him exactly, although closer acquaintance had not increased her desire for his company, but it was more to avoid his derision of her optimism that she evaded any intimate discussions.

Now, she made an impatient gesture and walked away, too disturbed over what had happened and its repercussions to pay any real attention to him. She didn't believe that Jeff had fallen out of bed. The bed he slept in was huge, and no way could he have tumbled over the edge. But something had incited those terrible cries, and she couldn't wait until the morning to find out what it was.

CHAPTER EIGHT

However, Keating barred her way when she arrived at the suite the next morning. 'Mr Korda is still sleeping,' he said, not allowing her to slip past him as she had done before. 'And, quite honestly, I think it would be safer if you didn't see him today.'

'Safer?' Sara stared at him. 'What do you mean?'

'I just think it would be unwise to upset Mr Korda any more than he's been upset already.'

'Will you stop calling him *Mr* Korda!' Sara snapped impatiently. 'And why do you think *I* might upset him? We're friends. He likes to see me.'

Keating drew himself up to his full height. 'I didn't want to say this, Miss Fielding, but it seems I'm going to have to.' He paused significantly. 'If you must know, I think you're to blame for what happened last night. If you hadn't come here interfering, Jeff would never have attempted what he did.'

She blinked. '*I'm* to blame!' she echoed. 'Why? What happened?'

Keating sniffed. 'Jeff had a fall—a serious fall. I'm waiting for Doctor Haswell now. It may be that he's suffered some further injury.'

She gasped. 'Jeff *fell*!' she exclaimed, remembering what Grant had said the night before. 'But how could he? It doesn't seem possible.'

'Well, it happened,' declared Keating firmly. 'And I think you should seriously consider the consequences of what you're doing in future. Jeff's paralysed, Miss Fielding. That's a fact. He tires easily; that's a fact, too. And encouraging him to watch moving pictures, that simply highlight his own limitations, is both reckless and cruel!'

Sara flushed. 'At least he's aware of what's going on

around him now,' she said, aware of the defensive note in her voice and despising herself for it. 'And I don't see how watching—moving pictures, as you put it, could cause him to fall out of bed.'

Now Keating frowned. 'Did I say he fell out of bed? I don't believe so.'

She hunched her shoulders. No, it was Grant who had said that. 'I assumed that was what you meant,' she mumbled, feeling like a schoolgirl. 'What did happen, then? Shouldn't he have been asleep at that time?'

'I settled him for the night at eight o'clock as usual,' reported Keating indignantly. 'You don't imagine I knew anything about what he was doing, do you? If I had—'

'But what was he doing?' Sara interrupted him wearily. 'How did he come to be out of bed? I assume he was out of bed when he fell.'

He hesitated. Then, apparently deciding that no stigma could attach to him for being honest, he said: 'He was trying to get to the bathroom, with the use of a pair of crutches.'

'What?' She knew a surge of excitement. 'You mean he was actually trying to do something for himself!'

'Oh, he did something for himself all right,' said Keating, not responding to her look of enthusiasm. 'He lost his balance as soon as he tried to stand upright, and he tumbled into that television set you had put at the foot of the bed.'

Sara swallowed. 'Is it broken?'

'What? The boy's leg, or the set?'

Her colour deepened. 'I meant the set, but of course, Jeff's leg is more important. It's not broken, is it?'

'You heard him yelling, didn't you?'

She nodded.

'Then decide for yourself.'

She put a hand against the wall beside the door and rested her forehead against her upraised arm. 'Do you think he'll be all right?' she asked miserably, all her earlier sense of achievement dissipating. 'Have you contacted—er—his father?'

'Not yet. I'll wait and see what Doctor Haswell says,'

replied Keating smoothly. 'And now, if you'll excuse
me . . .'

'Of course.' Sara half turned. 'You will—you will let me
know what the doctor says, won't you? And if Jeff wants to
see me——'

'I suspect that may not be likely,' returned Keating, with
evident satisfaction. 'Jeff was fairly voluble last night, and I
got the impression that you were the last person he wanted
to see,'

'Even so . . .' Sara was insistent.

'Oh, very well.' He gave her his word. 'But I should
seriously consider my position, if I were you, Miss Fielding.
After what happened last night, your services may no
longer be necessary.'

Of course, Grant sympathised with her. 'I did warn you,'
he remarked smugly, coming across her curled up on one
of the lounges by the pool, her face drawn with
concentration. 'I mean, let's face it—the *fuss* he made . . .'

'Well, if he's broken his leg,' said Sara worriedly. 'Is
Doctor Haswell here yet? Have you seen him?'

'He's up there now,' Grant told her carelessly, taking the
chair beside her. 'Why don't you go and put on your
bikini?' He touched her jean-clad thigh. 'I might join you.'

She flinched away from his probing hand, and he scowled.
'For goodness' sake!' he muttered. 'Lighten up, will you?
You're acting like there's been some kind of tragedy! The
kid tried to get out of bed and he fell. So what? It happens
to us all.'

Sara glared a him. 'You're so insensitive!'

'Practical,' he amended shortly. 'No matter how long you
sit here brooding over past mistakes, you won't make a
scrap of difference to Jeff's condition. Personally, I think
you ought to be glad it happened. It saves you wasting any
more time on the awkward little creep!'

She turned away from him, but as she did so, a shirt
sleeved man in his fifties emerged from the house and
walked towards them. Doctor Haswell? she wondered
anxiously, and springing to her feet, she went to meet him.

'You must be Miss Fielding,' he said as she approached.
'I'm Jeff's doctor. And you're the young woman, I hear,

who's responsible for Jeff's cuts and bruises.' He smiled, but Sara was too tense to notice.

'Is that all?' she exclaimed, pressing her hands together. 'There are no broken bones, or anything like that?'

'No.' Doctor Haswell smoothed the thinning hair on his pate. 'Apart from a few minor contusions, there's no damage done.'

'Oh, thank goodness!'

Sara was fervent, but the doctor wasn't finished yet.

'In any case, I wanted to see you, to speak to you myself,' he added. 'I wanted to congratulate you for achieving the impossible. Six weeks ago, I'd never have believed that anyone could pull Jeff out of his apathy.'

She coloured. 'To what end?' she muttered self-consciously. 'I don't suppose Jeff would agree with you. Like you said, I'm to blame for what happened.'

'*I* wouldn't exactly use those words,' retorted Doctor Haswell drily. 'I'd say you should take the credit for what happened. Don't take any notice of Alan Keating—he always fusses like a mother hen. Jeff is okay. He's making progress.'

Sara shook her head. 'You didn't hear the noise he was making last night——'

'That's right,' Grant intervened from his seat beside the pool. 'Howling like a banshee, he was, Doc. I bet old Cora thought the zombie was out to get her!'

Doctor Haswell listened tolerantly, then turned back to Sara. 'I shouldn't worry too much about what you heard,' he said gently. 'Most of it was probably frustration at his own inadequacy. And at being found out.'

She stared at him. 'You think he's done something like this before?'

'I'd say it's probable. He was a little distance from the bed when he fell, and I doubt he could have achieved so much at a first attempt.'

She caught her breath. 'Do you think it's possible he has some feeling in his legs?' she exclaimed.

'Hey, come on!' The doctor gave her a rueful smile now. 'I'm not talking miracles here. Somehow—we don't know how—Jeff dragged himself out of bed, and tried to make his legs support him. They wouldn't—that much is obvious. What is exciting is that he actually made the effort.'

Sara sighed. 'I see.'

'Don't sound so down-hearted! It's a great breakthrough.'

'For you, perhaps. Not for Jeff,' said Sara sadly. 'Is there no possible chance of him regaining the use of his legs?'

Doctor Haswell hesitated. 'Six weeks ago, I'd have said no chance at all.'

'And now?'

'Now? Now, I'd say it was highly unlikely.'

'His injuries were that bad, hmm?'

'Well, his spinal cord wasn't severed, if that's what you mean. But his back was broken, and the nerves were irreparably impaired.'

'I see,' said Sara again. 'And no one's ever recovered from that kind of paralysis.'

'I didn't say that.' The doctor sighed now. 'Let me explain: when Jeff first had the accident, which was about nine months ago, the prognosis was not unfavourable. Oh, I'm not attempting to minimise his injuries. They were— and are—quite formidable. But had Jeff been prepared to co-operate, had he had some faith in the powers of rehabilitation, we might be some way now towards handling his condition.'

'But Jeff wasn't co-operative.'

'That's an understatement!' exclaimed Grant scornfully, but this time Doctor Haswell was not diverted.

'No,' he said, 'Jeff was not co-operative. In fact, he showed no interest at all in living.' He paused. 'Were it not for the fact that Link was able to afford to employ a team of medics to work on him day and night, I really think he might not have survived those first crucial days.'

'But why?' Sara was confused.

'Who knows?' Doctor Haswell spread his hands. 'It would seem Jeff had everything to live for. But that's the way it is sometimes.'

'Poor little rich kid!' taunted Grant from his chair. 'Don't I get sick of hearing that?'

'Then don't listen,' retorted Sara, turning on him. She resumed her questioning. 'Are you saying Jeff's paralysis could be psychosomatic?'

The doctor shook his head. 'Oh, no. The nerves were damaged all right, we have evidence of that; he's never likely to stagger out of bed one day and confound us all. But, given time, and therapy, he could have learned to do things for himself—and used his crutches with rather more success.'

'You're speaking in the past tense. Isn't it possible now?'

'Anything's possible—if Jeff is willing to let us help him. Naturally, these months of inactivity have made the job that much more difficult, and it may be he'll never regain lost ground. But we could try.'

'If Jeff was willing.'

'If he was willing,' he agreed.

Sara's shoulders sagged. 'Then why isn't he?'

'Well,' Doctor Haswell was reassuring, 'you have set the wheels in motion, at least. That's something. When I speak to Link, I'll be sure and tell him what you've done.'

Sara's smile was forced. 'I wish you wouldn't.'

'Why not?'

'Because she's afraid he might come down here to see for himself,' remarked Grant laconically. 'I think Link scares her.'

'He does not!'

She was instinctively defensive, but Grant was not convinced. 'Well, you looked pretty scared to me the last time he'd been talking to you,' he observed carelessly, and she realised he had mistaken panic for intimidation.

'I don't think Miss Fielding has any reason to be afraid of Link,' put in the doctor now. 'I'm sure he'll be as delighted as we all are that Jeff has shown some initative at last.' He paused. 'I hope you're going to keep up the good work.'

Sara shrugged. 'According to Mr Keating, Jeff blames me for what happened to him. He said he didn't think he'd want to see me again.'

The doctor nodded. 'That sounds like Keating.'

She moistened her lips. 'Don't you think it's true, then?'

'Oh I wouldn't be at all surprised if Jeff had said something of the sort,' responded Doctor Haswell, and Sara's spirits plummeted. 'But that's not to say you should pay too much attention to it. After all, I doubt if he was enthusiastic about seeing you in the first place.'

Her brow furrowed. 'You really think I should see him whether he agrees or not?'

'I think you may have to,' confirmed the doctor ruefully. 'Jeff's his own worst enemy, and that's who you've got to fight.'

'But what about Mr Keating?'

'Alan Keating doesn't employ you; Link does,' responded the doctor firmly. 'My information is that you've been given a free hand with the patient. Unless I decide to the contrary, I want you to exercise that privilege.'

It was easier said than done. Given Jeff's attitude, Keating evidently thought he had every right to bar her from seeing his patient, and when Sara presented herself again, just before lunch, he was no less belligerent than before.

'I don't take my instructions from Doctor Haswell,' he declared, when she mentioned what the doctor had said. 'Mr Korda—Mr *Lincoln* Korda, that is, is my employer. Until he knows—and endorses—what's been going on, I insist that you leave Jeff alone.'

Over lunch, Sara considered her options. She could wait until the following day and hope that Jeff might have changed his mind by then, which didn't seem likely. Or she could delay any further action until Keating's day off, in the hope that she could then gain entry as before. Though, knowing her adversary as she was beginning to, she suspected he would put off any free time until the present crisis was over. Or, finally, she could attempt to force her way into the suite, maybe even asking Grant to help her. But, none of these alternatives appealed to her, and she unconsciously betrayed her frustration in a long-drawn-out sigh.

'You know, you're going to have a few grey hairs before you leave here,' commented her companion drily. 'What's wrong now? Did Jeff throw another tantrum?'

Sara looked at Grant doubtfully and then, realising she couldn't bottle it up any longer, she explained what had happened. 'So you see, I don't know what to do,' she finished unhappily. 'That suite is like a fortress, with Keating acting as overlord!'

'Why don't you phone Link?' Grant suggested at once, helping himself to a peach, and she frowned.

'Could I?'

'Why not?' he shrugged. 'I do it all the time.'

'I know, but——'

'But what? It's an emergency, isn't it? I'll get you the number, if you like.'

Sara hesitated. She knew that half of Grant's eagerness to help stemmed from a desire to score against Keating. The two men barely tolerated one another at the best of times, and she couldn't deny that in the beginning, Keating's attitude had been unbearably supercilious. However, since her erstwhile success with Jeff, he had a lot more free time on his hands, and because he had had to offer his services elsewhere, Grant had taken a delight in baiting him with it.

Now she looked troubled. 'What do you think Mr Korda will say?' she asked, her own pulses racing at the thought of making the call. She hadn't spoken to Lincoln since that evening on the terrace, and looking back on it from a distance of two weeks, she was half inclined to believe she had imagined what had happened.

'Speak to him and find out,' suggested Grant, with a shrug, but his eyes were intent. 'What's the matter? Are you afraid to do it? I thought you told Doc Haswell you could handle Link.'

'I don't think I said that exactly,' said Sara, with some embarrassment. 'All right. All right, I'll speak to him. When do you think I should do it? When you call him this evening?'

'There's no time like the present,' drawled Grant, and she guessed he was enjoying her confusion, too. 'Come on. You can use the phone in Link's den. I guess you've never been in there, have you?'

Her nervous smile was non-committal, but she looked round the not-unfamiliar environs of Lincoln's study with some apprehensiveness. She remembered the room only too well from the never-to-be-forgotten night of her arrival, and she smoothed the grain of the leather-topped desk with reminiscent fingers.

In the event, Grant made the call for her, and only when Lincoln's secretary came on the line did he hand the receiver to her. 'Her name's Olivia Simons,' he hissed, his palm covering the mouthpiece, and Sara nodded gratefully as he let himself out of the room.

But Lincoln wasn't there. In spite of Sara's fervent attempts to locate him, his secretary had no definite information as to his whereabouts. 'I know he had a luncheon engagement, Miss Fielding,' she replied regretfully, 'but Mr Korda did not leave a number where I could reach him. Shall I ask him to ring you, if he does come back in to the office? Or I could leave a message with his answering service just in case he doesn't come back today.'

'Oh, no. No, that won't be necessary,' murmured Sara hastily, half relieved at the reprieve. 'I—er—Mr Masters will be speaking to him later. I'll ask him to deliver my message.'

Grant was philosophical when she found him on the terrace.

'I guess you're going to have to leave Jeff to his own devices for today,' he declared, not without some satisfaction. 'It sounds as if Link is occupied with something—or someone—more attractive than business, hmm?' He gestured towards the pool. 'Why don't we follow his example?'

Sara had to admit that the idea was inviting, but right now the beauty of her surroundings had never meant less. It was ridiculous, she knew, but Grant's careless remarks concerning his employer's activities had scraped a nerve, and excusing herself on the pretext of changing into her swimsuit, she left him and went up to her room.

She spent some time tidying her room and washing those items of her laundry she preferred to attend to herself. She left them to dry on the towel rail in the bathroom, and then seated herself on her balcony, prolonging her isolation. An oil tanker appeared on the horizon, its massive decks unmistakable even from a distance, but it came no nearer the mainland, and she wondered if it was on its way to Cuba. Closer at hand, a handful of seabirds were squabbling over the remains of a shellfish, which had been washed up by the tide, and immediately below her windows, Grant sprawled on a sunbed beside the pool. It was all very peaceful and civilised, she reflected broodingly—except there was nothing particularly soothing in the thought of Jeff trapped in his room. He was as much of a prisoner of his own frustrations as if Keating had actually locked his door with a key.

It was late afternoon when the drone of a low-flying aircraft disturbed her meditation. Looking up, she saw the chrome and silver livery of a sleek executive jet heading towards the air-strip at the other side of the island. As she watched, its under-carriage lowered to break its speed, and she realised with sudden apprehension that it was going to land.

Sara had not seen the aircraft Lincoln Korda used to fly back and forward to New York, but she had little hesitation in deciding that this must be it. Contrary to her suppositions, it seemed, he had not been spending the afternoon with a woman. He had been flying south to see his son. Doctor Haswell must have phoned him, after all? He must have decided she might need some support in her dealings with Keating and Jeff.

The aircraft had disturbed Grant, too, and he grunted and sat up, shading his eyes to watch the jet making its approach. 'Hot damn!' he muttered, and then slanting a glance up to Sara's balcony he pulled a wry face. 'Looks like you're going to get to speak to Link in person,' he added, revealing that he had been aware of her presence all along. 'You'd better come down now. I'd guess it's you he wants to see, not me.'

Sara didn't answer him, though she did beat a hasty retreat from the balcony. She, too, suspected Lincoln might be expecting an explanation of the previous night's events, and she wanted to be ready for him this time.

Her hand was not quite steady as she secured the coil of silky hair in a knot on top of her head. It would have been easier to braid it as usual, but for once she wanted him to see her as an equal, instead of a contemporary of his son's. So far, he had always caught her at a disadvantage. This time she was determined to erase that previous image.

Of course, it did cross her mind that her desire to gain his approval was not just a matter of pride. As she stroked eyeshadow on to her lids and applied a tawny gloss to her lips, she was not unaware of the light tremor in her fingers. After all, she was not so blasé that she could dismiss what had happened between them without feeling some emotion. He had kissed her! Even if she had provoked him— unwittingly or otherwise—he had taken her in his arms and made passionate love to her, and she was not indifferent to the change this must have wrought in their relationship. She wasn't sure what she expected exactly; she wasn't even sure how she wanted him to react. But she had to feel she was looking her best, even if he chose to ignore her.

A lemon-yellow camisole dress completed her ensemble. The lace-edged straps exposed her shoulders and the golden tan that was so attractive on her pale skin, and she viewed her reflection composedly before descending the stairs. She intended to be there, on the terrace, when Lincoln arrived. She intended to behave as if his arrival had not taken her by surprise, and that she had made no especial effort on his behalf. She wanted to tilt her head casually, and greet him from the depths of a sun-lounger. She wanted him to be the intruder, and herself the established occupant of his house.

But, as she stepped out on to the patio, she realised she had taken just a little too long over her appearance. She emerged into the sunlight at the same moment that Lincoln appeared at the end of the terrace, and she guessed he had strolled round from the front of the house. The jacket of a navy blue suit was looped over his shoulder, the collar of his shirt loosened and the tie pulled down in deference to the heat of the afternoon. He looked as dark and disturbing as ever, and Sara struggled to control her colour as he looked in her direction.

However, before she could formulate any kind of greeting, a second person appeared behind him. Small and slim and dark, also, Lincoln's companion was a young woman, not much older than herself, Sara estimated, and all her good intentions dissolved in a wave of indignation. The girl's bloused leather flying suit and the fur jacket draped casually about her shoulders were so obviously expensive, much like the girl herself, thought Sara tensely, but it was the look of indulgence that Lincoln bestowed upon her as she confidently caught his arm that caused Sara the most irritation. If he was truly concerned about his son, why had he brought his mistress with him? she asked herself bitterly, not so naïve that she couldn't recognise their intimacy for what it was.

To her relief, it was Grant who filled the role of welcoming committee, allowing her to remain in the background as he went to greet his employer. She would have withdrawn altogether had it not looked so obviously ill-mannered, and she reminded herself it was for Jeff's sake that she was here at all.

'Hey, Rebecca!' exclaimed Grant, identifying the young women by his words. 'This is an unexpected pleasure. Come, sit down. Link didn't tell us he was bringing you.'

'Link didn't know,' admitted the girl slyly, and to Sara's mortification, she seemed to rub herself against him as she said the words. 'I persuaded him to let me join him,' she added, her eyes drifting to Sara rather speculatively as she spoke. 'Grandpa's still in New York, but I was desperate for some sunshine!'

'Well, you got it. I hope it was worth the trip,' remarked Lincoln, extricating himself from her clinging fingers and tossing his jacket on to a chair. Then he levelled his intent gaze at the young woman standing in the shadow of the house. 'Hello, Sara. Are you waiting to speak to me?' He frowned. 'Is everything all right?'

Sara wondered how he dared ask that after what had happened at their last meeting, but it was obvious it had meant nothing to him. And by his attitude, he was inviting her to resume their previous relationship, probably bringing Rebecca Steinbeck with him just to prove his point.

Her mouth was dry, but she refused to let him see how he disconcerted her. Instead, she held up her head and said stiffly: 'I suppose that rather depends how you look at it. I assume you've spoken to Doctor Haswell. He will have told you what happened. And I want you to know I accept full responsibility—'

'Wait a minute!' Lincoln's intervention was harsh and swift, and she wondered if for a moment he had misinterpreted her words. She hoped he had, she thought savagely. It would serve him right if she embarrassed him now, in front of his—*friend*. 'Run that by me again,' he

added, taking the steps necessary to narrow the space
between them, halting with one hand raised to support his
weight against one of the creeper-hung posts of the balcony.
'Why would I have spoken to Haswell? Do I take it that
something has happened?'

Sara swallowed, her composure wilting. 'You don't
know?'

'Does it sound like it?' Lincoln was watching her with
narrowed eyes. 'What am I supposed to know?'

She took a deep breath, fixing her attention on the
exposed vee of brown skin visible above his tie. She knew
this wasn't the moment to think of such things, but she
couldn't help remembering the sensual pressure of his
mouth on hers, and the muscled urgency of his thighs
against her own. If she looked at him now, she was afraid
of what he might read in her face, and she had to force
herself to answer him with equal detachment.

'You didn't get any message, then?' she queried,
endeavouring to behave as if he had never laid a hand on
her, but his muffled oath brought her unwary gaze to his.

She need not have worried, however. The expression in
his eyes was far from indulgent, and his: 'Will you get to
the point?' was uttered in an almost threatening tone.

'All right.' Sara made a helpless gesture to hide her
resentment. Rebecca Steinbeck was staring at her with
unconcealed impatience, and she realised her prevarication
was only increasing her dilemma. 'Jeff tried to use his
crutches last night and fell,' she explained hurriedly. 'I did
try to ring you to tell you myself, but your secretary didn't
know where you were.'

'Last night!' exclaimed Lincoln blankly, and Sara sighed.

'No, this afternoon,' she corrected him, dreading the
inquisition she was sure was to come. 'It—it's created a
problem, you see. I wanted your endorsement before going
any further.'

He straightened then, the proof of his own reaction
evident in the sudden pallor of his skin. 'Did I hear you
correctly?' he asked at last. 'Did you say Jeff actually tried
to use crutches? My God! When was this? Did you say last
night?'

'Yes.' Sara moistened her lips. 'He—he'd got out of bed.

Doctor Haswell thinks it might not have been the first time.'

'God!'

Lincoln was obviously astounded, but she had no time to assimilate his reaction further before Rebecca intervened.

'Would you mind if I asked Cora to take my bags up to my suite, darling?' she asked, in a plaintive tone. 'I'm sure you're dying to hear all about Jeff, but I'm truly desperate for a shower. I want to get out of these clothes and into something more—comfortable. If you don't mind . . .'

'What?' It was obvious from the dazed look on Lincoln's face as he swung round to face the other girl that he was still absorbed with what he had learned. But he quickly recovered his good manners. 'I'm sorry,' he exclaimed, pushing long brown fingers through the virile thickness of his hair. 'Of course. I'll have Thaddeus take them up right away.' He glanced back at Sara, and now his expression was cool and controlled. 'I guess we'll have to continue this later,' he added, taking the hand Rececca held out to him, and shaking his head as if to clear it. 'Until later. Grant.' He inclined his head. 'Sara.'

They went into the house, leaving Sara feeling cold and bereft. Once again their conversation had been inconclusive, she thought tensely. And once again, she felt as if she had come off worst.

CHAPTER NINE

GRANT was in the hall when Sara came down for dinner that evening.

'We're having drinks outside,' he told her wryly, guiding her through the French doors of the dining room. 'A cosy little foursome, wouldn't you say? Or perhaps you wouldn't.'

Sara looked up at him warily. 'Is Miss Steinbeck staying here, then?' she asked, in an undertone. 'I thought her grandfather owned a house in Miami. Isn't that what you said?'

'Oh, there's a house all right,' conceded Grant, with some irony. 'An enormous place overlooking the bay. However, you heard the lady say her grandfather is still in New York. I guess she thinks it's more fun to stay here. And more—convenient, hmm?'

Sara looked away from his sardonic face. Grant might know nothing of her infatuation with Lincoln Korda, but he knew women, and it amused him to stir her resentment. He must know she was on edge over her dealings with Keating, and he evidently enjoyed reminding her that Lincoln considered Rebecca Steinbeck's comfort was more important than her own.

A more galling discovery was that they were first down. Lincoln and his guest did not appear until some fifteen minutes later, and then they arrived together, which to Sara's mind was significant. Tonight, the dark girl was wearing a backless gown of silver moiré, with a cuffed collar and long batwing sleeves. It made Sara's cream silk shirt and pants look very ordinary, but there were only a limited number of changes Sara could ring with her wardrobe. Besides, she told herself impatiently, what did it matter what she wore? No one was going to look at her with Rebecca Steinbeck in their sights. Which was just as

well, she decided grimly. Any involvement with Lincoln
Korda could only mean trouble, and she didn't think she
could handle him in any case. With her hair plaited and
coiled in a coronet on top of her head, she looked neat,
but not exotic, a fair description of her looks as compared
to the American girl's.

'Are we late?' Rebecca asked coyly, as Grant gallantly
took charge of the drinks, and as she went to join him,
Sara was briefly alone with her employer.

'I'm sorry our conversation was interrupted earlier,' he
remarked, joining her as she hovered somewhat nervously
near the rim of the pool, and Sara shrugged.

'It doesn't matter,' she said, watching the progress of a
leaf that had fallen into the water, but Lincoln was insistent.

'It does,' he said. 'And can't you look at me when I'm
talking to you, dammit? After the way you behaved this
afternoon, I'm beginning to believe you're avoiding me.'

She moved one slim shoulder. 'Oughtn't you to be
looking after your guest, Mr Korda?' she enquired,
examining the contents of her own glass, and with a
muttered imprecation, he moved away.

The conversation became general, although Sara took
little part in it. She was relieved that Grant proved a more
than adequate substitute, and by the time they went in for
dinner, Lincoln's face had lost its grim intensity.

For her part, Sara had enough to do in controlling her
errant attention. In spite of herself, her eyes were constantly
drawn to Lincoln's dark-clad figure. Although he was not
wearing a dinner jacket this evening, the dark blue corded
velvet which had taken its place was just as attractive, and
the lazy grace of his movements was a constant source of
illicit pleasure. Or was it pain? she wondered tensely, as a
shivering spasm invaded her stomach. She had only to
think of him with Rebecca Steinbeck for the melting fluidity
of her bones to harden into brittle relics, and she was
unaware he was speaking to her until Grant's fingers jogged
her arm.

'Link was asking if there's something wrong with your
steak,' he remarked, with heavy cynicism, and Sara's lids
fluttered wildly as she struggled to compose herself.

'What? Oh—oh, no. No, there's nothing wrong with it,'

she said hastily, aware of Rebecca's resentment that she should be neglected, even for a moment. Her eyes flickered over Lincoln's sombre face, some distance from her at the end of the table. 'I'm—not very hungry, that's all.'

His lips tightened. 'If you're worrying about Jeff, forget it,' he advised her bleakly. 'I was going to wait until after dinner, but I've spoken to Haswell, and I'm content that he knows what he's doing.'

Sara knew a brief spark of indignation. '*He* knows what *he's* doing?' she echoed disbelievingly, meeting his gaze with the shield of her anger to protect her, and he sighed.

'All right. *You* apparently know what *you're* doing,' he amended evenly. 'Hell, anyone who can get Jeff to do something for himself has to be applauded!'

Sara bent her head. She had half hoped he would argue with her. It would have given her a way to expunge a little of her frustration. But he didn't, and she was obliged to mumble: 'Thank you,' as she nudged the stem of watercress which had adorned her steak around her plate.

'What's so amazing about Jeff learning to use crutches, darling?' Rebecca enquired at that moment, evidently determined to retain Lincoln's attention whatever the cost. Talking about his son might not be wholly to her liking, but Sara could see she resented the fact that someone else had captured his interest.

'I did tell you Jeff had refused to respond to therapy,' Lincoln reminded her drily, and Rebecca pulled a face.

'Well, yes, I know you did,' she defended herself swiftly, 'but surely it was only a matter of time before he realised it was his only option.'

He regarded her unsmilingly. 'You don't know Jeff, Rebecca. Options don't mean much to him.'

'It's not my fault I don't know him,' she responded, adopting an aggrieved air. 'You don't know him all that well yourself!'

There was an ominous silence after this remark, and Sara, catching Grant's eye, saw the gleam of malicious amusement that was lifting the corner of his mouth. He was enjoying this, she thought angrily, and although she had no reason to feel any sympathy for her employer, she did.

'It's not easy for anyone to get to know Jeff,' she inserted quietly. 'Accidents affect different people different ways. A few—a very few—find the strength to overcome their disabilities without any outside influence, but most people need all the patience and understanding they can get.'

'I don't need a sermon. I know how difficult it must have been for Link,' retorted Rebecca, resenting her intervention, but now Lincoln himself broke in.

'Whether or not it's been difficult for me is not in question here,' he exclaimed harshly. 'What Sara's saying is the truth. Jeff's taken his injuries badly, and until she came he wouldn't even look at a wheelchair. Now, apparently, he's actually attempting to get out of bed, and it annoys me that she thought I might be angry because he's got a few cuts and bruises.'

Sara's lips parted. 'You approve?'

'Do you doubt it?' His grey eyes were coolly intent.

'I wasn't sure.' She swallowed. 'Mr Keating——'

'You'll get no more obstruction from him,' said Lincoln flatly. 'I've threatened to take him back to New York if he refuses to co-operate. I don't think he will.'

'Well, I think Michelle should be held responsible,' said Rebecca firmly, evidently deciding she was having no luck with her previous method of approach. 'I mean, Jeff can't have had much of a life with her all these years, can he? I heard that there was a rumour going around that the crash wasn't exactly an accident——'

'Where did you hear that?' Lincoln did not try to conceal his anger now, and Rebecca hurried to defend herself once again.

'Oh, I don't know, darling,' she protested, shaking her head. 'You know how these rumours get around. No one admits to starting them, but they're there anyway. And you did intimate to Grandpa that Jeff had—well, attempted to take an overdose . . .'

'That's different,' said Lincoln harshly. 'For God's sake, he's only nineteen, Rebecca! How would you like to be paralysed, confined to a wheelchair, compelled to use sticks for getting around the rest of your life? Don't you think, in those circumstances, a feeling of hopelessness would be quite natural?'

'Don't get angry with me, Link darling,' Rebecca pouted

sulkily. 'It's not my fault that Jeff's—the way he is.' She shrugged. 'As I said, Michelle——'

'Let's leave Michelle out of this, shall we?' Lincoln pushed back his chair and got abruptly to his feet, just as Vinnie appeared with a tray of coffee. 'I'll take mine in the den,' he declared, walking past her to the door. 'Join me in fifteen minutes, Sara. I want to talk to you before I leave.'

'You're not leaving tonight, Link!' Rebecca exclaimed in dismay, but he barely glanced her way.

'I did warn you this was only a flying visit,' he remarked ironically, halting in the doorway. 'And you're welcome to stay, if you want to. My house is your house, isn't that what they say down here?'

The atmosphere after he had departed was, if anything, even more charged than before. Rebecca's jaw was compressed with a mixture of frustration and fury, and the looks she kept casting in Sara's direction would have fuelled a furnace could their power have been harnessed. It was obvious she needed someone to blame, and Sara was the equally obvious choice.

'I suppose you think you're very clever, don't you?' Rebecca demanded of the younger girl, as soon as Cora had left the room. 'How did you persuade Jeff to get off his back, I wonder? Do paraplegics have sexual urges? I'd really like to know.'

'Becca!' said Grant warningly, but Rebecca was indifferent to anyone's feelings but her own.

'No, I mean it,' she persisted maliciously. 'There has to be a reason why Sara has succeeded when everyone else has failed. And she is rather attractive, don't you think, even if she wouldn't win any prizes for deportment!'

This unsubtle reference to her lameness brought a hot flush of colour to Sara's cheeks, but before she could say anything, Grant intervened. 'You really are peeved, aren't you, Becca?' he mused infuratingly, 'What's the matter? Can't you stand the competition? Or are you afraid Link will see the attraction, too?'

As Rebecca was formulating a suitable retort, Sara decided she had had enough. 'It's all right, Grant,' she said evenly, getting to her feet. 'Miss Steinbeck can think what she likes about my association with Jeff. I don't mind. In fact, it's quite a compliment, considering she has problems with perfectly normal relationships!'

'You *bitch*!'

Rebecca was incensed, and Sara steeled herself for the stream of abuse she was sure was to follow. But, as if realising she was unlikely to enhance her image by acting like a fishwife, Rebecca thought again, and a veneer of sophistication descended on her features.

'I'm sure you realise I shall have to tell Mr Korda of your quite—unprovoked rudeness,' she declared, reaching for her wine and taking a studied sip. 'You shouldn't think because you've aroused some latent spark of paternity in Link that you're indispensable. A few well-chosen words— at the right time, of course, if you get my meaning—and you could find yourself on a plane back to England.'

Sara folded her napkin and laid it on the table with a quite remarkable show of calmness; remarkable, because inside she was a quivering mass of jelly. 'If Mr Korda gives me notice, then that's his decision, isn't it?' she said steadily. 'And now, if you'll excuse me . . .'

It wasn't until she was closing the door of her room that she remembered Lincoln had said he wanted to see her in fifteen minutes. It was already almost fifteen minutes since he had walked out of the dining room, and the prospect of meeting him now, in her present state of nerves, was barely feasible. How had she dared to speak to Rebecca like that? she asked herself miserably. However provocative the other girl had been, she was a guest in this house. Sara was not. She was an employee, nothing more, and just because she was allowed to live like a member of the family was no reason to behave like one. Rebecca was right. She had been rude; unforgivably so. And if Lincoln was persuaded to fire her, she had only herself to blame.

But for the present, she had the coming interview to face. She would need all her wits about her if she was to meet his coolness and detachment in equal measure. He obviously expected her to take her cue from him, and if she wanted to help Jeff she had to put her own emotions aside. Besides, nothing momentous had happened, she argued for the umpteenth time. She had provoked him, that evening on the terrace, much as she had provoked Rebecca a few minutes ago; only in Lincoln's case, his reaction had been typically chauvinistic.

With this conclusion ironed out in her mind, Sara added a touch of powder to her cheeks, to subdue their hectic colour, and tucked an errant strand of red-gold silk back into place. Then, resigned to the fact that she still looked disturbed, she left the room again before she could lose what little courage she had.

She was halfway downstairs when she saw Rebecca going into Lincoln's study. Her sandalled feet had made little sound on the treads, and she guessed the other girl was unaware of her observation. But the fact remained, Rebecca was now closeted with her employer, making sure he heard her side of the story before he heard Sara's, she guessed. Still, whatever her purpose, Sara could not intrude without encountering more hostility, and with a feeling of frustration, she turned back. He would have to send for her, she decided, re-entering her own room and closing the door. He could hardly expect her to hang about downstairs, waiting for Rebecca to leave.

An hour later, Sara looked at her watch with some misgivings. Either he had forgotten all about the summons he had issued earlier, or he expected her to make herself available when he was free. But how was she supposed to know when that was? There was no chance that Rebecca might inform her when she was leaving, and short of watching the door to his study, she was helpless. Of course, she could go down and press her ear to the panels in the hope of hearing some sounds from within, but she could imagine the reaction if someone caught her at it. She had thought she might hear Rebecca come upstairs, or voices even from the hall, but the house was silent. It was barely ten o'clock, but it could have been midnight, and she sighed in frustration at the remembrance that Lincoln was leaving in the morning.

Leaving her seat in the blue and cream luxury of the sitting room, she opened her door and stepped out into the corridor. Wall-lights burned all night in their sconces along the wide hallway, and there was no sense of the lateness of the hour as she walked towards the galleried landing. Below, in the hall, no one stirred, but there was a line of light beneath Lincoln's study door, and abandoning discretion, Sara knocked.

Predictably, there was no reply, and she expelled a quivering breath. Asleep or—*asleep*, she pondered uneasily, reaching for the handle. Oh, please, let him be alone, she added, and silently opened the door.

The room was empty. A brief glance around elicited the information that although Lincoln had evidently been here— there was a coffee cup and a glass holding down the papers on his desk—he was no longer in residence. Was he coming back? she wondered. The lamps still burning seemed to indicate that he was. Or had he simply left them for Cora or one of the other servants to extinguish? Did someone as wealthy as Lincoln Korda care about conserving energy?

Closing the door again, she chewed thoughtfully at her lower lip. What should she do? Leave him a note? Apologise for not keeping their appointment, but explain that she had seen Rebecca going into his room and she hadn't wanted to intrude? There was something about putting her excuses into words she didn't like, and she finally decided it was the thought that Lincoln might suspect that that was exactly what they were. Would he believe her? Or would he assume she was simply avoiding him again?

The draught of warm air that swept about her ankles at that moment ended her speculations. A door banging and the unmistakable smell of the ocean alerted her senses, and she had no time to co-ordinate a course of action before Lincoln turned the corner and saw her. He had evidently been swimming. His dark hair was plastered slickly to his head and his feet were bare. For the rest, a navy-blue towelling bathrobe was tied loosely at his waist, and the towel he had used to dry himself hung carelessly over his shoulder.

If she was startled at seeing him, he was no less surprised to find her outside his study door. The dark brows arched enquiringly, almost as if he had not issued that summons earlier, she thought crossly, trying to control her racing pulses. There was even the suspicion of a frown in the downward tilt of his mouth, and she wondered if he imagined she had deliberately delayed this meeting.

Sara spoke first, compelled to say something to justify her position. 'I—er—I've been waiting to see you,' she murmured stiffly, pushing her hands into the pockets of her pants. 'I didn't know you'd gone out.'

'How could you?' Lincoln's voice was cool. 'But aren't you a little late? I believe I said nine o'clock, not a quarter after ten.'

She sighed. 'I did come at the proper time, but you already had a visitor,' she replied. 'Naturally, I assumed you'd let me know when you were free.'

'You assumed that, did you?' There was irony in his voice. 'It didn't occur to you that as you had the prior claim to my attention, you could have let me deal with my—visitor, as you put it?'

'I didn't think you'd want to be interrupted.'

'Didn't you?'

'No.' Sara squared her shoulders. 'In any case, I'm here now, Can we talk?'

'Like this?' Lincoln's mouth twisted. 'It may have slipped your notice, but I've been swimming.'

'I do realise that.' She held up her head. 'Tomorrow, then.'

'No. Tomorrow I shall be in New York,' he answered, shaking his head. Then, evenly: 'You'd better come up to my suite. We can talk while I get changed.'

She stared at him. 'I don't think that's at all suitable.'

'No?'

'No.' She could feel her colour deepening. 'Mr Korda——'

'Oh, call me Link, for God's sake,' he muttered impatiently. 'We're not exactly strangers, are we? That's one of the things I want to talk to you about, and perhaps it would be as well if we spoke somewhere privately. My suite seems the most logical place.'

'I don't think so.'

'Why?' His nostrils flared. 'You're not afraid of what I might do to you, are you? You can always scream, you know. If what I hear is true, Jeff's yelling woke the whole household.'

Sara pursed her lips. 'Mr Korda——'

'Do you want to keep this job?' he snapped suddenly, and she flinched.

'Of course.'

'Then follow me,' he ordered, and strode away towards the stairs.

Lincoln's rooms were, as Grant had told her, in the opposite wing from that of his son. Lights had been left burning there, too, and their huge pleated shades illuminated a comfortable sitting room, with ivory-silk walls, highlighted by misty Japanese prints, and squashy striped sofas, in shades of apple green and ice-blue leather. The carpet was silk, too, and led into the adjoining bedroom, but Sara resolutely seated herself in the sitting room. Even being here, in Lincoln's apartments, was nerve-racking enough, without the added trauma of seeing where he slept. She had been half afraid they might find Rebecca already in residence after the way she had behaved earlier, but that particular fear was unfounded. Evidently the other girl had decided not to push her luck, although she could well be waiting for Lincoln to join her in her rooms after his swim.

'I'm going to take a shower,' he remarked now, flicking a switch that brought music from a concealed hi-fi system flooding into the apartments. 'Make yourself at home. I won't be long.'

'Thank you.'

Sara's response was clipped, but she couldn't help it. Lincoln was unloosening the cord of his bathrobe as he walked through to the bedroom, and her eyes were drawn compulsively to the lean expanse of chest exposed by the parting panels. He was not a particularly hairy man, as she already knew, but she had glimpsed the arrowing curls low on his stomach. And although she fought the image, she couldn't help the unbidden thought that he might not have been wearing anything else.

The sound of running water assured her that he was at least taking his shower, and deciding she was behaving like a schoolgirl, she left her seat. The music was soothing, a delightful sonata by Chopin, that Sara recognised from her days of classical ballet training. Giving in to an urge to exercise her abilities, she allowed herself a little pirouette, only to falter badly when her ankle refused her weight.

'Damn,' she muttered, recovering her balance, and limping to the archway that divided the two rooms, she used the pillar to support her weight as she massaged her ankle.

It was inconceivable that she shouldn't allow herself to glance into Lincoln's bedroom then. She would not have been human had she not been curious, and as she had come so far . . .

Setting her injured foot back on the floor, she gazed around the spacious apartment. As in the sitting room, the walls were once again hung with Italian silk, this time in a more restful shade of amethyst. There were a pair of matching armchairs, a writing desk and a glass-topped table, and an enormously big colonial four-poster, spread with a soft satin coverlet. The room was comfortable, without being feminine, the pale cream carpet underfoot the most obvious touch of luxury.

The temptation to feel the softness of the carpet beneath her bare foot was irresistible, and easing off her sandal, she allowed her toes to curl into its silk pile. There was something almost sensual in that tentative contact, and she was so absorbed with what she was doing, she didn't notice that the water had stopped running. The first intimation she had was when the door to the adjoining bathroom opened, and she froze ignominiously when Lincoln came out.

She was half afraid he might be naked, but he wasn't. He was in the process of tying the cord of a wine-coloured dressing gown, and judging by the way it clung to his damp flesh, she suspected it must be silk, too.

He paused for a moment when he saw her, his gaze taking in the hastily withdrawn foot, and the sandal which refused to slide back on to it. Then, crossing his arms, he said flatly: 'Not so indifferent, after all, hmm?'

Sara sighed. 'What can I say? I was curious. You were in the shower, and——'

'—and you thought you'd have a look around.'

'I wasn't nosing.'

'I never said you were.'

'No.' She conceded that was true. 'I—it's a beautiful house. You must be proud of it.'

'Proud?' His brows arched. 'I should be, perhaps, but I'm not. This was Michelle's father's house. I can't forget that.'

'Do you want to?' It seemed natural to ask him.

Lincoln shrugged. 'I had no animosity towards the old man, only towards his daughter. But perhaps they were too closely allied.' He broke off, as if just realising to whom he was speaking. 'Anyway, you're not interested in my hang-ups. I suppose you expect an apology.'

'An apology?' For a moment, Sara was confused. Then she bent her head. 'If you mean about—about what happened a couple of weeks ago, it doesn't matter.'

'What else do you think I meant?' he demanded, and she thought how incongruous it was they should be standing talking here, in the bedroom, as if it was quite acceptable to do so.

'I—nothing.' She glanced behind her. 'Shouldn't we go into the other room?'

He ignored her request, taking up a silver-backed brush from the bureau and using it to smooth the unruly tangle of his wet hair. Because they were wet, the ends of his hair overlapped the collar of his dressing gown, causing a darkening dampness of the cloth. It was an incredibly personal thing to do, implying an intimacy which they did not share, but Sara couldn't help watching him, and feeling an involuntary reaction.

'Tell me about Jeff,' he said, playing with the brush in his hands. 'Haswell seems to think you're achieving some kind of miracle. I'd like you to tell me how you're doing it.'

Sara swallowed. 'I don't do anything much,' she murmured deprecatingly. 'We talk, that's all. About anything and everything.'

'Just like that.'

'Well . . .' she hesitated. 'It wasn't so easy in the beginning, of course. He—Jeff, that is—he suspected I was some kind of doctor; a psychiatrist, I think. When I told him I used to be a dancer, I don't think he believed me. Then, when he did, he thought I'd come to patronise him.'

'Yes, Jeff would think that.' Lincoln frowned. 'Go on.'

'There's not much more to tell. I suppose I had to get him to trust me. I think he does—or did! When I learned what he'd been doing, I was absolutely amazed.'

'But flattered, surely. He must think something about you to try and prove himself to you.'

Sara felt the rush of colour to her cheeks. It was no use. With this man, she had no defence.

'I think he's begun to believe there is a life to be lived outside the four walls of his bedroom,' she offered carefully. 'But watching television could have done that.'

Lincoln shook his head, dropping the brush back on to its tray. 'Do you know how often I've tried to get him to have a television in his room?' he demanded. 'He wouldn't even listen to me. Now I go away, and not only is there a television, but a video recorder, too.'

She took a deep breath. 'I hope—I hope his fall hasn't changed his mind.'

'You haven't seen him since it happened?'

'No.'

'No, Keating stopped you, didn't he?'

'Well, he did say *Jeff* didn't want to see me,' she admitted honestly. 'Apparently he blames me for what happened.'

'Mmm,' Lincoln nodded. 'But you don't intend to let that deter you.'

'Not if Doctor Haswell gives me his support. Oh,' she made a rueful gesture, 'and you, of course.' But as she said this, she remembered what Rebecca had said, and she wondered if this was his way of getting round to that particular obstacle.

'I shouldn't have thought my support would mean that much to you,' he ventured quietly. 'After what happened between us, I wouldn't blame you if you had little faith in my judgement.'

'Oh?' Sara cast another rueful glance over her shoulder, realising that in replacing his hairbrush on the bureau, he had lessened the distance between them. 'I don't know what you mean.'

'Yes, you do.' He was patient with her. 'I shouldn't have touched you—we both know that. All I can say in mitigation is that somehow it got out of hand. After the way I had accused you of—well, provocation, it was pretty pitiful that I should be the one to take advantage of you. I'm sorry.'

'I've told you, it doesn't matter,' she murmured awkwardly. 'I've—forgotten all about it.'

'Have you?' His tone was dry. 'How convenient for you.'

Sara drew another breath. 'Is that all?'

'I suppose so.'

But when she bent to restore her sandal to her foot, he came towards her, so that when she straightened, there was barely a yard between them. 'Don't take any notice of what Rebecca may say,' he added, removing a long tawny hair from the collar of her shirt and stretching it between his fingers. 'She—well, she can be vicious.'

'Yes.' Sara's heart was beating so fast, she had difficulty in saying anything.

'Yes.' Lincoln looked down at the silky strand he was holding and nodded. 'As you noticed, she came to the den earlier.'

Sara's tongue circled her dry lips. 'I know.'

'Do you know what she said?'

She shrugged. 'I can guess.'

'You'd probably be right.' He looked at her and his eyes were disturbingly intent. 'It seems Rebecca resents your being here. Your success with Jeff notwithstanding, I think she'd do almost anything to force you to leave. Including telling me what you think of the relationship she has with me.'

She gasped. 'I didn't——'

'Didn't what?'

'Discuss your relationship with Miss Steinbeck.' Sara's face burned. 'I was rude, but not about that. She—well, she implied some things about Jeff, and I retaliated, that's all.'

'What things?'

She looked away. 'Does it matter?'

'I think so.'

'Oh—well, it was just something about him being— attracted to me. It was a lot of nonsense.'

The hair snapped and Lincoln dropped it on to the carpet at their feet. 'I see.' He frowned. 'But that's not so outrageous, surely. I dare say Jeff is attracted to you.'

Sara sighed. 'It was the way she said it.'

'Ah.' He inclined his head. 'Rebecca can be a little—
outspoken at times.'

Sara forced a tight smile. 'Can I go now?'

'Have I upset you?'

'No . . .'

His face darkened. 'It seems I have. Look,' he paused to
take a breath, 'I'll wait and leave in the morning. That
way, I can take Rebecca back with me. Okay?'

'It's nothing to do with me.' All she wished was that the
interview was over. 'If that's all . . .'

'Oh, for the Lord's sake!' He expelled his breath heavily.
'What do you want me to do?'

'Me?' She stared at him blankly. 'I can't tell you what to
do. If you *want* to take Miss Steinbeck back with you, then
that's your—your prerogative.'

'My prerogative!' She could feel his eyes boring into her.
'Such a long word to imply something entirely different.
What do you really think of our relationship, I wonder?
Has Grant been regaling you with the saga of the de Veres
and the Kordas?'

Her guilty expression was answer enough, and Lincoln's
lips twisted. 'So now you know my assertion about being a
married man was a defensive mechanism.'

'Mr Korda——'

'Link!'

'Mr Korda—I don't think we should be having this
conversation.'

'Why?'

'Why?' She looked at him imploringly, and then wished
she hadn't. His eyes were too shrewd; too watchful; too
observant; too distractingly dangerous to her peace of mind.
'Please—I should be going——'

'Don't you want to know why I lied?'

'Why you lied?' Sara swallowed convulsively. This was
getting out of hand. 'I—don't think that's necessary.'

'Nevertheless, I'd like to tell you.'

'Mr Korda——'

'It's quite simple really,' he said, giving her a rueful
smile. It was the first time he had smiled at her without
sarcasm, and her heart flipped a beat. 'After Michelle and I
separated, I got involved in series of—what shall I call

them?—unfortunate situations. They were my indiscretions, of course. I'm not blaming anyone else. The truth is, I went a little wild, and there are always women willing—— Anyway, since I learned some sense, it's become second nature to me to keep most members of your sex at arm's length, and if that sounds abominably conceited—well, it's not meant to.'

Sara managed to nod. 'I understand.'

'Of course,' he went on, just when she was beginning to breathe again, 'that's no excuse for the way I treated you. Even if I felt I had some provocation.' His eyes darkened perceptibly. 'Were you Antony's mistress?'

She took an involuntary step backward, and came up against the solid curve of the archway. 'Antony's mistress?' she echoed, foolishly, wincing as the post dug into her spine. For a moment, she couldn't remember who 'Antony' was. Then, as she reminded herself that he meant *Tony*, his expression changed.

'Did you hurt yourself?' he exclaimed, coming towards her as she endeavoured to step away from the jamb, and her involuntary denial was silenced by the searching gentleness of his hands. Half turning her away from him, he probed the small of her back with tender fingers, finding the sore spot and massaging it expertly.

'Better?' he asked, when she couldn't suppress the sigh of pure relief that escape her lips, and she nodded.

'Much better,' she admitted, and his hands stilled abruptly as she looked up into his face.

She was held, sideways, between his hands, and although she knew she ought to move away from him, she couldn't. Her gaze was caught and held by the sudden penetration of his, and almost imperceptibly the mood changed.

His eyes moved from her face, down the slender column of her throat to the dusky hollow just visible below the lapels of her shirt. Because he was holding her sideways, he could look down the vee of her shirt, and her flesh tingled warmly beneath that pervasive appraisal. She knew a quite incredible desire to feel his hands all over her body, and her skin felt almost sensitized with the urgency of that need.

'You don't hurt anywhere else, do you?' he asked,

noticing the sudden spasm that crossed her face, and she shook her head.

'No!'

'Are you sure?' With unhurried deliberation, his hand moved from her waist in front, up over the tense frame of her ribs, to the swelling curve of her breasts. 'You don't hurt here—or here,' he murmured, his palm caressing each swollen bud in turn, and then sliding inside the neckline of her shirt to find the silken softness of her flesh.

'Oh——' Her breath caught in her throat at the sensuous exploration of his hands, and his breathing quickened in concert, as he bent his head towards her. 'No,' she protested, turning her head away, but he wasn't listening to her. Whatever thought had been in his mind when he asked her about his brother, her clumsy stumbling had erased it. Touching her had aroused other feelings, and she was as guilty as he was for not getting out of here while she could.

His mouth at the curve of her jawline was incredibly sensual, his tongue touching her skin, letting her feel its heat and its wetness. She wanted his tongue in her mouth, she thought dizzily. She wanted to wind her arms around his neck, and press herself close against him; so close he could feel her heart beating, so close she could feel his stirring maleness between them.

'Oh, God, Sara,' he muttered, feeling her weakening resistance, and sliding his arm around her waist, he pulled her fully against him.

His mouth sought hers then, satisfying that alien part of herself that had wanted this to happen, while his hand at the back of her head tore impatiently at the coronet of braids that confined her hair. With an urgency that bordered on violence, he loosened the pins and threaded his powerful fingers throught its length, winding its brilliance around her neck and delighting in the intimacy.

'I want you,' he muttered, burying his face in its silken curtain, and she was too inflamed to do anything but acquiesce. She wanted him, too, she thought incredulously, and nothing else seemed of half so much importance.

The sound of the outer door to Lincoln's apartments opening and closing did not immediately register. Lincoln was kissing her, his hands on her hips were eliciting a quite

uncontrollable response to his arousal, and all outside
influences had ceased to exist. She was lost in a world
where nothing mattered but that he should go on touching
her and caressing her, and devouring her with his lips, and
when he abruptly put her from him, she whimpered in
dismay.

'Please . . .' she breathed, her confused senses still
refusing to accept that he had rejected her, and with a
groan of impatience, he put a finger to his lips. Then,
stepping past her, he went into the sitting room.

'Link?'

The doubtful enquiry was spoken in Rebecca's unmistakable tones, and Sara felt a wash of cold sanity sweep over
her. Dear God! she thought in agony, as trembling fingers
sought to restore her gaping shirt to rights. She had now
indentified the sound that had echoed in her subconscious.
She never thought she would have reason to feel grateful to
Rebecca Steinbeck for anything, but she was. And she had
been right all along. Lincoln had arranged to see his
mistress after his swim. Only she had forestalled him, and
now Rebecca had come to find out what was going on.

She glanced despairingly about her. She was trapped.
Unless Lincoln took Rebecca back to her own apartments,
they would be coming in here soon, and she would be
caught, like a fly in honey. Only she didn't like her
metaphor: more like a fly in a web of deceit, she thought
bitterly. And how would Lincoln explain her presence,
without resorting to more deception?

CHAPTER TEN

'I HAD to see you—to speak to you before you left,' Rebecca was saying now, and although Sara couldn't see them, she could imagine the dark girl winding herself about him. Her voice was so persuasive, so confident—husky with the urgency of a passion long denied. Sara would have done anything not to listen to it, but she didn't have much choice.

Lincoln's response was less encouraging, however. 'You shouldn't have come here, Rebecca,' he said, and Sara took a shaking breath. How ironic it would be if by involving himself with both, he had successfully alienated either!

'I had to.' Rebecca's tone was tearful now, hinting of a different interpretation. 'I couldn't bear to let you go away, thinking of me as you do. It's not my fault I care so much about you. You don't know what it's like to——'

'Not now, Rebecca!' Lincoln sounded distinctly unfriendly. 'Look, we'll talk again tomorrow. I'm not leaving until the morning. You can come back with me, if you like.'

'I can?' There was a pause. 'Then why can't we——?'

'No, Rebecca!'

'Why not?'

Her eagerness was mortifying, and Sara had heard more than enough. If only there was some way she could get out of here, she thought desperately. If only she had the nerve to walk out now and call his bluff, and let Rebecca see what kind of man he was. But, although the sound of Rebecca begging Lincoln to make love to her was anathema, the idea of exposing herself to the other girl's scorn and ridicule was even more unthinkable. Nevertheless, she refused to listen any longer, and treading silently across the carpet, she opened his bathroom door and stepped inside.

The atmosphere in the bathroom was still moist and steamy from Lincoln's shower, although a fan humming softly in the background was doing its best to clear the air. It was a huge bathroom, illuminated by lights concealed below a cornice set up near the ceiling. A large step-in tub and a smoked-glass shower compartment were divided by a collection of ferns and climbing plants with wide, spiky leaves, and misted mirrors threw back her reflection from a dozen different angles.

There was something intensely personal about being in his bathroom, she realised uneasily. The razor he had evidently used earlier was still lying between the twin hand-basins, and the towels he had soaked in drying were strewn about the floor. The navy robe he had worn after his swim was deposited on the lid of a laundry basket, and as there was no sign of a discarded pair of shorts, she was left to wonder if he had been wearing any.

But at least she could hear nothing but the hum of the fan in here, she acknowledged with satisfaction even if the thought of spending an unspecified period in his bathroom filled her with dismay. Perhaps she should take a bath, she mused wryly, trying to lift her spirits. But nothing could erase the image of what she was trying to avoid.

'Sara!'

She heard Lincoln call her name before the door behind her opened and he appeared. It happened so quickly, she half thought he had told Rebecca she was here, and was summoning her to join them. The prospect of that was so distasteful to her, she remained silent, and only when he opened the door and she saw the empty bedroom beyond did she begin to hope that he had succeeded in getting rid of the girl.

'What are you doing in here?' he demanded, stepping back to allow her to emerge into the bedroom again, and Sara flushed as she came forward.

'I could have been taking a bath. It would have been all the same to you,' she retorted, deciding the best method of defence was attack. 'Do you usually walk into bathrooms unannounced? Or as it was me, didn't you think it mattered?'

Lincoln's mouth compressed. 'Would you believe me if I told you I was half afraid you might have gone?' he asked quietly. 'I wouldn't have blamed you—Rebecca is hardly discreet.'

'How could I go?' Sara argued hotly. 'I may be unimportant, but I'm not exactly invisible!'

'What do you mean?'

She caught her breath. 'You—you and Miss Steinbeck, that is—were between me and the door!'

'Oh!' Lincoln nodded now. 'You didn't realise there was another door.'

'Another door?' squeaked Sara in dismay. 'Where?'

'There,' said Lincoln carelessly, gesturing across the room.

It was a humiliating discovery to learn that the door she had thought must lead into his dressing room actually led into the corridor. She wondered if he thought she had known about it all along, and had gone into the bathroom to pretend she hadn't. Of course, there might even be a second door out of the bathroom for all she knew. Oh, why hadn't she considered that possibility? Instead of putting herself in such a position!

'How foolish of me,' she murmured now, her brief spurt of defiance evaporating. 'I'm sorry.' Her voice was stiff. 'I suppose you think I was eavesdropping.'

'Hardly.' His mouth turned down at the corners. 'Besides, there was nothing private about our conversation.'

'Miss Steinbeck might not agree with you.'

'*Miss Steinbeck* was simply concerned in convincing me that she's not the cold-hearted bitch she appeared earlier,' said Lincoln shortly, and Sara bent her head.

'I don't wish to discuss it.'

'No, nor do I,' he agreed levelly, 'but I do want you to understand her motives.'

'They're really nothing to do with me,' she insisted, wishing she had never mentioned Rebecca, but Lincoln wasn't finished.

'Rebecca obeys her grandfather in all things,' he added quietly. 'Michael would like her to be the second Mrs Korda. Do I make myself clear?'

Sara drew a painful breath. 'You don't have to explain anything to me.'

'Damn you, I know I don't! I just wanted——'

'Any feeling you have for Miss Steinbeck, or she for you——'

'This has nothing to do with Rebecca's feelings. God, I don't care about Rebecca's feelings right now. Only yours!'

'Mine?' Sara lifted her head then, but the brilliance of his eyes was too intense. 'I—it's late. I've got to go.'

'Why?'

'Why?' She glanced longingly towards the archway into the sitting room. 'Well, because—because I do.'

'Because Rebecca interrupted us, and your narrow little mind can't cope with that kind of complication,' he corrected her flatly. 'Okay. Okay, goodnight.'

'Goodnight.'

She turned to go, but as she reached the arch that divided the rooms, she hesitated. The choice was hers now. She could leave if she wanted to; he had evidently lost all interest in her. But this time pride resisted his propensity to have the last word.

Speaking over her shoulder, she threw his taunt back at him. 'You didn't actually expect to take up where you left off, did you, Mr Korda?' she enquired acidly, and rejoiced in his audible intake of breath.

'What I expected—or didn't expect, for that matter—is not a subject for discussion,' he told her civilly. 'Go to bed, Miss Fielding.'

But Sara couldn't leave it there. 'You did expect to go on, didn't you?' she accused him, finding it easier to talk when she wasn't looking at him. 'You're incredible! You're making love to one woman, when another arrives and professes her undying love; and you're so full of yourself that when you've got rid of the second, you expect the first to be waiting in eager anticipation! My God, it's barbaric!'

'It wasn't like that, and you know it,' said Lincoln wearily, and she could hear the taut frustration in his voice. 'I am far from full of myself, as you put it, and I was not—*making love* to you. When I do, you'll know it.'

Sara gasped, and couldn't resist a glance over her shoulder then. 'Don't you mean *if*? she demanded indignantly, and with an impatient sigh he came after her.

'No, I mean when,' he retorted harshly, halting right behind her, and it took an enormous effort of will power not to lose her cool and run.

'I want an apology,' she declared, hardly knowing what she was saying, in the raw panic of the moment. But the words spilled out, and she stiffened automatically when his hands gripped her shoulders.

'An apology?' he echoed incredulously, jerking her round to face him, and forced to support her words or look foolish, she nodded. 'An apology for what?'

'For—for taking advantage of our situation,' she invented hurriedly, realising she was pushing him just a little too far. Frustration was rapidly giving way to a desire for vindication, and the smouldering impatience in his eyes gave them a strangely sultry appearance.

'For taking advantage of our situation,' he repeated bleakly, his hands digging into the slender bones of her shoulders. 'Are you serious?'

Sara faltered, torn by the scowling disbelief in his gaze and her own uncertainty. 'Well, what would you call it, then?' she mumbled, wishing she had never started this, and with a smothered oath Lincoln pulled her into his arms.

'How about—an irresistible attraction?' he muttered, his lips against the side of her neck, and without giving her time to recover from the unexpectedness of his caress, he covered her mouth with his.

She could hear the acceleration of his heart, as his arms closed about her. For all he had acted so confidently, she sensed the lingering doubts he cherished, and that made him vulnerable. And perhaps that was why she couldn't push him away. There was something incredibly satisfying in the knowledge that she had the power to arouse this man, and for all her grand intentions, she felt her resistance give.

Her hands, which until then had been crushed between them, now slid around his waist, and then she was pressing herself against him, her breasts flattened by his chest, her hip bones melting into the potent urgency of his. He was all bone and muscle, no trace of fat anywhere. She could feel every flexing angle of his body, and the palpable weakness in her legs was only equalled by the sharp constriction in her stomach.

'Rebecca means nothing to me,' he told her roughly, his hands parting the buttons of her shirt from their holes, enabling him to stroke the creamy skin of her shoulder with his tongue. 'Once—once before, I got involved with a woman to facilitate her family's needs, but it won't happen again, I

promise you.' His fingers found the lace-trimmed slip of
cotton that comprised her bra and pushed it carelessly aside.
'My whole life until this point seems to have been made up
with doing things for other people. This . . .' his teeth
enclosed the engorged nipple that nudged his lips, 'this . . . is
for me.'

Sara shivered. She was afraid he was moving too fast for
her. The searching hunger of his kiss had left her weak and
aching for more, but the intimate caress of his hands reminded
her of her own inexperience. This was no fumbling youth she
was tangling with. This was a man, with a man's needs and a
man's expectations, and although she desperately wanted to
prove herself, she trembled before the commitment.

Yet she didn't stop him when he slid the shirt from her
shoulders and allowed it to fall to the floor. Nor did she
object when her bra followed its path, exposing her more
fully to his gaze. His eager mouth was on hers, his tongue
igniting a flame that was searing in its heat, and her tremulous
inhibitions were consumed in the fire.

Besides, he had loosened the belt of his robe so that her
breasts were teased by the hair-roughened skin of his body,
and when he gathered her closer, not even the twin thicknesses
of her trousers and panties could prevent her from feeling the
swollen evidence of his desire. Her hands were making an
involuntary exploration of their own, sliding inside his robe to
spread her palms against the silky hollow of his spine. The
texture of his skin was smoother there, and still a little moist
from his shower, much different from the taut curve of his
buttocks and the thickening hair that marked their joining
with his thighs. Meanwhile, Lincoln's lips were beating a
sensuous path across her breasts, and upwards to the sensitive
curve of her neck and shoulder, and she was almost mindless
with delight. But when he grasped her hand and pressed it
down between them, close against the throbbing source of his
manhood, she was shocked into the realisation of how far
they had gone.

'No—we—I can't,' she protested feebly, recoiling from the
fiery heat of his flesh, but Lincoln wasn't taking her objections
seriously.

'We can. We're going to,' he added huskily, and swinging
her up into his arms, he carried her to the bed.

She panicked when he drew her silk trousers and the diminutive scrap of cotton underneath down her legs, but then he was beside her on the bed, and the naked weight of his body was a powerful intoxicant. She had to tell him, she thought anxiously, but the knowledge that if she did so he would in all probability leave her created a dilemma she was not equipped to handle. Instead, she lay like a statue, steeling herself not to respond to the searching pressure of his mouth.

'Sara—for God's sake, Sara,' he groaned, sliding his hands up and down her body, trying to instil some feeling into her, but she refused to meet his gaze. It was taking all her will power not to submit to the urgency of his hands, and when he bent his head to dip his tongue into the hollow of her navel, she arched convulsively.

'That's it,' he breathed, against her stomach, feeling her fluttering pulses jerking to life beneath his tongue, and against any defence Sara could raise, her body began to move with him. It was like an instrument in the hands of an expert, she fretted, struggling to hold on to her sanity, and Lincoln's husky words of approval were an added provocation.

'I want you, and you want me,' he told her thickly. 'Don't you?' he demanded, threatening to follow his fingers with his lips, and with the hot length of him pulsing against her, how could she deny it?

'Yes. Oh, *yes*,' she admitted weakly, and parting her legs with one of his, he knelt across her.

The temptation was still to fight him. He was so big and powerful, and although she had always believed that when this moment came, she would be ready for it, she wasn't. She didn't know what he expected of her; she had never had to face the simple practicalities of making love. And when he cupped her rounded rear and brought her to him, she felt as helpless as a baby in his hands.

But it was when he thrust inside her that she reacted. There was a searing pain when he penetrated the protective membrane, and she couldn't deny the choking sob that escaped her lips, or prevent her hands from pressing frantically at his chest. Her recoil was unmistakable, and Lincoln's eyes sought her face in disbelief.

'God,' he groaned. 'Why didn't you tell me?' but Sara's resistance had ceased as the pain subsided. It was too late now to regret what had happened, and his angry condemnation was just a futile waste of words.

'It doesn't matter,' she mumbled, feeling ridiculously immature, but his expression did not change.

'I thought——'

'I know what you thought,' she interrupted him unhappily, wishing he would just go on and get it over with, but with an oath of self-disgust he drew away from her.

'God,' he muttered, sitting up, with one leg beneath him, the other drawn up to provide a resting place for his chin. 'You should have stopped me! Why didn't you?'

Contrarily, now that he had withdrawn from her, Sara knew a sense of bereavement. 'What's the matter?' she asked, unaware of her own provocation as she propped herself up on her elbows. She wetted her lips. 'Was I so bad?'

'Don't talk rubbish!' he muttered, gazing at her broodingly. 'You should have told me you were a virgin! God, I didn't know there were any of them still around!'

She quivered. 'Is it a crime?'

'Yes,' he retorted coldly, and then, seeing her wounded expression, he shook his head. 'No,' he sighed wearily. 'No, it's not a crime. Not in normal circumstances, that is. Only these are hardly normal circumstances, are they? I'm no white knight, Sara. I'm not the man who should have—destroyed your innocence. Some place, somewhere, there's the man who deserves to be the first. But not me. *Not me!*'

Sara absorbed this in silence. Lincoln looked so grim; so frustrated. She almost felt that it was her fault for not being what he expected, and she desperately wanted to reassure him that she had been as much to blame. Besides, if she was completely honest, she would admit that what had happened had not changed her feelings towards him one bit. He was still the only man she had ever wanted to make love with, and there was a bitter-sweet poignancy in the intimacy they had shared.

With a feeling of inevitability, she moved then, scrambling up to kneel behind him. With her breasts warm against his shoulders, she slid her arms around his neck, and pressed her lips to his cheek.

'Don't!' he muttered, but his intention to escape her clinging arms went wrong, and she ended up in his lap, her arms still round his neck. *"Sara——"*

'Well, I'm not now, am I?' she protested obliquely, and he frowned.

'Not what?'

'Not strictly a virgin; not any longer,' she informed him huskily, sliding her hand along his jawline. 'Don't you think that's rather a waste?'

'Sara!'

But she could feel the instantaneous reaction of his body beneath her thighs, and when he lifted his hand to remove hers, she took it to her breast. 'Don't you want me?' she asked, her cheeks turning pink at such wanton behaviour, and with an agonised expellation of his breath, Lincoln closed his eyes.

'Don't I want you?' he echoed, opening his eyes on a grim laugh. 'Dear God, Sara, of course I want you, but——'

'But nothing,' she interrupted him gently, taking him with her, back against the satin coverlet, and the sensuous softness against her thighs cushioned what came after . . .

There was daylight beyond the fine silk curtains at Lincoln's windows when Sara awakened. Sunlight was causing tiny threads of light to pierce their ivory folds, glinting on the brass rails at the foot of the bed, and sending rainbow slivers across tumbled sheets.

For a moment, she was puzzled by her surroundings. The lilac-coloured walls were not familiar, and nor was the bed. But as she moved and discovered her own nakedness, memory flooded back, and with a feeling of anticipation she turned her head.

However, she was alone. The place beside her had been occupied; that was evident from the dented pillows and twisted sheets. But Lincoln had announced the night before that he was leaving for New York today, and a quick look at her wristwatch confirmed her worst fears. It was almost nine o'clock! Not late by normal standards, perhaps, but when she considered that Lincoln usually left at seven, it was far too late to hope that they might see one another before he departed.

And she had wanted to see him. With a feeling of delicious

lethargy, she rolled on to her stomach and buried her face in his pillow, remembering his lovemaking with a clarity that defied expression. But, she acknowledged, after a few mindless moments, after what had happened last night, she could no longer delude herself about her feelings for him. Crazy—*hopeless*, she derided, her exhilaration evaporating—as it was, she was in love with him, and she had to face the painful fact that he didn't feel the same. Oh, he was attracted to her, he had said so. He had wanted her. But she was just one of many women he had made love with, while she knew she would never want anyone else.

It had all proved so fantastic. What had begun as an unmitigated disaster had become something so right, so perfect, that even Lincoln had not seemed able to get enough. He had been unable to leave her alone, and it had been almost morning before they fell asleep in one another's arms.

Sara shook her head. And to think that she had invited him to resume his lovemaking with something akin to martyrdom! She had been quite prepared to stifle her suffering so that she might make him happy. She had never expected to respond in the way she had, and instead of him hurting her, he had taken her to paradise.

From the moment he entered her, she had felt her senses stirring, her muscles rushing to enfold him within their silken sheath. If was if they belonged together, she had thought at once, and there had been something so wonderful about feeling him move inside her. There was no pain, only an intense pleasure; a feeling of anticipation that this was what she had been waiting for all her life.

He had been so gentle to begin with, she remembered, his own pent-up hunger held in check until she could share it with him. He hadn't rushed her or got impatient with her, even though he must have suffered agonies of frustration. Instead, he had used his quite extraordinary skills to give her satisfaction, and by the time he reached his climax, she had been bucking under his hands.

After that, of course, he had not been so gentle. The sensuous play of tongues became only a prelude to what came after, and Sara remembered she had been just as eager to experiment with her body. She recalled, with some embarrassment now, how he had rolled her over on to her

stomach, and let his lips trail the length of her spine. She had
discovered she had nerves in places she had not known
existed, but when she had tried to do the same for him the
results had been electrifying. She could still taste him on her
tongue, and she expelled her breath luxuriosuly, remembering
his passion.

It had been so beautiful, she thought blissfully. He had
been beautiful, a darkly passionate god, who had brought her
to a complete awareness of her own sexuality. She had
thought she was cold; she wasn't. In Lincoln's hands she was
liquid gold. She had discovered the true sensuality of her
nature, and if it had been a little disconcerting to find
scratches on Lincoln's back, he hadn't seemed to mind. They
had been a source of amusement to him, and he had assured
her they didn't hurt much. Besides, they had been worth it;
she was quite fantastic, he told her, burying his face between
her breasts. And although she had thought it couldn't happen
again, it had . . .

But what now? she wondered painfully, forced to face the
fact that not once had Lincoln mentioned any permanency in
their relationship. And, as if to reinforce that realisation, he
had left her as she slept, probably to forget all about her until
he returned to Florida again.

And that was what she had to consider, she reflected now,
sitting up in the huge bed. If she stayed here, if she continued
her efforts on Jeff's behalf, she was tacitly accepting that
when Lincoln came to see his son, she would be available.
Was that what she wanted? She knew that it was not.

The sound of someone entering the other room sent her
scuttling for cover. Even if, by some miracle, it should be
Lincoln, the idea of confronting him, topless, was too daunting
to consider. But it wasn't Lincoln, it was Cora, carrying a tray
set with breakfast.

'Good morning, miss,' she greeted the girl casually, drawing
back the curtains with her free hand, before bringing the tray
to the bed. 'Mr Link gave orders to bring you breakfast at
nine-thirty. It's a little bit before that, I know, but I thought
you might be eager to get in to see young Jeff.'

Red with embarrassment, Sara struggled up against the
pillows, tucking the sheet beneath her arms. 'I could have got

up for breakfast, Cora,' she mumbled awkwardly. 'Um—this is very kind of you. I don't know what to say.'

'Don't say nothing,' declared Cora cheerfully, not a bit put out at finding the girl in her employer's bed. Did he make a habit of it? wondered Sara uneasily, and then dismissed the idea as being unworthy.

'I hope you don't think——'

'I don't think nothing either,' retorted Cora, before she could finish. 'Now, you tell me what you want to wear, and I'll get your clothes from your own room and bring them to you.'

It was a quarter to ten when Sara presented herself at Jeff's door. A swift shower, in the unfamiliar luxury of Lincoln's bathroom, had cleared the cobwebs, and if she was still not sure of what she was going to do in the future, she had decided to shelve it for today. Besides, work was what she needed, to take her mind off Lincoln, and being with his son was probably the next best thing.

Alan Keating was non-committal when he let her in. 'I'm sorry I'm late,' she apologised, feeling obliged to make some explanation, and his careless shrug was hardly an acceptance.

She felt ridiculously nervous as she walked into Jeff's bedroom. She hadn't been in here since he had had the accident with his crutches, and although it was only two days ago, it seemed like an eternity. At first glance, everything appeared normal, but she noticed at once that the television had been removed. The blinds, too, which she had succeeded in raising a few inches, were back in their lowered position, and Jeff himself lay motionless between his cotton sheets.

She moved round the bed so that he could see her, not saying anything initially, allowing him to make the first move. And she didn't have to wait long for him to make it. His eyes flickered, as if some sixth sense had warned him he was no longer alone, and his mouth compressed sullenly as he met her uncertain gaze.

'What do you want?'

Sara sighed. 'Isn't that a rather pointless question?' she asked quietly, and his lips twisted.

'It all is, isn't it?' he demanded. 'Pointless, I mean. My being here, your being here, the whole unholy mess!'

She moved a little nearer. 'You're not telling me to get

out, then?' she ventured, torn by the lines of bitterness beside his mouth, and he shrugged.

'Would it do any good if I did?' he grunted. 'No, why should I? I don't have the means to eject you. I can't even eject myself.'

Sara shook her head. 'That's not what I want to hear, and you know it.'

'Sorry.'

'Jeff, for goodness' sake! I think I'd rather have you snarling at me than giving in like this. I thought you had some spirit. What's happened? What's gone wrong?'

'As if you didn't know!'

She came closer and with a helpless gesture, seated herself on the edge of his bed. 'Do you want to tell me about it?'

'No.'

'Then *will* you tell me about it?'

'There's nothing to tell. I'm a cripple! That's it—period.'

Sara took a deep breath. 'That's not what Doctor Haswell says.'

'What does he know?'

'He knows about you. He knows about cases like you.'

'*Cases* like me!' Jeff grimaced, and Sara wished she could call the word back. 'Yes, that's what I am—a case!' he added harshly. 'A suitable case for treatment, wouldn't you say?'

She hesitated. 'Your feeling sorry for yourself isn't going to help. Doctor Haswell says that your attitude can be psychologically bad for rehabilitation.'

'Rehabilitation,' he echoed. 'You know all the words, don't you? Well, here's another one—*paralysed*, right?'

'What about—lazy?' suggested Sara quietly. 'Or indolent? Or—morally insensible?'

'You——' Jeff struggled up on his elbows, and then, as if realising what she was trying to do, he slumped again. 'All right,' he said carelessly, 'I'm probably all those things. That's why people get tired of me. You will too, you'll see.'

She gazed at him. 'What an opinion you have of us, of your family! Your father doesn't get tired of you. He loves you.'

'Does he?' He didn't sound convinced. 'Dad loves me so much, he chucked me out when I was seven! So much for my family. Let's talk about something else.'

Sara bit her lip. 'Jeff—Jeff, your parents separated when you were seven. Naturally your mother took you with her. That's the usual way of things when young children are involved.'

'Even if I didn't want to go, and she didn't want to take me?' He regarded her pityingly. 'Look, we don't talk about my family, right? I don't even want to think about them.'

She hunched her shoulders, unable to make any sense of what he had said. But he was right. If he hadn't wanted to go, and Michelle hadn't wanted to take him, why had Lincoln insisted that he lived with his mother?

With a dismissive gesture, she put that particular problem aside for the present and said gently: 'So tell me what went wrong the other night. Mr Keating said you fell. Did you hurt yourself?'

'What do you think?' His face darkened. 'I smashed the television! So much for rehabilitation, wouldn't you say?'

Sara shrugged. 'That's not rehabilitation, and you know it. You need help to achieve that kind of success. What I can't understand is why you won't let anyone help you. If you really wanted to get out of that bed, you'd struggle to find a way.'

Jeff glared. 'Oh, yes? I was waiting for the amateur prognosis! If it was up to you, you'd have me bowling about in a wheelchair. Well, I'm not ready for that kind of existence. And what's more, I don't think I'll ever be.'

CHAPTER ELEVEN

IT WAS nearly lunchtime when Sara went downstairs. Moving somewhat disconsolately, she made her way out on to the patio, welcoming the heat of the sun on her head and bare arms, like a benison to banish the chill of the morning.

It had not been a good morning. Struggling to make conversation with Jeff, she had known the same sense of inadequacy she had felt during her early days at Orchid Key. But at least then, she had not had the spectre of the success she had achieved to taunt her, and although she had stayed with him for the usual length of time, that had been mainly to prevent Keating from gloating that he was right. It was true, though. Jeff's attitude had changed, and it was daunting to imagine how long it might take to regain that lost ground—if, indeed, it could be regained at all.

Of course, her worries over Jeff had succeeded in masking her own problems. For the past couple of hours, she had managed to put all thoughts of Lincoln Korda to the back of her mind, and if she couldn't prevent herself from thinking about him now, at least that particular problem did not demand an immediate solution.

The heat on the patio was intense, and Sara felt a wave of weariness sweep over her. She was so tired, she thought, with some perplexity, and then was glad she could blame the sun for her suddenly deepening colour. And why not? she reflected unhappily. No wonder she felt so depressed. She had had a very restless night . . .

'You look grim,' a voice commented drily, and she saw Grant rising from his seat beside the pool to come and meet her. 'Tough time, eh?' he added, adjusting the waistband of his shorts. 'Well, you were warned.'

Sara stifled an impatient rejoinder. It would be too easy to argue with Grant in her present mood, and right now, she

141

didn't need another argument. 'I can handle Jeff,' she retorted, avoiding his outstretched hand, and then caught her breath instinctively, when a second voice remarked softly: 'I'm pleased to hear it.'

It was Lincoln who spoke, and she jerked round abruptly to find him seated at the table behind her. The shady canopy had shadowed the man, and the briefcase and papers on the glass-topped surface in front of him, and her heart pumped rapidly at the realisation that he had apparently ducked his New York meeting.

But it wasn't just that thought that caused the sudden moistness in her palms, and sent the blood rushing fiercely through her veins. It was the knowledge that Lincoln was here, not in New York, and that she might have to face her decision sooner than she thought.

'You've seen Jeff,' he said now, getting up from his chair and coming towards her, and she knew a quite ridiculous desire to run. It didn't seem possible that she and this man had just spent the night in each other's arms, and his cool, controlled expression gave the lie to her chaotic thoughts. Unlike Grant, he was wearing cream cotton trousers and a short-sleeved shirt, and although his attire was not formal, no one could be in any doubt as to his superiority. It was something about his manner, something about the way he moved and spoke, that defined his precedence. And that was why Sara had to steel herself to face him. It did not seem conceivable that she could stay here now. He probably wouldn't want her to, she reflected, as he dismissed Grant with a casual gesture. He probably regretted last night just as much as she did. Or did she? She wasn't absolutely sure.

'What happened?' he asked, as Grant disappeared into the house, and looking up into his dark disturbing face, Sara was amazed anew at his capacity to hide his real feelings.

'With Jeff?' she asked unnecessarily, giving herself time to gather her thoughts, and at his brief nod: 'Not a lot.'

'You did see him, though?'

Lincoln was persistent, and she knew a stirring sense of injustice. Last night—last night he had made love to her, for heaven's sake! Didn't that mean anything to him? Had he no feelings?

'Yes, I saw him,' she said now, forcing herself to move past

him, removing the necessity to look at him at all. 'He's—
morose; uncommunicative. In spite of what I said to Grant
I'm not at all sure I can repair the damage. He seems to have
lost heart.'

'That has happened before.' Lincoln spoke tersely. 'You're
not giving up, are you?'

'Giving up?' Sara cast him an indignant look over her
shoulder. 'How do I know that my being here has achieved
anything? Jeff might have been attempting to use his crutches
for months, not just weeks!'

He swore then. 'You know that's not true,' he exclaimed,
overtaking her as she walked across the patio and blocking
her path. 'I told you last night, we hadn't even been able to
get him to have a television in his room, let alone anything
else.'

Sara concentrated on the toes of her sandals. 'The
television's gone now.'

'I know.' Lincoln expelled his breath impatiently. 'It was
damaged when he fell. Another set is available, as and when
you can persuade him to have it.'

She caught her breath. 'And if I can't persuade him?'

'You will.'

'What makes you so sure?' She looked up at him then,
stung by his complacency. 'I may not be here.'

His eyes narrowed. 'What do you mean?'

'What do you think I mean?' She bolstered her failing
courage with an effort. 'I have to go back to London some
time. Christmas will be here soon. I've been here over a
month.'

'I know exactly how long you've been here,' Lincoln
informed her flatly. 'I just didn't realise there was a restriction
on the length of time you stayed.'

Sara held up her head. 'I can't stay here for ever!'

'I wouldn't have called one month for ever,' he retorted
bleakly. 'Tell me, this sudden desire to leave wouldn't have
anything to do with what happened last night, would it?'

'Last night?' She repeated his words uncertainly, and his
voice hardening, Lincoln intervened.

'Don't tell me you've forgotten what happened last night,'
he snapped, thrusting his hands into his pockets, as if to quell

an uncontrollable urge to shake her. 'We spent the night together, remember? In my bed?'

Sara's shoulders jerked. 'I hadn't forgotten.'

'No, I didn't suppose you had.' He stared at her grimly. 'That's what all this is about, I suppose.'

'What all what is about?'

'This sudden desire to return to London,' he grated harshly. 'These threats you've been making concerning Jeff's treatment. What do you want from me, Sara? A promise that it won't happen again?' His lips twisted. 'Or a marriage proposal?'

She choked. 'You can't be serious——'

'It was a clever ploy, I'll give you that,' he went on, as if she hadn't spoken. 'A rather sophisticated form of blackmail, wouldn't you say? Make it worth my while, or I'll withdraw my—what shall we call them?—services?'

'You—you——'

Unable to find words to voice her contempt, Sara swung away from him then, but before she had taken a dozen steps, his fingers grasped her arm. Curling about the soft flesh above her elbow, they arrested her progress, forcing her to turn and face him if she wanted to pry them loose.

'Okay, okay,' he muttered, as she struggled to tear his fingers from her arm, 'I take that back. You're not blackmailing me. Not consciously, at least.' He winced. 'For the Lord's sake, Sara, that hurt!'

'I'd like to hurt you a whole lot more,' she told him tearfully, and with a muffled oath, he released her.

'Listen to me, will you!' he exclaimed, before she could walk away. 'All right, I'm sorry I said what I did. I didn't mean it. Does that satisfy you? Put it down to—frustration! I'm not used to being in a situation like this.'

'Do you think I am?'

'I'm in a better position than most to know you're not,' he retorted, bringing a hot flush of colour to her cheeks. 'So,' he sighed, 'is that why you wanted to leave? Because of what happened?'

'No!'

Lincoln hesitated. 'You don't hate me, then?'

'No.' Sara turned away from him, unwilling for him to see how much his words disturbed her.

'But you don't want to repeat the experience,' he suggested

quietly, and taking her cue from him, she shook her head. 'So . . .' He was silent for so long, she wondered what he was thinking. But then he appended, '... you'll stay.'

She moistened her lips. 'I don't know.'

Impatience stirred in the lighter depths of his eyes. 'Why not?'

'It's not that simple,' she murmured unsteadily, knowing there was nothing simple about this whole situation. 'I—I just don't know if I can help your son.'

'Let me be the judge of that.'

'Do you think you have that right?' she asked huskily, and he swung her round to face him with ungentle hands.

'What did you say?'

'I said, do you think——'

'Damn you, I know what you said!'

'But you asked——'

'I asked what you said, I know. What I should have said was: what do you mean?'

Sara quivered. 'Why—why did you abandon your son when he was seven years old?' she asked, hearing the words, yet doubting her own temerity in using them. Whatever was she thinking of? she fretted. It would serve her right if he threw her into the pool. However worthy her motives, it was nothing to do with her. She had taken momentary leave of her senses, and retribution was bound to follow.

But Lincoln's voice was expressionless when he answered her. 'Who told you I did?' he asked evenly, and Sara realised then that as with Jeff, she would have preferred his anger.

'Um—Jeff,' she admitted honestly, too startled by his response to equivocate. And Lincoln nodded as she spoke, as if he had already guessed her informant.

She took another breath. 'Is it true?'

'That I ordered Jeff to leave with his mother?' His face grew cold and withdrawn. 'Yes, it's true. And I'd do the same again, in similar circumstances.'

Sara shook her head. 'You can't mean that!'

'Can't I?' His lips twisted. 'Well, I'm afraid I do. You don't understand, do you?'

She frowned. 'But surely you know what it did to Jeff!'

'What it did to Jeff?' Lincoln snorted. 'I know what it did to me!'

Sara blinked. There was something she was missing here. 'But then why——?'

'It's a long story,' he interrupted her harshly. 'And not one I choose to tell you right now. The decision's yours. Either you stay or you don't. It's up to you. I'm not baring my soul to persuade you!'

The next few days were not easy ones for Sara. She was caught in a trap of her own making, and although common sense adjured her to leave, emotion compelled her to stay. And it was not just the feelings she had for Lincoln that made her choice so difficult. She had grown genuinely fond of his son, and the idea of leaving Jeff to turn in even more upon himself did not bear thinking about.

But it wasn't easy going on as before when she discovered Lincoln had decided to stay for a few days. 'I guess Becca got her own way, after all,' Grant commented to Sara, when he learned what was happening. 'But hell, there's no reason why Link shouldn't take a break. He's got some good men working for him. It's time he learned to delegate.'

For her part, Sara tried to avoid conversations about her employer. And he was still her employer, in spite of what had happened. She also did her best to avoid both him and Rebecca, and she was most at ease when Lincoln took his guest away from the island.

Breakfasts were no problem, of course. She had taken to having a tray in her room, and her mornings spent with Jeff were free of any outside influence. Lunch these days was usually a buffet, provided, so Grant told her, for Lincoln's benefit, enabling him to eat when he chose. Lincoln apparently worked mornings in his study, and Sara managed to snatch a sandwich or a salad without encountering any awkward moments.

But afternoons were not so uncomplicated. Sara, who had been accustomed to spending the hottest part of the day by the pool, couldn't always find excuses to keep herself indoors, and Grant would have got suspicious if she had shunned the sun completely.

All the same, it was incredibly difficult for her to appear quiescent when Lincoln was stretched out on a cushioned lounger only feet away. Particularly as Rebecca took every opportunity to display her prior claim. She was constantly flirting with him, or touching him, or drawing his attention to her, and Sara grew hot and angry at the thought that he knew she could hear them.

Yet, in spite of everything, she stayed on, numbing her mind to the kind of relationship Lincoln might be sharing with Rebecca, and concentrating her efforts on his son. The most important thing was proving to Jeff that people cared about him. And at least his father's continued presence meant that he spent more time with the boy.

Then one morning, towards the end of the week Lincoln had spent at Orchid Key, she arrived at Jeff's apartments to find Keating was not in attendance. It was most unusual. He invariably let her into the suite, and she was surprised when she found the outer door open and no one about. For an awful moment she wondered if Jeff had had a relapse in the night and been rushed into hospital, but then she heard voices from the bedroom and realised Keating must be with him. Crossing the sitting room, she tapped lightly at the bedroom door, only to be momentarily struck speechless when Lincoln opened the door.

'Come in,' he said, stepping back to allow her to enter, and because she could hardly refuse him, she found herself doing as he said.

But it was hard to speak to Jeff with his father at her side. Heavens, it was hard enough to look at him, when her eyes were continually drawn to the dark-clad figure at the end of the bed. It was the first time he had worn a dark suit since he came here, and she was painfully persuaded he had come to say goodbye.

Jeff, meanwhile, was regarding the two of them with watchful attention. Propped on his pillows, his pale face almost a match for the crisp white cotton, the contrast between him and his father had never been more marked, and ignoring her own feelings, Sara felt her heart go out to him. In consequence, when Lincoln spoke to her and she was forced to look at him, her eyes were bright with accusation.

'I beg your pardon?'

'I said—I'd better get going,' said Lincoln levelly, meeting her hostile gaze without resentment. 'If you'll both excuse me . . .'

'You're leaving?'

The indignant words were out before she could prevent them, and a line appeared between Lincoln's brows. 'I have to return to New York this morning, yes,' he conceded politely. 'I thought Grant might have told you. Rebecca is leaving with me.'

'No. No, I didn't know,' said Sara tautly, and then, realising that Jeff's interested gaze was upon them, she struggled to compose herself. 'Well . . .' she bared her teeth in the semblance of a smile, 'I hope you have a safe journey.'

'I would have told you myself, if I'd thought it would mean anything to you,' said Lincoln in a low voice, and she wondered with some amazement if he had forgotten his son was listening. 'I have to attend a board meeting this afternoon,' he added, apparently indifferent to her signals. 'And unfortunately it's not something I can lay off on anyone else.'

'What a shame!' she sympathised, her eyes darting pointedly from his face to the bed and back again. 'Well, I'm sure we don't envy you having to go back where it's cold and damp, do we, Jeff? I—er—I saw the weather forecast on television last night, and I believe they said the temperature was something like minus three degrees.'

'It doesn't make much difference to me,' remarked Jeff without emotion, but his eyes belied his bored expression. For the first time in days, he was actually showing some interest in something, Sara realised anxiously. But what he was thinking, and how it might affect him, was just another worry to add to all the rest.

'You'll be—all right, won't you?' Lincoln asked now, and Sara drew a steadying breath.

'I'm sure Jeff is going to be just fine,' she said, deliberately misinterpreting his words. 'Er—say goodbye to Miss Steinbeck for me, will you? I don't think I'll have a chance to see her before you——'

'I don't think he means me, Sara,' drawled Jeff, at her elbow. He had levered himself up on to his arms and was regarding her now with malicious enjoyment. 'Why don't you tell the man to get lost? Or would you like me to do it for you?'

'Just keep out, Jeff, will you?' exclaimed Sara revealingly. And then, turning to Lincoln, she spread her hands. 'I think you should go, Mr Korda. I don't think this conversation is getting us anywhere.'

Lincoln's lean features hardened. 'If you say so.' He looked at his son for a long moment, and then walked towards the door. 'Okay.' He rested one hand against the side of the door. 'I'll see you two later.'

He let the door swing to behind him, and feeling the need to ascertain that he had actually gone, Sara went to close it. Then, turning, she rested her shoulders against the panels.

'You enjoyed that, didn't you?' she demanded, losing her temper with her charge for the first time since their initial encounter, and Jeff slumped back against the pillows.

'Why not?' he countered, adopting a defiant tone. 'It's not my fault if he fancies you. You should have let me tell him to——'

'Don't say it!' She thrust herself away from the door and came towards the bed. 'You know nothing about me or your father, and I should have thought you were a little old to play stupid childish games!'

Jeff scowled. 'I notice you don't deny it.'

'Deny what?'

'That the old man fancies you!'

'He's not an old man,' said Sara automatically, and then wished she hadn't when he crowed in triumph.

'You see,' he sneered, 'you can't deny it. I saw the way you looked at him. I may be stupid, but I'm not blind!'

Sara's hands clenched. 'You like hurting people, don't you?' she exclaimed. 'That's how you get your kicks. I should have realised. We were getting along too well before, weren't we? When you had that little mishap, it must have pleased you no end. At last you could blame someone else for your own ineptitude!'

'That's not true!'

He was defensive, but she had no sympathy for him. 'It is true. That's why you've let me come here every day, trying every way I knew to get you to show some interest in living again. It wasn't good enough to send me away. There wasn't any fun in that. No, you had to have me sitting here, making amends, feeling guilty, giving you a fillip every time I opened my mouth!'

'No——'

'No?' Her lip curled now. 'But you've just proved it. The way you treated your father just now. The way you speak about him makes me sick! He could tear you into strips if he wanted to, but he doesn't. He's trying, if you could but see it, to make amends for the past. He loves you. He wants to be your friend. And all you do is feel sorry for yourself.'

'Whose fault is that?' muttered Jeff sulkily, and Sara heaved a sigh.

'I suppose there are faults on both sides,' she admitted wearily, realising it was the first time she had acknowledged that there might be another side. 'But you make everything harder. Not only for him, but for yourself.'

He hesitated. 'Have you ever met my mother?'

'No.' She felt her colour rising. 'What has that to do with anything?'

'You don't know her, then?'

'No. How could I?'

Jeff shrugged. 'I don't know. I just wondered.' He paused. 'How long have you known Dad?'

He had not called his father 'Dad' before, and Sara was almost afraid to answer him, in case she said the wrong thing. 'Oh, just since I came here,' she answered cautiously. 'Why? What does it matter?'

'So you've never talked with him—really talked with him, I mean?'

'About what?'

'About me. About my mother.'

Sara shook her head. 'No. I've told you, it's——'

Jeff nodded. 'I didn't blame him, you know,' he broke in ruefully. 'Not at first anyway. I suppose I didn't really understand what was happening to begin with, but even when I did, I didn't blame him. Michelle's not the constant type—I could see that. What I couldn't see was why he blamed me as well! What did I do? Why did he turn against me?'

Sara felt the remaining vestiges of her anger drain out of her. That was a question she couldn't answer, and like Jeff, she couldn't understand it either.

'Who knows?' she said now, not making the mistake of lying to him. 'I expect he had his reasons. But you're here now; isn't that what matters? When you really needed him, he came through.'

Jeff didn't answer her. He seemed lost in thought. But Sara had a curious feeling that the morning had not been wasted after all. She was almost inclined to believe their argument had cemented the cracks in their relationship, and she felt distinctly brighter when she went down for lunch.

The next morning, she had another surprise waiting for her when she arrived at Jeff's apartments. The wheelchair, which she had previously seen on the patio downstairs, was standing in the middle of Jeff's sitting room, and she gazed at it disbelievingly when Keating let her in.

'He asked for it to be brought upstairs,' said Keating shortly, when she cast an incredulous look in his direction. 'Don't ask me why. It's nothing to do with me.'

Shaking her head, Sara let herself into the bedroom, only to stand and stare at the sight of Jeff, sitting on the side of the bed, trying to haul a knitted jersey over his head. His pyjamas had been discarded, and a pair of jeans and a cotton tee-shirt had taken their place. And presently, he was endeavouring to push his arms into the sleeves of a cashmere sweater.

In spite of her excitement, she was half afraid to move in case he noticed her intrusion and took exception to it. But a moment later he looked up and saw her, and a becoming wave of colour swept up his cheeks. 'Well,' he growled, 'don't just stand there—come and help me! Keating is no good. He fusses over me like I'm a baby!'

'And whose fault is that?' enquired Sara drily, coming to perch on the side of the bed and guide his arm into the sleeve. 'There. I bet that feels good, doesn't it? You know, I didn't realise how handsome you are until now.'

'Rubbish!' he muttered, but she could tell he was flattered. Besides, it was true. The sweater and jeans gave substance to his wasted frame, and without the bony hollows in his neck to detract from his lean features, he definitely stood a second glance.

'Did you send for the wheelchair?' Sara ventured, feeling her way, though she guessed it was not something Keating would have done alone, and Jeff nodded. 'So,' she smiled, 'what's the action?'

'The action?' He grimaced. 'Something tells me I'm going to be exhausted by the time I get into the chair. But I might get a chance to try and move it. Even if it is just around the room.'

She bit her lip. 'I could wheel you down——'

'No!'

'No?' She swallowed. 'I'm sorry, I thought——'

'I know what you thought.' Jeff spoke abruptly, but then he sighed. 'Look, I know you mean well, Sara, and I'm grateful to you honestly. For—for everything. But I have to do this my way. I don't want anybody *wheeling* me around. I want to wheel myself.'

'All right.' She stood up. 'So—shall I get Keating?'

'What for?'

She faltered. 'To—to help you into the chair, of course!' she murmured, and he smiled.

'Just get the chair, will you?' he requested gently, and ignoring Keating's disapproving gaze, Sara did as he suggested.

It was nerve-stretching watching Jeff's efforts to lever himself into the wheelchair. To begin with, he forgot to put the brake on, and when he tried to use the arm as a crutch, it moved away from him. Sara felt as if it was her fault the chair had moved, causing him to teeter for an awful moment between chair and bed. She should have put the brake on for him, she realised, but when she started forward, his expression drove her back.

The second time, he made sure the brake was secure, and this time his attempt to use the chair as a support was more successful. But it still took a tremendous effort of will to shift his useless legs off the bed, and she had to steel herself to remain motionless when she desperately wanted to help.

'Would you rather I left you alone?' she asked once, and Jeff paused in his manoeuvrings and regarded her, red-faced.

'I guess you'd like to get the hell out of here, wouldn't you?' he countered, and Sara didn't bother to deny it. 'Anyway, I'd prefer you to stay,' he added, resuming the rocking motion which he hoped would eventually enable him to swing out into the seat. 'If you go, Keating will come back, and right now I need encouragement, not his procrastination.'

He succeeded in levering himself into the wheelchair a few minutes later. Even so, there was a heart-stopping moment when Sara thought his efforts would come to grief. The weight of his body on his arms seemed almost too great for the weakened muscles to handle, and for what seemed an inordinately long period of time, but which was probably only a few seconds, he looked as if he was going to end up on the floor. But then, controlling his wobbling arms, he threw himself forward, and much to her relief—and his, no doubt— he lodged on the edge of the seat.

'I made it!' he muttered unsteadily, and then, more confidently: 'I made it!' and unable to resist the temptation, Sara ran to give him a swift hug.

'Yes, you made it!' she exclaimed, feeling a swelling of emotion in her throat. 'Oh, Jeff, I'm so pleased for you! And this is only the beginning.'

'Is everything all right here?'

Keating's voice from the doorway brought Sara up with a start. Wiping a surreptitious tear from her cheek, she turned to face the man, guessing as she did so that he had never been in any doubt. He just wanted to know what was going on, she bridled, but almost immediately she stifled her resentment. It was only natural that Keating should be concerned, she told herself reasonably. He had been looking after Jeff ever since the accident, and he was bound to be apprehensive when something so arbitrary was taking place. All the same, she wished he had knocked before opening the door. Although she had only been hugging Jeff, Keating's air of disapproval made her feel as if she had been caught in some illicit act.

'Everything's fine,' Jeff answered him now, his hands groping for the brake and releasing the wheels. 'How's that?' he asked breathlessly, rolling the chair across the carpet. 'Step out of the way, will you? I want to go into the next room.'

CHAPTER TWELVE

In the days that followed, any lingering doubts Sara had had concerning her justification in being here were dispelled. If nothing else, she had been instrumental in getting Jeff to leave his bed, and Doctor Haswell was lavish in the praise he bestowed upon her.

'You know, I always thought Antony Korda was a bit of a poseur,' he told her ruefully, 'but I've been forced to revise my opinion. Sending you out here was an inspiration! I must remember to shake his hand, next time his camera brings him Stateside!'

Keating was predictably less enthusiastic, although he evidently approved of his patient's change of attitude. Sara guessed what galled him most was her involvement in Jeff's improvement. He still resented her intervention, and the fact that Lincoln had taken her side.

Of Lincoln himself there was no word. Doctor Haswell had wanted to ring Jeff's father and tell him how his son was progressing, but Jeff had asked him not to. 'What's to tell?' he had argued, when Sara had suggested his father should be told. 'I can sit in a wheelchair! So what's new? Wait until I've gotten used to getting in and out of it. There's no point in making a fuss over something so trivial.'

Sara decided there was no point in pursuing the topic. Besides, if she was honest, she had to admit she had no desire to precipitate Lincoln's return to the island. His presence created too great a disturbance in her life, and so long as he wasn't here, she didn't have to think about him.

Of course she did. Most particularly when she went to bed at night. It was impossible to slide between the sheets without thinking about Lincoln's lean muscled body next to her own, and the treacherous emotions he had made her feel could not so easily be dismissed. Sometimes the memories caused her breasts to harden, and an actual physical ache throbbed between her legs. On those occasions, it was incredibly difficult to sleep at all, and in the morning she could see revealing little smudges beneath her eyes.

But luckily, during the day, Jeff's activities submerged all other feelings. Much to Keating's—and, she was sure, Grant's—chagrin, Jeff soon got bored with staying indoors. Once he was up, once the shades were lifted, he embraced his freedom with both hands, and Sara was beside him when he went downstairs for the first time.

Nevertheless, Sara did have some bad moments when Jeff wheeled himself out on to the sun-drenched patio. In spite of the progress that he had made, she wasn't at all sure how he would react to this new environment, and she remained in the shadow of the balcony as he took his first breaths of salt-laden air.

And then he turned and looked over his shoulder, and she knew it was going to be all right. 'It's a long time since I looked at this view,' he said, beckoning her towards him. 'Almost twelve years, to be exact. Amazingly enough, it hasn't changed.'

Sara expelled her breath, unaware until then that she had been holding it. 'Did you think it would?' she ventured softly, and he cast her a rueful glance.

'I was afraid it might,' he admitted, resting his elbows on the arms of the wheelchair. 'So much else has. I guess it didn't seem conceivable that this place would stay the same. I used to love it here. That's why I shut myself away upstairs. I didn't want to remember, I just wanted to forget.'

'And now?'

'Now?' he grimaced. 'Now, I've got to remember, haven't I? Haswell says the only way to cope with the present is to accept the past. It happened. I can't change it. All I can hope to change is the future.'

With Christmas only a couple of weeks away, Sara had a letter from Vicki. She had eventually written to her friend, explaining what was going on, but apart from a card, sent during a modelling assignment in Paris, Vicki had not replied. Now, however, she wrote to say that she hoped

Sara didn't mind, but she was going away for the festive season. 'I'm spending Christmas in a château in the Loire valley!' she explained, emphasising her words with underlinings and exclamation marks. 'Believe it or not, but I'm staying with a real-life French count! And not an impoverished one either! His family have vineyards; acres of them, or is it hectares? Anyway, he wants me to meet his parents, so maybe this is it? I'm holding my breath!'

Sara had to smile. Vicki wrote as she spoke, and Sara could sense the other girl's excitement. And why not? she reflected ruefully. Christmas at a French château sounded incredibly romantic. Maybe Vicki was serious this time. It certainly sounded as if she was. But she couldn't help thinking how much she would miss her if Vicki went to live in France.

Jeff had become a regular occupant of the patio, and he and Sara spent most mornings there now, instead of in the artificial coolness of his apartments. She had even persuaded him to use a cushioned lounge chair to sunbathe, instead of his wheelchair, though so far he had resisted her efforts to get him to wear shorts. She knew he was self-conscious about his legs, and didn't press him. But sometimes she sensed his raw frustration when the sun became too hot.

Then, one morning, returning from a stroll along the beach before breakfast, she heard the sound of someone in the pool. For a moment, the sight of that slick wet head reminded her of the time she had mistaken Lincoln's dark colouring for Jeff's. But this time she didn't jump to that conclusion. Instead she sauntered across the patio area, steeling herself for the encounter, only to gaze disbelievingly into Jeff's excited face.

'Hi,' he greeted her breathlessly, clinging to the side of the pool with his arms along the rim. 'Surprise, surprise!'

Sara shook her head. 'What are you doing?'

'What does it look like I'm doing? I've been swimming, of course.' He pulled a face. 'Well, kind of,' he amended. 'But it feels pretty good.'

'Oh, Jeff!' She squatted down on her haunches beside him and shook her head. 'That's marvellous! Marvellous! I don't know what to say!'

'How about—I told you so?' he suggested drily. 'You knew that sooner or later I'd have to take my clothes off!'

'But how did you——?'

'Believe it or not, Keating's been helping me,' Jeff admitted. 'This is my third swim, actually. But I wanted to be more proficient before asking you to join me.'

Sara expelled a trembling breath. 'And it feels good?'

'Bloody good!' he assured her firmly, and then, pushing himself away from the side, he floated lazily out into the middle of the pool. 'Aren't I clever?' he demanded and she nodded. 'I guess when Christmas is over, I might let Haswell fix up some therapy, too. What the hell! What have I got to lose?'

And, in the days that followed, Sara was reminded of the realisation that once one set a snowball rolling, it quickly became an avalanche. She was delighted with his progress, of course. How could she not be, when everything she had ever hoped for Jeff was coming true? But she couldn't deny the troubling sensation that time was running away with her, and that every advance he made was one step nearer her own departure.

A week before Christmas, she prevailed upon Grant to take her across to the mainland, so that she could buy some cards for her friends back home, and a few small gifts. She bought a silk scarf for Grant, and a tie for Keating, and after some consideration, some cassette tapes for Jeff and a personal hi-fi on which to play them. The shops in Cypress Beach were expensively dressed in festive garb, but Sara felt a faint nostalgia for cold weather and a touch of snow. It didn't seem the same, shopping in a chemise dress and strappy sandals. Or maybe it was just her present mood.

When Grant spoke to Lincoln that evening, he asked to speak to her. Grant came to find her as she was changing for her evening swim, and she knew a sense of unease as she wrapped a robe about her bikini-clad body.

'What does he want?' she asked Grant, as he escorted her downstairs, and the man shrugged.

'Who knows?' he countered, leaving her at the study door. 'If he wants me again, I'll be outside. Don't look so worried. He probably wants to congratulate you.'

She closed the study door behind her before picking up the phone. 'Yes?'

'Sara?'

'Yes.' She moistened her lips. 'You wanted me?'

'That's a leading question,' said Lincoln flatly, and then, before she could retaliate, he added: 'I wanted to know if you'd any plans for Christmas. I mean, if you want to go back to England for the holiday, I shall quite understand.'

Her stomach hollowed. 'I—er—I hadn't thought——' she stammered helplessly. 'If that's what you want——'

'What I want doesn't come into it,' Lincoln broke in quietly. 'I just thought I ought to broach the subject with you. Your staying at Orchid Key has been pretty much taken for granted. But I realise you may have other commitments.'

Sara tried to think. What did he mean? Was this a polite way of asking her to leave? In spite of her earlier nostalgia, the idea of going back to London had never seemed less appealing, and with Vicki spending the holiday in France, the flat would be cold and uninviting.

'Will you—I mean, do you intend—that is, would you rather I went back to England?' she ventured. 'I suppose, if you're going to be here . . .'

'. . . you'd rather not,' he finished for her grimly. 'I quite understand.'

Sara caught her breath. 'That wasn't what I was going to say.'

'No?' he sounded sceptical.

'No.' She paused. 'I just thought—if you were bringing some friends—or family——'

'What family?' Lincoln sounded bleak. 'My brother, as you know, lives and works in London. I have no other close relatives. And my wife—my ex-wife—has just informed me she's getting married again.'

'Oh!' Sara swallowed. 'I'm sorry.'

'Why? Because you think it may upset Jeff?'

'No! That is—well, I don't know how Jeff will take it. I just meant——'

'You surely didn't think it might upset me?' he exclaimed impatiently. 'Sara, all it means to me is that I shall no longer have to pay an extortionate amount of alimony!

Anything else is quite out of the question. I thought you knew that.'

'Yes.' Sara nodded. But she still had doubts. He must have loved Michelle once, or why had he married her?

'Anyway,' he continued now, his low attractive voice lifting the hairs on the back of her neck, 'it might be as well to warn Jeff. Michelle might just decide to introduce his new stepfather to him.'

'Here?' Sara could hear the way her voice had risen.

'It's possible,' Lincoln said laconically. 'You don't sound enthusiastic.'

'I'm not,' Sara admitted honestly.

'Can I ask why?'

'Well . . .' she lifted her shoulders, 'she hasn't shown any interest in Jeff's condition for the past six months, has she?'

'Nor did I—for twelve years,' he reminded her drily.

'That—that was different.'

'How?'

'Oh . . .' Sara sighed, 'he was healthy then. I suppose—I suppose he didn't really need you. But after the accident, when he did need you—you were there.'

'That wasn't why,' said Lincoln quietly, and she frowned.

'What do you mean?'

'What I say. The accident—brought us together. But only indirectly.'

She was confused. 'But I thought . . .'

'I know what you thought.'

She wetted her lips. 'And you're not going to tell me about it.'

'Not now,' he conceded flatly, 'So—let's talk about why I rang, hmm? First of all, I'd like you to spend Christmas on the island, if you have no other plans. Okay?' He paused. 'And now, tell me about Jeff. I've spoken with Haswell, of course, and he's kept me informed of his progress, but I want to hear it from you. Is it true that he can swim?'

'I think Jeff hoped——'

'——to keep it from me; I know,' he sighed. 'But surely you can understand how impossible that was. I'm responsible for him. I have to know his day-to-day development.'

Sara hesitated. 'I think Jeff might find that hard to believe.'

The pregnant silence that followed this statement was eloquent of his feelings, and it was some time before he said tersely: 'I thought we just covered that.'

She caught her lower lip between her teeth. 'I don't believe we discussed Jeff's feelings at all.'

'Sara——'

'Well, it's true. Surely you must see that so much of Jeff's progress is dependent on his psychological condition. Right now, he's excited with his success. But when he has to face therapy, when he realises the barriers . . .'

She heard his indrawn breath. 'And what do you think I can do?'

'You could be there. You could share it with him. You need to talk to your son, Link. Sooner or later, you've got to.'

'And how am I supposed to do that? Jeff doesn't want to talk to me.'

'Well, that's because——'

'Because what?'

'Because—because he doesn't understand about—about you and Michelle.'

'Do you think he could?'

'I think so.'

'What faith you have!' he jeered sardonically.

'Well . . .' Sara refused to be deterred, 'there are always two sides to every situation.'

'I'm flattered!'

'If you'd stop being so sarcastic, you might learn something,' she exclaimed impulsively, and then her shoulders sagged in helpless frustration. 'Oh, what's the use? You won't——'

'What makes you think Jeff would listen to my—side, as you put it?' Lincoln interposed harshly. 'Twelve years is a long time out of anybody's life. I know.'

'You could try,' she insisted huskily. 'Will you?'

'And we'll all live happily ever after!' muttered Lincoln, with bitter irony. 'Okay, Sara, I'll see you on Christmas Eve. Until then—take care, mmm?'

The days to Christmas seemed to drag, and Sara knew it was because she was counting the hours until she would see

Lincoln again. It was crazy, she knew. Their conversation had done nothing to solve her uncertainties about their relationship. But they had communicated about Jeff, and she wanted desperately for them to be friends again.

Jeff himself was getting stronger all the time. Doctor Haswell said that swimming was a therapy, and every day Jeff spent a little longer in the pool. The sun, too, was playing its part, and he had lost that pale and pallid complexion. Only the thinness of his legs betrayed his condition, and they had strengthened in the warm healing water.

Because he was stronger, Jeff now joined Sara and Grant for dinner most evenings. He even watched Sara sometimes, when she went for her nightly swim. With Grant's assistance, she had arranged for a ramp to enable Jeff to wheel himself down on to the beach, and although the sand made movement hazardous, he enjoyed the small freedom. She guessed it was only a matter of time before he suggested joining her, but she didn't know how he would fare in the rougher waters of the ocean.

That was something his father could decide, she thought with some satisfaction, the evening before Lincoln was due to arrive. As she plunged into the waves, she felt distinctly more optimistic for the future, and she felt sure that if Lincoln and his son could communicate, half Jeff's problems would be over. She was still no nearer to understanding what had gone wrong between them, but she was convinced that time was all they needed.

About a quarter of a mile out from shore, she turned on to her back and allowed herself to drift with the tide. It was so good to feel the heat of the day seeping from her body. It had been a humid afternoon, and she was not surprised to see purplish clouds massing on the horizon. Cora had warned that the weather might be stormy the following day, and Sara hoped urgently that it would not delay Lincoln's arrival. The plane he used seemed so small to combat the elements. Yet Grant had told her that it was just as stable as some of the bigger jets.

All the same, the weather in New York had been wintry. Low temperatures, and a biting wind, had produced a flurry of accidents, and on the nightly news Sara had seen a handful of cars that had been overturned. It had made her wish he was here already, and that the hazards of the journey could be behind him.

She was beginning to feel cold, as much with her thoughts as with the temperature of the water, she believed, but all the same, it was time to get back. She wanted to give herself time to shower before dinner, and she planned to do her nails before meeting Lincoln tomorrow.

However, when she pushed herself upright and looked about her, she saw she was much farther out than she had intended. The stronger current had swept her beyond her normal limit, and although she wasn't frightened, it was a little daunting to face such a long swim back.

Still, she could see the beach in the half light, and if she was not mistaken, Jeff was sitting in his chair waiting for her. It was somewhat reassuring, knowing he was there, watching her. He might not be able to offer her any assistance, should she need it, but at least he could call for help if he saw she was in difficulties.

She sighed. Now why had she thought of that? she wondered impatiently. She had been swimming every night for weeks, without the slightest need for anyone's assistance. So why should she need assistance now? She was being foolish; and unnecessarily pessimistic. Just because she was feeling the cold, for once, there was no reason to believe she was going to get into difficulties.

All the same, she swam back towards the shore with more enthusiasm than she usually experienced. She knew she was eager to get back to the beach again, and the abrasive rub of a dry towel. She couldn't wait to feel the enveloping warmth of a sweater about her shoulders, and the prospect of a hot shower before dinner had never seemed so attractive.

The pain in her calf struck when she was still about a hundred yards from the shore. She had had cramp before, but never so violently, and the initial shock sent her floundering. Her nose and mouth filled with water, and the sudden shortage of air caused a tight constriction in her lungs. For a brief period she was actually under the water, and the thundering in her ears made her head ache.

She fought back to the surface, gulping as her lungs filled

and the spasm receded. Dear God! she thought, struggling to remain calm, at least the pain had gone. But the leg still felt weak, and she had the horrible suspicion that if she used it again, the spasm would return.

It was about this time that she became aware that someone was calling to her. She thought she must have been listening to the sound for some time before it registered, but when it did, she looked towards the shore and saw Jeff waving at her.

'Are—you—o—kay?' he shouted, his voice almost carried away by the wind, and Sara knew a momentary fear. How soon could Jeff get help to her if she started to flounder? she wondered. In five minutes? Ten? Longer? How long could she stay afloat with that crippling gripe in her muscles? And what was the point of staying afloat if the tide simply carried her beyond their sight?

Such thoughts were foolish, but it was remarkably difficult to feel optimistic in her present plight. Without wasting her strength by replying to Jeff, she merely gave him a reassuring wave in answer. 'I'm okay,' she said, if only to prop up her own spirits, and refusing to give in to panic, she started to swim again.

Her muscles contracted only a few yards farther on, and this time the pain attacked her ankle as well. Already weakened as she was by the cold, which seemed to be spreading to every extremity of her body, the injured ankle was a natural casualty. Her foot felt frozen, the toes locked in agony, and she threshed about frantically, striving for stability.

Jeff was shouting again—at least, she thought he was. Or maybe the voices she could hear were in her head. She wasn't absolutely sure of anything at that moment. It was taking every ounce of strength she possessed to keep herself afloat. If only it wasn't so cold, she thought despairingly. The numbing chill that was gripping her was taking her will to save herself away . . .

CHAPTER THIRTEEN

AN HOUR and a half later, Sara faced Doctor Haswell's reproving gaze from the comfort of her bed. Her teeth had only just stopped chattering, and in spite of the warmth of the night, the bed was packed with blankets and hot water bottles.

'Well, that was a silly thing to do, Sara,' he said, folding his stethoscope away, but although his expression was reproachful, nothing could hide the twinkle in his eyes. 'You could have drowned! If Jeff hadn't been there, watching you . . .'

'But he was there, wasn't he?' mumbled Sara, shivering as she remembered those awful moments in the water. 'I'll never be able to thank him enough. I thought I was going to die!'

'It was a distinct possibility,' said Doctor Haswell sharply. 'You were practically unconscious when they pulled you out of the water. Still, I suppose we ought to be thankful. You certainly achieved something tonight!'

She trembled. 'Is—is he all right?'

'Jeff?' Doctor Haswell grimaced. 'Well, he's lucky to be alive too.'

'I know. But is he all right? Will this make any difference to him?'

'All the difference in the world, I should think,' remarked Doctor Haswell drily. 'Jeff used his legs tonight, Sara. He actually managed to use them to keep you both afloat. He's proved that with time—and effort—he may eventually walk again.'

Sara caught her breath. 'I can't believe it!'

'I think we all feel that way.' Doctor Haswell gave her a rueful smile. 'After all these months without hope, none of us can take it in.'

164

'But—how did he get into the water?'

'He overturned his chair on to the sand, and dragged himself down the beach.' Doctor Haswell shook his head. 'He was desperate. He could see you were in difficulties, but he couldn't make anyone in the house hear. Thank God Link arrived as he did, or we might have had two tragedies on our hands!'

She blinked. 'Link—Link's here!'

'How do you think they got you out of the water?'

She put up a trembling hand to her temple. 'But—I thought—Jeff——'

'Jeff managed to reach you and keep your head above water, but he didn't have the strength to get you back to shore. The tide was too strong. It was carrying you out. I guess that was how you got into difficulties in the first place.'

Sara stared at him. 'I had no idea . . .'

'No. Well, as I said a few moments ago, you were virtually unconscious when Link reached you. I doubt if you had the ability to distinguish between Jeff and his father.'

She absorbed this new development with some apprehension. 'And is he—is Link, I mean—is he very angry?'

'Angry?' Doctor Haswell looked surprised. 'No, I wouldn't say he was angry. Impatient, perhaps. Concerned, definitely. But not angry.'

'But doesn't he blame me?' Sara shifted a little anxiously. 'I mean if I hadn't gone swimming——'

'Which I understand you do every evening.'

'—Jeff would never have risked his life.'

'Or discovered his own abilities,' he reminded her gently. 'Sometimes it takes something like this to make the breakthrough. Jeff knows that. And so does Link.'

Sara quivered. 'I don't remember much beyond the point when Jeff reached me. I remember him talking to me, telling me it was going to be all right. But I was so cold . . .'

'The first stages of hypothermia,' said Doctor Haswell grimly. 'You're lucky to be alive, and that's what matters. Believe me, Link's pretty pleased about that.'

Sara's tongue circled her upper lip. 'Will—will you thank him for me? Will you thank both of them?'

'I think you're going to be able to thank him yourself,' said the doctor drily. 'He's waiting for me to finish my examination, and then he wants to see you. But don't be alarmed, he's not looking for a fight.'

Sara wondered. She also remembered that he had not planned to get here until tomorrow. Thank God he had, she thought fervently. For all their sakes!

The tap at the door a moment later took Doctor Haswell across the floor to answer it. 'Oh come in, Link,' Sara heard him say warmly, and she hunched the covers beneath her chin as he walked towards the bed.

She could imagine how she must look to him, she thought unhappily. With her hair roughly dried and caught back with an elastic band, and her face still white and exhausted. Why was she destined to face him at a disadvantage? she fretted. If only once in her life she could have the upper hand.

'Hello, Sara.'

She looked up when he spoke to her, and she was surprised to see he looked a little less assured than usual. Maybe his strenuous swim had taken something out of him, too. Or was it something else? Michelle's proposed marriage, for example?

In any event, his black shirt and matching pants had taken every ounce of colour out of his face, and if he was excited about his son's unexpected bravery, it wasn't evident. He looked exhausted, drained; and his hand was not quite steady as he pushed back his still-damp hair.

'Hello,' Sara answered, as Doctor Haswell paused in the open doorway.

'I'll see you two later,' he said, as if aware that his presence was superfluous, and Lincoln lifted his head and nodded his thanks as he halted beside the bed.

'So,' he said, as the door closed behind the physician, 'how do you feel?'

'Um—warm,' said Sara awkwardly, indicating the layer of blankets on the bed. 'I—er—I don't know how to thank you. Between you—you and Jeff—you saved my life!'

'Thank God!' said Lincoln heavily, and much to her

surprise, he sank down on to the side of the bed. 'God, you don't know what I went through when I saw you two out there. I've had some bad moments in my time, but that must have been the worst!'

'I'm sorry——'

'You're sorry?' He stared at her unsmilingly. 'What did I tell you about swimming at that time of night?'

'I know.' She avoided his eyes. 'I was stupid! Don't worry, I won't do it again.'

'You won't.' Lincoln drew a steadying breath. 'After this little escapade, I'll see to that. Even if I have to leave orders to that effect.'

'All right.'

Sara was beginning to feel that Doctor Haswell had been a little optimistic in his assessment of Lincoln's reaction. He had said Lincoln wasn't angry, but he was. She could feel it. And what was more, he resented the danger she had represented to his son.

'Do you realise what could have happened if I hadn't turned up as I did?'

'Of course I realise it.'

'You were frozen!'

'I know that.'

'Whatever possessed you to go out so far?'

'I didn't go that far.' Sara sniffed. 'The tide must have carried me out.'

'Thank God Jeff was there.'

'Yes.'

'He was a bloody marvel!'

She trembled. 'I know.'

'Anyway,' Lincoln seemed to gather himself, 'you're alive, and that's what matters. Anything else doesn't bear thinking about.'

'No.'

He took a breath. 'So—you'll know what's happened, not just today, but during the past couple of weeks, puts a different light on Jeff's situation.'

Sara stiffened. 'It does?'

'Of course. Jeff's whole attitude has changed. In January, Haswell's hoping he'll agree to go to a rehabilitation centre in California. They've had some pretty good results in recent years, and now that Jeff's willing to co-operate . . .'

'I see.' She knew the words were adequate, but the pain she felt inside her made anything more impossible.

'You approve, don't you?' he asked, and realising he must not suspect her real feelings, she nodded.

'Of course.' She cleared her throat in an effort to dispel the quavery note from her voice. 'That's wonderful news.'

'Is it?' He frowned. 'So why do I get the impression you're not too happy about it?' And when she persisted in evading the penetration of his gaze, he captured her chin between his fingers and turned her face towards him. 'Come on! What's wrong? You look like you're going to cry. Aren't you happy for him?'

'Don't be silly!' With an effort, she escaped his hands and turned her head away. 'If I seem—wishy-washy, it's because I'm tired. It has been an—exhausting day.'

'Don't I know it?' Lincoln spoke vehemently. 'Sara, you were unconscious when I took you from the water. For heaven's sake, I thought you were dead!'

She swallowed. 'Well, I'm not. And—and I do realise what it means so far as Jeff is concerned——'

'I'm not talking about Jeff now,' said Lincoln grimly. 'I'm talking about you! And God help me, if you don't look at me soon, you may wish you had drowned out there!'

Sara's breath caught in her throat at his words, and almost involuntarily she turned her head on the pillow. In the light from the lamp burning on the bureau, she caught a strange glimpse of some naked torment in his eyes, but then, without another word, he got abruptly to his feet.

'I'd better go,' he said, and now he avoided her eyes as he walked towards the door. 'Sleep well!' he added, his voice terse and strained. 'No doubt we'll talk again in the morning.'

'Wait!' Now it was Sara's turn to prolong his visit. 'I—er—I thought you said you weren't coming until tomorrow,' she offered pointlessly. 'Isn't that what you told me?'

'I changed my mind—thank God!' His voice was flat now. 'Okay?'

'Because of the weather?' she persisted, and as she

turned, the covers exposed the narrow straps of her nightgown.

'The weather had nothing to do with it,' retorted Lincoln shortly, propping his shoulder against the door. 'I came because I wanted to be here. For the first time in years, Orchid Key is not somewhere to avoid.'

'Oh!' Sara felt the faint surge of excitement she had experienced when he said the weather had had nothing to do with his early arrival subside. 'Does that mean you and Jeff are friends again?'

He sighed. 'Is that all that matters to you?' he demanded. 'That Jeff and I should become friends?'

She hesitated. 'It is important.'

'Oh, I agree. Goddammit, do you think I don't want to be friends with my own flesh and blood?'

'I don't know, do I?' she muttered, burrowing back beneath the covers. If she wasn't careful, this conversation was going to deteriorate into another argument, and right now she didn't think she could take it.

There was silence for so long, she became half convinced he must have left without her notice. But when she eventually permitted herself a glance over her shoulder she saw he was still there, propped against the panels.

'All right,' he said at last, straightening to walk back to the bed, 'I guess I'll have to tell you, won't I? Okay.' He lifted his shoulders. 'The reason I—I threw Jeff out, all those years ago, was that Michelle—Michelle told me I wasn't his father.'

Sara was stunned. 'But you are!'

'I know that now,' said Lincoln wearily. 'I didn't then.'

'But how could you doubt——?'

'Quite easily,' he said bitterly. 'Jeff was six weeks premature. I didn't think anything about it at the time, but later on, Michelle used that to convince me that Jeff wasn't my son.'

'Oh, *Link* !' Sara was appalled, and she was hardly aware that she had used his name in her anguish. 'But—how——?'

'There were men,' said Lincoln flatly. 'It was a reasonable assumption that one of them had been Jeff's father. Michelle wanted to hurt me, and she knew of no better way.'

Sara caught her lower lip between her teeth. She wanted to ask if he had loved his wife. She wanted to ask about their marriage, but of course she couldn't. He was not telling her these things because he cared for her; he was simply satisfying her curiosity about his relationship with his son. But that was something she could ask him.

'The accident,' she said. 'I suppose when Jeff had the accident, Michelle had to tell you——'

'Well, it wasn't quite like that,' said Lincoln heavily, pushing his hands into his trousers pockets. 'Jeff needed a blood transfusion, and they didn't have a donor. It turned out he and I share a fairly rare blood group, so Michelle was forced to contact me.'

Sara moved her head against the pillow. 'And that was when——'

'Yes.' Lincoln's jaw compressed. 'That was when I learned I'd wasted twelve years of my son's life.'

'You hadn't wasted them. Michelle had!'

He heaved a sigh. 'I should have had more sense than to believe her. My God, for months I was tormented by the look on Jeff's face when I told him he was leaving. I ruined everything. Who knows, if it wasn't for me, Jeff might have never had the accident.'

'That's not true!' Compelled by a force stronger than herself, Sara pushed herself up right in the bed, uncaring that the cool night air was chilling her flesh, and bringing a wave of goose bumps to cover her skin. 'Link, Michelle took Jeff away. It's she who is to blame.'

'I think you'd better lie down,' said Link, avoiding a direct answer. Coming closer to the bed, he bent to draw the covers up to her shoulders. 'You don't want to risk pneumonia,' he added, waiting for her to settle back against the pillows. 'Now you know the truth, you can stop speculating—hmm?'

Sara sighed. 'I'm all right.' She touched his hand as it rested against the quilt. 'Um—thank you for telling me.'

"Sara!"

There was an element of impatience in his voice now, and although she was far from satisfied with the situation, she obediently subsided against the pillows. Link tucked the covers about her, avoiding her eyes as he did so, but as he was about to straighten up, she found her voice again.

'Did you—did you love her?' she asked huskily, unable to prevent the words, and with a muffled groan he sank down on to the bed again.

'Sara, Sara,' he muttered, 'This is neither the time nor the place for us to have this conversation.'

She swallowed. 'Why not?'

'Because I'm still suffering the after-effects of what almost happened this evening,' he retorted thickly. His hand brushed the curve of her cheek and then withdrew. 'You almost died tonight, Sara. I need to come to terms with that before I can offer you an unemotional explanation.'

'So you did love her,' she said unevenly. 'I thought you must have. You're not the sort of person——'

'Will you be quiet?' His hand moved to cover her mouth, and then, as if unable to withstand the need to touch her, he cupped her face between his palms. 'I married Michelle because I *thought* I loved her,' he told her emotively. 'Within six months I'd realised my mistake. I don't think she ever loved me. What I had mistakenly assumed was affection was nothing more than a desperate attempt to save her father from prison. The old man was a lawyer, and he'd been defrauding his clients for years. Michael Steinbeck warned me that she—and her mother—would do anything to get the charges dropped. I didn't believe him. Not immediately, anyway. By the time I did, Jeff was on the way, and I was foolish enough to hope that a child might make all the difference.'

'Oh, Link!'

Sara's lips trembled, and as if unable to resist the temptation, he lowered his head and stilled their tremor with his mouth.

'I'm sorry,' he muttered after a moment, when his uneven breath was moistening the curves and hollows of her ear. 'I did warn you not to press me tonight. Nerves have a habit of manifesting themselves in so many different ways, and right now I'm not exactly in control.'

'Link——'

'No, listen to me,' he insisted, drawing back so that he could look into her face. 'There's something else I want to say to you. Something I want to ask you. I was going to wait until you were up and about again, but what the hell! Tonight must be my night for confession.'

'To ask me?' Sara quivered.

'Yes.' Link sighed. 'I have a—proposition to put to you. I don't want you to answer me tonight. I want you to think about it very carefully before you give me your reply.'

'A proposition?' Her heart was pounding. Was it possible? Oh, God, she hoped so!

'As you know,' Link began, 'we're all hoping that Jeff will go to California in January, which means—well, your job here will be finished, right?'

'Right.' Sara could scarcely voice the word.

'So,' Link was smoothing her cheeks with his thumbs, but she thought he was scarcely aware of doing so, 'when that time comes, when Jeff doesn't need you any more, I want you to come to New York.' He hesitated. 'To work for me.'

CHAPTER FOURTEEN

THE PHONE was ringing as Sara came into the flat, and she kicked off her shoes as she went to answer it. Her feet were aching with the effort of walking from one job interview to another, and the weakness in her ankle had never felt more pronounced.

'Hello,' she said, picking up the receiver, and she could hear the lacklustre quality of her voice. It was probably the reason why she had failed half a dozen interviews already this week, she reflected wryly. Nobody wanted a secretary who showed so little enthusiasm for the job.

'Sara!'

The male voice was faintly familiar, and she struggled to identify it. One of Vicki's friends, she decided. Since her friend had become engaged to her French aristocrat, there had been several calls from erstwhile boy-friends wanting to know what was going on.

'Yes,' she said now. 'Who's that? I'm afraid Vicki's not in at the moment.'

'I don't want to speak to Vicki. I want to speak to you.' The man sounded impatient now. 'This is Tony Korda, Sara. Surely you remember me!'

How could she forget? She took a steadying breath before replying. 'Oh—Mr Korda,' she said composedly. 'Er—of course I remember you. I expect you're wondering why I haven't been in touch with you since I got back. Well, things have been rather hectic here, what with Vicki's engagement, and my looking for another job——'

'That wasn't why I rang.' Tony's terse words broke into her nervous babbling. 'I want to see you, Sara. Is there any chance that you could have dinner with me this evening?'

'Dinner!' The word was almost squeak, and Sara tried to recover her equilibrium. But to have dinner with Lincoln's

173

brother was the last thing she wanted to do, and it was difficult to sound indifferent when her heart was palpitating so badly. 'I—er—I'm afraid——'

'It is important, Sara,' he interrupted her again. 'Look, I know Vicki's in Paris at the moment. If you won't have dinner with me, couldn't I at least come round and see you for half an hour?'

'Come round?' Sara knew she was repeating herself, but it was such a shock to hear from him.

'Yes.' Tony was determined. 'I think you ought to know, there's been a—hitch in Jeff's recovery. I'd like to talk to you about it. What do you say?'

She put a confused hand to her head. 'What kind of a hitch?'

'I'll tell you when I see you. Can I come round?'

In the thirty minutes Tony said it would take to get from his studio to the flat, Sara made a few improvements to the living room. It was days since she had dusted or vacuumed, but she was suddenly glad to have something with which to fill her time, and when Tony rang the bell downstairs, she was reasonably pleased with her efforts. She checked her own appearance after speaking to him on the intercom, and while he came upstairs, she restored her hair to a semblance of its usual neatness. The narrow skirt and sweater she had worn to her interviews was plain, but attractive, and only the hollows beneath her eyes betrayed a certain fragility she could not disguise.

'Sara!' Tony exclaimed, when she opened the door to his knock. 'How good of you to see me.'

Sara could have said that he hadn't given her much choice, but instead she made a deprecating gesture and offered him a drink. 'I'm afraid it has to be sherry,' she appended ruefully. 'We don't appear to have anything else. Do you mind?'

'Sherry's fine,' Tony assured her, and eschewing her offer of a seat on the couch, he perched rather restlessly on the arm.

Sara, pouring their drinks with a somewhat unsteady hand, noticed that he looked tired, too. The tinted brown hair was showing definite signs of grey, and there was a nervous twitch at the corner of his mouth which she was sure had not been there before.

Handing him his drink, she said: 'What's the matter with Jeff? Please—tell me! We write to one another, you know, and in his last letter he sounded so optimistic. I thought everything was going so well.'

Tony took a sip of the sherry, then he said flatly: 'It is. Jeff's fine.'

Sara blinked. 'What did you——?'

'I said, Jeff's fine,' he said swiftly. 'It's Link I want to talk about, but I guessed if I told you that, you wouldn't agree to see me.'

Sara's legs were suddenly not strong enough to support her. 'I beg your pardon?' she whispered, and then sank down weakly on to the edge of the couch.

'I said——'

'I heard what you said,' she exclaimed tremulously. 'Tony, if this is some joke——'

'Joke!' he snorted. 'I wish it were!'

Sara shook her head. 'What can you possibly want to tell me about—about your brother?'

He regarded her steadily. 'That he's ill! That he won't see a doctor! That I'm worried sick about him!'

She blanched. 'Ill? How ill? What's wrong with him?'

Tony sighed. 'I thought you might be able to tell me that.'

'Me?'

'Yes, you. According to Jeff, you're the only one who might know.'

Sara gulped. 'That's ridiculous!'

'Is it?'

'Of course. I—your brother's illness is as much of a shock to me as it is to you.'

Tony hesitated. 'And you can think of no reason why he should be drinking himself to death, hmm?'

'Drinking himself to death!' She caught her breath. 'You're not serious!'

'Oh, I am.' Tony was frighteningly solemn. 'Again, according to Jeff, it all began when you walked out on him. Don't you think that's a coincidence?'

She gasped. 'I—I didn't walk out.' She shook her head. 'As you've just said, Jeff was going to California. My job—such as it was—was over. I—I just came home, that's all.'

Tony studied the liquid in his glass. 'As I understand it, Link asked you to stay. To go to New York with him.'

Sara stiffened. 'Did Jeff tell you that, too?'

'He offered you a job, didn't he?'

'Why ask me? You seem to know all the answers.'

'And you refused it. Even though, as you've just told me on the phone, you're still looking for employment.'

She straightened her spine. 'That's my affair.'

'Hmm.' Tony was thoughtful. 'And it didn't occur to you that that was a strange thing for Link to do?'

'What?' Sara was bewildered.

'To offer you a job.' He hesitated, then went on: 'Forgive me, Sara, but you're not exactly executive material. I mean, all right, you can type and do general office duties, but you're not the kind of career female Link would normally employ. Believe me, his staff are hand-chosen, graduates all of them, with the kind of academic background he himself has. You—well, your talents lay in an entirely different direction, didn't they? Until—until fate intervened.'

Her face burned. 'That's true, of course, but——'

'I'm not belittling your efforts, Sara, honestly. The work you did with Jeff was nothing short of miraculous. He appreciates that—we all do. But Link's offer—that was something else.'

She trembled. 'I—I don't know what you mean.'

'The fact remains, Link is sick. Are you going to take the chance that you might not be the only person who can help him?'

'That's not fair!'

Tony regarded her shrewdly. 'But you do care about him, don't you?' He shook his head. 'You know, when Jeff first put the idea to me, I thought he had to be wrong. Now—now, I can see he was a lot more perceptive than I gave him credit for. For God's sake, why did you leave him?'

Sara got abruptly to her feet. 'What do you expect me to do?'

He hesitated. 'Go and see him.'

'Jeff?'

'Link,' he said laconically. 'Don't play games, Sara. This is too serious.'

'But what if you're wrong?' she persisted. 'What if it's someone else?' She paused. 'Rebecca, for example.'

'The Steinbeck girl? Don't be foolish. Link's had plenty of opportunities to marry her. For God's sake, it was what the old man wanted. But it wasn't what he wanted.'

'And Michelle?'

'Michelle means nothing to him. I could have told you that three months ago.'

'Then why didn't you?'

'Perhaps because I didn't want you to get hurt,' said Tony drily. 'How was I to know that my hitherto sensible brother might possibly be attracted to a girl young enough to be his own daughter?'

Sara's flight landed in New York in the early afternoon, local time. It was an afternoon at the beginning of February, and New York was as cold and damp as it can be at that time of year. A chill mist hung over the river, and along the sidewalks, ice glinted on frozen pools. Even the tugs' sirens had a mournful air, and to Sara, who had never visited the city before, the gloominess of the day only accentuated her mood. She felt decidedly apprehensive when she emerged from the arrivals hall and summoned a taxi.

Tony had told her she would find Link at his apartment, but Sara had insisted on checking into a hotel before going to see him. After all, he might refuse to speak to her, and she had no intention of standing in some strange foyer with her suitcase, only to be turned away by a smug commissionaire.

Lincoln had apparently not been into his office for days, but, with her luck, Sara thought he might well have changed his mind today. She had decided to phone his apartment before actually visiting the building. It was all very well for Tony—and Jeff—to say confidently that Lincoln *would* want to see her. But they wouldn't have to face the humiliation if somehow they were wrong.

As they crossed the river, the imposing skyscrapers of Manhattan briefly claimed her interest. The familiar skyline, seen in dozens of films and television programmes, was just as impressive as she had expected. But her attention span was short, and aside from speculating how many floors above the street level Lincoln's apartment might be, her thoughts soon returned to the reason she was here.

What if Lincoln wasn't at his apartment? What if he wasn't even in New York? How far was she prepared to go to see him? And what was she going to say to him when she did?

Tony had arranged for her to stay at the hotel he generally used when he was in New York. The Pierre wasn't far from

Lincoln's apartment, and a uniformed bell-boy showed her into a pleasant room that overlooked the park.

'Is that Central Park?' Sara asked him, looking down on the tops of trees, bare now of all their greenery, and the young man nodded.

'That's right,' he said. 'And over there, that's where they have outdoor concerts in the summer time. You staying that long, Miss Fielding? Or is this just a business trip?'

She smiled. 'In a manner of speaking,' she murmured, sorting through her dollar bills to give him a tip. 'There you are. And thank you.'

'Thank *you*, Miss Fielding,' he responded happily, slipping the bills into his pocket. 'Now, you have a nice day, you hear? And anything you want, you just ask for me.'

After he had gone, Sara returned to the window, but the scene outside no longer had any appeal. Behind her, the telephone was waiting, and without giving herself time to have second thoughts, she crossed the room and picked up the receiver.

The phone seemed to ring for a long time before it was answered, and when the connection was made she was on the point of ringing off. But she hung on as a familiar voice gave the number, and she realised with a panicky sense of alarm that Lincoln himself was at the other end of the line.

'Hello,' he said, when there was no immediate response to his pronouncement. 'Can you hear me?' And she realised, with uneasy conviction, that he didn't sound at all as if he'd been drinking.

She had to answer. Either that or ring off and accept that she was too cowardly to go through with it. In which case, she had flown over three thousand miles for nothing, and wasted the fare Tony had insisted on financing.

'Lincoln?' she said, in a thready voice, and then more firmly: 'Link? It's me, Sara. How are you?'

The silence that met this announcement was even more nerve-racking than the first. She had committed herself now, and there was no way she could back out without making some explanation. He would know she was in New York. There had been no time lapse on their conversation, and there was none of the singing on the line that sometimes characterised transatlantic calls. She couldn't even pretend she was calling from England,

and just at that moment, she wished desperately that that was where she was.

'Sara,' he said at last, and she breathed an uneasy sigh for the detachment of his tone. 'This is an unexpected—surprise.'

She noticed he didn't say *pleasure*, but what could she expect? After all, he had no way of knowing why she was here. She could, conceivably, be on holiday—*at this time of the year?*—or accompanying an employer, she argued with herself.

'Do you—er—do you mind me calling?' she ventured weakly, then chided herself for her chicken-heartedness. What possible response could he make to a question like that? She should have asked if she could see him, she told herself impatiently. She had to be positive, or she was going to get nowhere.

'What I'm wondering is how you got this number,' replied Lincoln after a moment. 'Perhaps you'd like to tell me that.'

Sara nervously cleared her throat. 'I—well, I could have got it from your office,' she demurred.

'I think not.' He was disturbingly grim. 'My office does not give my private number to anyone without my consent, and I am quite certain I did not authorise you that privilege. So—I must assume Antony is responsible. I don't think even Jeff would trespass upon my privacy.'

She felt as if he had struck her. 'All right,' she said, struggling to keep the tremor out of her voice. 'So what if Tony did give me the number? I'm here in New York to see you. I could have just come to your apartment without warning you first.'

He took a swift intake of air, then said: 'Do you imagine it's as simple as that? Sara, this is New York, not Leamington! We have security guards here.'

'I know that.' In truth, Tony had told her she would have to check in with the commissionaire first. She paused. 'Does that mean you would have refused to see me?'

There was another ominous silence, then he said wearily: 'What are you doing here, Sara? Who sent you? Don't tell me you just decided to surprise me, because frankly I won't believe you.'

'Why?' She had to force herself to go on. 'Why shouldn't I want to see you? I thought we were—friends. At least, that was my impression when you offered me a job.'

'The job's filled,' said Lincoln flatly, and Sara had to grab hold of the back of a chair to support herself. 'I'm sorry. If that's why you came, you've had a wasted journey. Give Antony my regards when you get back to London.'

'Wait!' She caught her breath. 'You're not going to see me?'

'What would be the point?'

She quivered. 'Don't you—*want* to see me?'

'No, damn you!' snarled Lincoln thickly, and her ear rang as the connection was heavily severed.

She looked at the phone for several seconds after replacing the receiver, as if half expecting it might ring. But of course, it didn't. Apart from anything else, Lincoln didn't know where she was. And Tony had said he would wait until she contacted him. She could do that now, she reflected bitterly. She could even take the evening flight home, if she chose to do so. But no, she decided, after a moment's consideration. She was too tired to go through the hassle of cancelling her hotel room and getting an alternative booking on the plane. For tonight, she would pretend that she and Lincoln were lovers, and at least the half mile or so between them was infinitely cosier than three and a half thousand miles.

With that decision made, she unlocked her suitcase and took out her toilet bag. Then, discovering the shower in the adjoining bathroom, she stripped off her clothes and turned on the jets. A fresh start was what she needed, she told herself firmly, and for the present she closed her mind to the emptiness of tomorrow.

She was tempted just to slip into her nightdress and dressing gown after her shower. With a towel tied sarongwise about her body, she sat at the vanity table brushing her hair. But the idea of her own company tonight of all nights was not appealing, and persuading herself that this might be the one and only chance she had to dine in New York, she determinedly put the temptation of room service aside.

Instead, she made a booking in the downstairs restaurant, and rummaging in her suitcase, came out with the simple black jersey gown she had brought for just such an occasion. Only she had thought she might be dining with Lincoln, she reflected painfully, before once again banishing such thoughts to the realms of her subconscious.

Her booking was for half-past seven, and in spite of the lateness of the hour in London, she felt artificially energised as she took the lift down for dinner. It was as if the things Lincoln had said to her had destroyed any chance that she might sleep tonight, and she didn't feel the least bit tired as she took her solitary seat.

The restaurant was elegant and discreetly lit, but she noticed she was the only person dining alone. She guessed the waiters were curious to know who she was and whether there was some exciting reason for her to be visiting New York at this time. If they only knew, she mused, before the hateful thought could be suppressed, and she deliberately ordered a gin and tonic to numb the edge of her humiliation.

The alcohol was soothing, and she emptied her glass while she studied the menu. The giant shrimps sounded interesting, and she decided to start with them. Then an entrecote steak, served with mushrooms, and a bottle of Californian wine, just to be cosmopolitan.

The waiter took her order, and Sara turned her attention to her fellow diners. They were couples, mostly. Evidently, the Pierre catered to a business clientele, for there was a predominance of men in the room. But when her innocent gaze encountered a less-than-innocent response, she hastily transferred her interest to the appointments of the table in front of her.

The shrimps were delicious, but her appetite did not do them justice. Likewise, the steak was returned to the kitchens half eaten, and she only managed one glass of the rich claret before her stomach revolted.

'I'm sorry,' she apologised to the head waiter, when he came to assure himself that she was not dissatisfied with the service. 'It must be jet lag,' she added, folding her napkin and getting to her feet. 'It wasn't anything to do with the food.'

They probably thought she was just another eccentric Englishwoman, she thought, as she rode the lift back to the fourteenth floor. Who else would order expensive food and wine like that, and then leave most of it?'

Her room was halfway along the carpeted corridor. The rooms were set in pairs off narrow foyers, double panelled doors with the numbers in gold lettering. She inserted her key in her own lock and entered the room swiftly. She was not unmindful of her vulnerability here, alone, in a strange city. Although the corridor had been deserted, she had had a faintly apprehensive feeling ever since she left the dining room. In consequence, she slipped the safety chain into place and turned the dead bolt before turning to face the lamplit room.

But when she did, her heart almost stopped beating. A man was seated in the armchair by the window, his head silhouetted against the lights of the city outside. Most of his body was in shadow, only his long legs, crossed at the ankle, protruded into the light. Her first thought was how casual he seemed, just sitting there, waiting for her, and then how stupid she had been to secure the door without first checking that she was alone.

Panic swept up into her throat, but before she could summon her legs into action or get some sound from her frozen vocal chords, he got to his feet. 'Don't scream,' he said, moving forward, and as she slumped against the panels behind her, Lincoln stepped into the light.

Her immediate reaction was one of tearful indignation. How dared he come here, scaring her half to death? she wondered resentfully. He must have known how terrified she would be. But hard on the heels of this thought came the incredulous realisation that he had evidently gone to the trouble of finding her, and why would he do that, after that stilted little conversation they had had earlier?

'I'm sorry if I frightened you,' he said, and as her panic subsided, Sara was able to look at him properly. At last she was able to see for herself why Tony was so concerned about him, for no matter how he had sounded on the phone, he looked awful. He was very pale, and haggard, with purplish pouches below his eyes. He looked every one of his forty years, and more besides, she reflected anxiously. Dear God! what was wrong with him? Why was he pushing himself like this?

'How did you know where I was?' she asked huskily, pushing herself away from the door. It was hardly important, but she needed time to think.

'Anthony usually stays here,' said Lincoln carelessly, pushing his hands into the pockets of the black leather jacket he was wearing. 'The management know me. When I asked the number of your room, I let them think we were related.'

'But how did you get in here?' Sara shook her head. 'Do you have a key?'

'The bellhop let me in. They said you were dining in the restaurant, so I said I wanted to surprise you. I'm sorry, but I'm not in the mood to exchange pleasantries over a dinner table.'

'You don't look as if you've eaten for days,' said Sara bluntly, noticing how his corded pants hung on his hips. 'For heaven's sake, Link, what have you been doing to yourself? And why wouldn't you agree to see me this afternoon?'

Lincoln pushed back an unruly swathe of dark hair with a hand that shook a little. 'Do you blame me?' he muttered, watching her with wary eyes. 'I'm not exactly fit to see anyone. I suppose Antony told you I've been feeling—under the weather.'

'Under the influence, more like,' she said shortly, noticing the faint slur that marred his speech. It had not been evident on the phone, but it was evident now. 'You've been drinking, haven't you? Isn't that rather stupid?'

His lips twisted. 'You were always direct, weren't you, Sara? That was one of your most disarming attributes!'

'Don't be sarcastic!'

'Well, don't you be so bloody pious, then. For God's sake, why have you come here? To make my life even more of a hell than it already is?'

Sara gulped. 'No.'

'But Antony did send you, didn't he? If I wasn't sure before, I am now.'

She frowned. 'Why?'

'This hotel. Your staying here. Antony booked it for you, didn't he? I'm surprised he didn't come with you.' He hunched his shoulders. 'I wish he'd mind his own bloody business!'

'Do you?' She gazed at him. 'And I suppose you wish he hadn't interfered over Jeff as well!'

'As a matter of fact,' said Lincoln savagely.

Sara flinched. 'You'd rather your son had become a—a cabbage?'

'I'd have seen that didn't happen,' he retorted harshly, but she couldn't let him get away with that.

'You weren't having much success when I arrived,' she reminded him unevenly. 'You couldn't even talk to one another! As I recall it——'

'All right, all right!' He clenched his fists. 'My God, you're determined to have your pound of flesh, aren't you? Okay. You persuaded me to tell Jeff the truth, and he believed me. I'm grateful for that. But I don't have to like it, do I?'

Sara dropped her keys into her bag and set the bag on the

bureau by the door. She was shaking now, but she was determined not to let him see how much he had hurt her.

'So,' she said, avoiding the accusing glitter of his eyes, 'why have you come here? If—if you hate me so much, why didn't you just ignore my call?'

Lincoln closed his eyes for a moment. 'I don't hate you,' he said wearily. 'I wish to God I did! My life would be so much easier if I could just put you out of it!'

She blinked. 'But—why? What did I ever do to you?'

He gave her a disbelieving look. 'You don't know?'

'No.' She was bewildered. In spite of what Tony had told her, she was out of her depth here. Did he care about her or didn't he? And if so, why had he offered her a job instead of telling her?

Lincoln stared at her like a hunted animal for a few tense moments, and then, abruptly, he turned away, looking round the comfortable hotel room with restless eyes. 'I need a drink,' he said thickly, his eyes alighting on the refrigerated bar. 'Give me your key.'

'N—no.' Sara refused to participate in his self-destruction. 'Link—Link, we have to talk. Please, won't you sit down. At least you could tell me what I'm supposed to have done.'

He regarded her coldly. 'You won't give me your key?'

'No.'

'Very well.' Pushing his hands back into his pockets, he brushed past her and walked towards the door. 'I'll go and get a drink some place else.'

'Oh, Link!' With a defeated little sigh, she went after him, and as he fumbled with the safety chain, she pulled her keys out of her bag. 'Here,' she said, 'take them. Just don't—don't shut me out again.'

Lincoln took the keys, but he didn't move towards the cabinet. 'Shut you out?' he echoed blankly. 'When did I do that?'

'This—this afternoon,' said Sara, remaining where she was with a great effort of will power. 'I thought you didn't want to see me. I was going to catch the evening flight home.'

His lips parted. 'And why didn't you?'

'Because—because I wanted to stay,' she stammered miserably. 'There! Now you can have the last laugh. I may have come here because Tony asked me to, but my motives weren't entirely unselfish.'

He stiffened. 'What are you saying? That you really wanted that job I offered you?'

Sara hesitated. 'If it's still vacant, yes.'

'Oh, Sara!' With a sigh, Lincoln thrust the keys she had given him into his pocket and ran unsteady fingers round the back of his neck. 'Look, I don't know how to tell you this, but—well, there was no job.'

'No?' She tried to hide the sudden surge of emotion that gripped her. 'But you said——'

'I know what I said,' he replied heavily. 'Oh, what the hell! You might as well hear it from me as from somebody else. I only pretended there was a job, to get you to come to New York. Once you were here, I was hoping I might persuade you to change your mind about—well, about our relationship.'

Sara quivered. 'Our relationship?' she echoed softly. 'I—didn't know we had a relationship.'

'No.' Lincoln's tone was flat. 'That's what I thought. Well . . .' he pulled the keys out of his pocket again and dropped them on to the bureau, 'I guess this is where I came in. Sorry about the intrusion. It won't happen ag——'

'Oh, Link!'

Her agonised cry of protest stilled his hands as he fumbled with the bolt, and her eager arms sliding round his waist from behind evoked a muffled oath. But Sara was no longer in any doubt that what Jeff had suspected, and what Tony had said, was true. Amazing—*incredible*—as it might seem, Lincoln did care about her, and whatever he wanted from her, she was more than willing to give.

'Oh, Link,' she said again, pressing her face into the hollow of his spine, 'don't go! Please, don't go! I need you!'

She could feel him trembling as he turned to face her, but the hands sliding over her shoulders were hungrily possessive. 'What did you say?' he demanded roughly. 'Do you really want me to stay? Or am I just another case you're going to try and cure?'

She sniffed a little tearfully now. 'Well, you are a case,' she told him huskily. 'And how do I know this isn't just the alcohol talking? For heaven's sake, why didn't you just tell me how you felt in Florida?'

'I could ask you the same question,' he muttered, pulling her against him. 'And why do you think I needed the alcohol? Sara—God! I thought I was only a substitute. I thought it was Jeff you cared about!'

'Jeff?' She gazed at him blankly. 'But you couldn't——'

'Oh, I could,' he assured her unsteadily. 'Keating told me he'd seen you in one another's arms. What was I supposed to think?'

Sara shook her head, remembering that occasion with disbelief. 'It wasn't like that,' she exclaimed fiercely. 'Jeff had just made it into his wheelchair for the first time. I hugged him, that was all. I hugged him! There was nothing sexual about it.'

Lincoln groaned. 'But you always kept me at a distance!'

'I thought that was what you wanted. After you accused me of trying to blackmail you——'

He shook his head. 'I apologised for that.'

'But I couldn't forget it.'

'You don't understand,' he said, his voice muffled by her hair, as he released the pins holding it in its knot and buried his face in its tumbling softness. 'That night—that night we spent together meant more to me than I wanted it to. I didn't want to get involved, and I guess I tried to convince myself that I could get over it.'

'But you stayed on,' she reminded him, drawing back to look at him, and he gave her a wry smile.

'With Rebecca,' he agreed emotively. 'I guess I was trying to prove my indifference. It didn't work.'

Sara's tongue touched her lips. 'Did you—did you sleep with her, too?'

'Will you believe me if I say no?' he enquired huskily. 'I'll be honest—I intended to. But every time I took her in my arms, I kept seeing your face!'

'Oh—darling——'

She put up her hand to touch his cheek, but Lincoln was not proof against such endearments. With an exclamation, he turned her palm against his mouth, and then, cupping the back of her head with his hand, he brought her lips to his.

After that, it was difficult to think of anything but the searching possession of his tongue in her mouth. He was hungry for her, and she desperately wanted to show him that she shared his need. With a complete abandonment of inhibition, she burrowed inside his jacket, parting the buttons of his shirt to press her burning face against his skin. It was so wonderful to be able to share these intimacies with him, and he parted his legs to draw her closer, letting her feel his urgent need.

His kisses deepened as his hands explored her body, finding the nub of her zip at her nape and propelling it surely downwards. Then, with his lips seeking the smooth skin of her shoulder, he swung her up into his arms, and presently the cool sheets that the maid had turned down for the night were at her back.

'Let me,' she whispered huskily, as he began to loosen his shirt, but when her hands encountered the swollen length of him, taut beneath the bulging cloth of his pants, he put her quickly aside.

'I can't let you,' he said thickly, unbuckling his belt and tearing open his zip to expose his throbbing manhood. 'There's only so much I can take, and right now I can't wait!'

'I can't wait either,' she breathed, opening her bra and tossing it aside as he came down beside her. But it was Lincoln's hands that disposed of her panties, and parted her legs for his possession.

It was quickly over. The thrusting invasion of his body soon brought them both a shuddering satisfaction, and Lincoln collapsed upon her only seconds after she had reached her climax. So much for a lingering reunion, she thought ruefully, but oh, how marvellous it had been! She had only been half alive since that night at Orchid Key. But now she felt revitalised in every nerve and sinew.

It was some minutes before Lincoln stirred, but when he did, it was only to prop himself up on his elbows. 'You see what you do to me,' he murmured, smoothing the moist hair back from her forehead. 'I'm sorry—I wanted to be gentle, but I'd waited so long . . .'

'I'm not complaining,' she teased, stroking a bead of perspiration from his temple. 'I got the feeling you needed me.'

'You'd better believe it,' he groaned, burying his face between her breasts. 'I love you! I just wish I believed this was as good for you as it is for me.'

Sara frowned. 'What do you mean? You must know I love you, too.'

'Do you?' He lifted his head again.

'How can you doubt it?'

'And you don't think I'm—too old for you?'

'Too old?'

'I saw the way you looked at me when you came in. You looked—shocked.'

'I was shocked,' she exclaimed, twining her fingers in the hair at his nape. 'Link, have you looked at yourself recently? You've got so pale and tired-looking. And you've lost weight.' She paused. 'Tony said you were drinking yourself to death.'

'An exaggeration, I think,' he said roughly, but when she reached up to rub her lips against his, he closed his eyes. 'Okay,' he added, opening them again, 'maybe I have been imbibing a little too freely, but hell—it was the only way I could live with myself!'

'If only I'd known,' she sighed.

'But that doesn't alter the fact that Jeff is more your age than I am.'

'So what?' She wound her arms around his neck now. 'I don't love Jeff. I love you! Are you going to let me stay?'

'Stay?'

Sara hesitated. 'That is what you want, isn't it? That I should stay with you?'

Lincoln regarded her warily, his lean attractive features mirroring a little of the tension they had exhibited earlier. 'Is that what you want?'

She blinked. 'Well, of course it is,' she stammered. And then, swallowing: 'What's wrong?'

He shook his head. 'Nothing.'

'Yes, there is.' She shook him. 'Link, you're shutting me out again. What did I say? Tell me!'

He rolled on to his back beside her and stared at the ceiling then. 'All right,' he said flatly. 'I had a more—permanent relationship in mind. But if you want——'

'A more permanent relationship?' she echoed, pushing herself up on one hand to look down at him. 'Do you mean—marriage?'

His eyes turned towards her, and she thought he had never looked more attractive to her. Their lovemaking had banished the defeated expression from his face, but now it was being replaced by a weary resignation. 'Yes,' he said. 'Old-fashioned, aren't I? But that's what I've been trying to tell you.'

Sara shook her head. 'You—want to—marry me?'

'Don't look so surprised. I may have had one unfortunate experience, but I'm not opposed to the idea.'

'Oh, Link!' Suddenly realising how shamelessly she was exploiting his need of her, she lowered herself against him, and with her mouth teasing his, she breathed: 'I'm not opposed to it either. I just didn't think you would want to marry me.'

His hands slid into her hair, almost pulling it away from her scalp as he forced her head upwards. 'What did you say?'

'You heard me,' she murmured painfully. 'Oh, darling, I'd marry you tomorrow, if I could. But not if you're going to scalp me every time I make a mistake.'

'Do you mean it?' With a disbelieving oath, he rolled over, bearing her back against the mattress. 'You do mean it!' he added, seeing the eager acknowledgement glowing in her eyes. He shook his head. 'Oh, Sara! What a lot of time we've wasted!'

There was a satisfying silence, and then Sara whispered huskily: 'We'd better not waste any more, hmm?'

'No chance,' Lincoln assured her, with a return of his usual confidence. 'I'll have to tell Antony—*Tony*—he can interfere any time he likes!'

ANNE MATHER began her career by writing the kind of book she likes to read—romance. Married, with two teenage children, this north-of-England author has become a favorite with readers of romace fiction the world over—her books have been translated into many languages and are read in countless countries. Since her first novel was published in 1970, Anne Mather has written more than eighty romances, of which over ninety million copies have been sold!

Books by Anne Mather

STORMSPELL
WILD CONCERTO
HIDDEN IN THE FLAME
THE LONGEST PLEASURE

HARLEQUIN PRESENTS

683—SIROCCO
715—MOONDRIFT
810—ACT OF POSSESSION
843—STOLEN SUMMER
869—PALE ORCHID
899—AN ALL-CONSUMING PASSION

HARLEQUIN ROMANCE

1631—MASQUERADE
1656—AUTUMN OF THE WITCH

Don't miss any of our special offers. Write to us at the following address for information on our newest releases.

Harlequin Reader Service
901 Fuhrmann Blvd., P.O. Box 1397, Buffalo, NY 14240
Canadian address: P.O. Box 603,
rt Erie, Ont. L2A 5X3

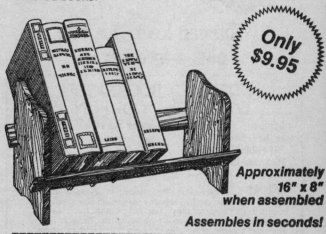

Can you keep a secret?

You can keep this one
plus 4 free novels